BRANDEN SYLVESTER

Black Thread

Renewal & Implications

This book is dedicated to my brilliant daughter Roxanne Layne, who brainstormed this story with me for countless hours.

And a very special thanks to Chandler for her wise counsel and clear guidance throughout the process, a true sweetheart and amazing woman.

And a huge Thank You! to my mother.

Contents

II   IMPLICATIONS

I

RENEWAL

Chapter 1

Gaeldritch sat in her timeworn rocking chair, the aged wood creaked softly against the solid stone floor with every subtle shift of her weight. Her eyes remained fixed on a small lantern that radiated a cold glow of pale blue light through its iron-framed, weathered glass panes—each pane distorted by countless years. The lantern rested a few feet in front of her on the cool, hard ground, a solitary beacon amid the surrounding darkness.

The heavy fabric of her black robe flowed around her like a cascade of living shadows, pooling at her feet with an almost sentient grace. With every measured sway of the chair, her feet tapped gently against the stone, producing a rhythmic, spectral cadence that seemed to echo the secrets of the silent chamber.

She was seated in a vast cavern, carved from rugged limestone by miners over a century ago. Long after those laborers had abandoned their work and their pickaxes fell silent, the Grand-Witch had claimed the old mine—its intricate shafts and meandering tunnels becoming her clandestine domain. The stone floors were etched with deep grooves and pockmarked with scattered holes, enduring reminders of the relentless pickaxe blows and hammered rail spikes of a bygone era. Beyond lay an endless network of passageways and natural caverns, interwoven with underground streams that had tunneled through ancient watercourses. Yet, in stark contrast to these damp, mysterious corridors, the expansive chamber where Gaeldritch sat remained remarkably bone-dry, elevated well above the waterline—a dry sanctuary amid a subterranean realm of moisture.

The lantern's faint pale light crept around the room as the flame inside flickered and back-lit the silhouettes of a gathering of listeners sitting on mats spread across the floor, their eyes fixed on Gaeldritch as she prepared to deliver her thoughts.

Her bony fingers—pale, sinewy, and abnormally long—rested upon the arms of her chair. The thin, calloused tips seemed to absorb the faint light that flickered through the cave, as though her flesh itself served as a conduit for the unseen energies drifting through the air.With a slow, deliberate exhalation, she turned her gaze toward them.

When she spoke, her voice was imbued with an unmistakable weight of command—a tone that brooked no interruption or distraction. She had a voice of one who had pierced beyond the veil and communed with forces beyond mortal comprehension, speaking as a master instructs an apprentice poised on the precipice of forbidden knowledge, their understanding delicate and tentative, teetering on the brink of revelation.

"All of you must heed this teaching, pay attention!" she began, her words slicing through the stillness. "I have heard some of you refer to our coven, yet you pronounce it incorrectly. Our coven is spoken with a hard 'O'—much like the word 'woven'—and not as 'kuh-vin,' which is the pronunciation used by the countless profane who truly know nothing of the arcanum. Our benefactor hails from ancient lineages, from the Gauls of over two thousand years past, and since those times, we have always pronounced our sacred order as he did then, as C-O-VEN, with a hard 'O'."

"The roots of our coven stretch even further back than ancient Gaul, where our order was even then called a C-O-VEN! So...you must show proper respect for our order and utter our words precisely, for if you cannot speak them correctly, you shall never harness the full power of our incantations. Do not mispronounce our spells! I admonish all of you now, speak with precision! There is no leeway to this command and mispronunciation will be met with dire punishment."

After a measured pause, Gaeldritch drew in a deep breath. "Now, with that clarified," she continued, "I wish to tell you about a creature very special to our coven."

"He has been known by many names throughout the ages," Gaeldritch murmured, her words carrying like a distant hiss in a tomb. "A creature of boundless strength—he is a being both relentless and resilient. Born from the foulest mixtures of organic matter, together with earth and water, shaped by the hands and mind of our visionary—our benefactor—whose alchemical genius breathed life—everlasting life—into that which would have died otherwise, but was instead granted immortality."

She leaned forward, her eyes gleaming with an eerie fervor.

"This creature is of the bog, and is no ordinary being," she continued, her voice admiring. "He exudes the blackest sludge from his very pores, thick and primal, as though he is the bog itself—indeed its essence pulses through his veins. At

5

night, he prowls unseen, performing his sacred duties beneath the shroud of darkness. Yet should the task require, he will move even in daylight, clinging to the edges of sight, slipping between shadows—distorting the light—as though the sun itself dare not acknowledge his presence."

She extended a hand toward a dark sack resting on the rock floor beside her, its surface woven from a pitch-black thread that seemed to devour the faint pale light.

"He carries sacred bags similar to this one," she intoned, her voice barely audible, yet still heard well, thick with reverence. "Woven from our black thread, a gift bestowed upon him centuries ago by our Grand-Weaver. Within these sacks, he secures bodies to provide for us the fats, phlegms, biles, and other excretions of the profane—the harvest that fuels our rites and provides the vital ingredients of our many concoctions."

Her voice softened, touched with an almost unsettling fondness. "He is beloved amongst us—an irreplaceable figure in the coven's circle. His work is tireless, his purpose un-wavering. Night after night, he travels vast distances unseen, and he brings us what we require—those raw elements from which we distill our power, the lifeblood of our sacred order."

She paused for a few moments and a profound silence settled over the chamber, thick and in awe.

Gaeldritch shifted in her chair, the wood creaking like brittle bones beneath her. With a slow, deliberate motion, she reached into the folds of her robe, retrieving a small jade-colored vial. She uncorked it with the ease of one who had performed the action countless times before, tilting it back and draining its contents into her mouth in a single, fluid motion. A brief flicker of something potent and unfathomable passed over her eyes—a momentary communion with forces unseen.

"Over centuries of time, he has been called many names—the Bog Man, the Sack Man, the Bogey Man, the Swamp Creature, Boggart, the Bog Bear...and many others." she went on, her voice now a low, intimate murmur. "Names used by the ignorant and the uninitiated, who perhaps caught a glimpse of him and lived to tell about it, those who cannot fathom what he really is. But we, in our coven, know his true name—he is Tum-Grissell—he is Abominatio! And he has served our coven faithfully for over eight hundred years."

She leaned forward slightly, her pupils glinting in the dim light. Then, with a voice like breath upon a tombstone, she whispered, like a snake hissing,

"*Ayduxia sakshi kachia*", an ancient phrase of admiration and adoration.

The words hung in the air like drifting smoke, weightless yet unshakable. Her gaze slid toward the darkened corners of the chamber, as if she could see Tum-Grissell at work, wading through the night, his heavy-weave sack made of black thread in hand, fulfilling his everlasting duty.

At last, Gaeldritch settled back in her chair, her breath slow and measured. The silence that followed was not empty—it was thick, pulsing with the weight of the unseen, the unheard, and a heavy stillness remained.

Chapter 2

J ust days after turning eight years old, Holly Childs felt like life couldn't get any better—it was the last day of school, and summer break had finally arrived. The June afternoon sun bathed her skin in warmth, while the air buzzed with the scent of wild grasses and blooming weeds swaying along the edge of the narrow road. As she walked home, everything in her life felt perfect.

Her book bag was lighter than usual, carrying only a few of her favorite books—collections of short stories—and some of her pencil drawings of birds. Everything else had been unceremoniously tossed into the trash the moment the final school bell rang.

Holly adored scary stories—tales of ghosts, vampires, and lurking creatures. She relished the thrill of the supernatural, much to the dismay of her classmates, who found her fascination strange. But Holly didn't care what they thought. Let them talk. She was content in her world of eerie shadows and thrilling mysteries.

She also loved birds. Whenever she had a quiet moment, she would draw them, their wings stretching toward the sky. Her mother, an avid birdwatcher, had taught her to admire their beauty, to find wonder in their movements and the freedom of their flight. Today, as she skipped along the pavement, she imagined them soaring high above her, dark shapes against the endless blue.

Holly always walked home from school alone, and she enjoyed the solitude. Her house stood beyond the old farms, along a road where the fields stretched wide, and only a handful of older houses dotted the land. On the walk home from school, unlike her classmates, who turned in the opposite direction toward their clustered neighborhoods, Holly veered off on her own, toward the quiet under open skies. She never cared for the constant chatter of the other children—always gossiping, always fussing about things that didn't matter to her. She preferred her own company, where her imagination could run free.

For her birthday, her mother had given her a new pair of shoes, and she loved them. She admired them as she walked, enjoying their look as well as the cushion the new soles provided on the hard pavement. Her brother, Thomas, had gifted her a watch and admonished her to never be late again—now that she could see the time, there would be no excuse for to stay outside too late. She liked it well enough, but the band felt tight on her wrist. Sweat gathered beneath it, and she was tempted to take it off, but she resisted. Instead, she focused her attention on the beauty around her.

Suddenly—

She heard a rustling.

Holly's steps faltered as the tall weeds beside her quivered. Her pulse quickened. Then, in an explosion of motion, a large, dark-brown German Shepherd burst from the thick weeds, landing heavily on the pavement behind her. It growled—a low, guttural sound—its claws clicking sharply against the pavement. Holly gasped, staggering back, her legs wobbling beneath her.

"Go away!" she shouted, her voice trembling.

The dog barked—a deep, menacing sound that sent a shiver of dread down her spine. It stared at her, its body tense, its gaze locked onto her as if she were prey. Holly's breath hitched. She glanced down the long street toward her house— her only hope was to reach the safety of home.

Panic surged through her. She turned and ran, her small legs propelling her forward as fast as they could. She had barely made it ten feet before the book bag slung over her shoulder yanked her violently backward, nearly pulling her off her feet. She whipped her head around—the dog had clamped its powerful jaws onto the bag, its teeth sinking deep into the fabric.

She screamed, trying to pull free. The dog growled, tugging and shaking the bag as if it were fresh prey.

With a desperate twist, she slipped the strap off her shoulder and tore away, leaving the bag behind. She didn't dare look back. She ran with everything she had, her heart hammering like a drum. The safety of her home was still far ahead—

Then—a yelp.

The barking and growling stopped.

The only sounds were her gasping breath and the rapid pounding of her feet on the pavement.

Holly kept running, lungs burning, legs aching, but confusion gnawed at her. Why had the dog stopped chasing her?

She slowed and finally stopped, doubling over with her hands on her knees, gasping for air. Fear pulsing through her, she hesitantly turned back toward the dog.

It lay there, motionless on the road.

Her book bag rested beside it. The dog's body was eerily still, its chest unmoving.

Holly stared, her breath caught in her throat. Moments ago, the dog had been relentless, mere seconds away from biting her. A strange chill slithered through her veins.

What had stopped the ferocious dog?

She needed her bag. Her books, her drawings—pieces of herself—were inside. Swallowing her fear, she stepped forward.

As she neared the dog, she saw it.

Blood. Dark and thick, pooling beneath the dog's head, seeping into the cracks of the pavement.

Her stomach twisted.

Just grab the bag. Don't think. Don't look. Just grab the bag and get home.

She reached down, snatched it up, and slung it over her shoulder.

Then—

A slight shift in the tall weeds.

She froze.

Oh no! Another dog?

Her wide eyes scanned the tangled grasses beside the pavement. There, just a few feet away, was something that didn't belong.

A shadow.

An unnatural darkness nestled in the foliage, its edges blurred, as though it bled into the light around it.

Holly's heart pounded.

What is that?

She squinted, struggling to make sense of the darkness. It was faded and blurry, almost like a dark-gray thunderhead sitting on the ground. Her mind couldn't comprehend what she was looking at. It looked like a patch of dark earth in deep shadow, but there were no trees to cast shade, and the sun beamed brightly overhead. There was no clear contrast between its dark edges and the surrounding daylight—only a strange gradient of blackness blurring into the light, unnatural, defying the logic of the afternoon sun.

Then—

From within the darkness, two eyes snapped open.

Holly's breath caught in her throat.

They were large. Alive. Watching her.

Their pupils were black as ink, the irises a deep, burnt orange, vibrant against the whites that surrounded them. The eyes stayed on her, unblinking, assessing.

And then—

They narrowed.

A surge of terror shot through her.

Holly stumbled back. Then, instinct taking over, she turned and ran.

She didn't look back. She couldn't. Her feet pounded the pavement, her book bag bouncing against her back, her pulse roaring in her ears. Tears blurred her vision, but she didn't stop. She couldn't stop.

The eyes—those terrible orange eyes—had stared into her eyes.

She finally reached her house, her safe haven, and scrambled up the front steps. She flung the door open, rushed inside, and slammed it shut with shaking hands. Her fingers fumbled over the deadbolt and twisted the knob—

Click.

Sealed inside, in safety.

Leaning against the door, her chest heaved, her breathing ragged and uneven. She felt lightheaded, sick to her stomach. She sank to the floor, arms wrapped tightly around her bag, her whole body trembling.

The image of those eyes—those inhuman eyes—burned into her mind.

Tears streamed down her face, her small body wracked with fear.

A scream tore free from her lips.

"Mom!" she cried, her voice cracking with desperation. "I need you, Mom!"

Chapter 3

Holly's mother, Hannah, dashed out of the kitchen, her apron still tied around her waist, her face creased with concern. "What's the matter, darling? What happened?!" she asked, her voice steady but worried as she took in Holly's tear-streaked face and heaving breaths for air.

Holly looked up at her mother, her words stumbling out between gasps. "I was walking home, and one of the farmer's dogs came out of the weeds and attacked me! It tried to bite me, Mom!" She held up her bag, showing the torn fabric, the unmistakable marks of teeth. "I ran, but... but then I looked back and the dog was dead. And... and I saw something else."

Her mother's face softened as she knelt down next to Holly and placed a comforting hand on her shoulder. "Something else?" she asked, her voice calm but edged with worry.

Holly nodded, her voice dropping to a frightened whisper. "It was a monster—a huge, dark monster in the weeds. It... it had orange eyes, Mom. They were looking right at me."

Her mother pulled her close, stroking her hair as Holly's sobs began to subside. "Oh, sweetheart," she murmured. "You are safe, trust me. No dog can harm you here, or anything else, for that matter."

She looked at the bite marks on Holly's bag, a flash of unease in her eyes before she turned back with a reassuring smile. "You're home now, calm down. I"ll visit with the Becksteads and the Holts and make sure their dogs will never be a problem again."

Holly hugged her mother tightly, trying to let her warmth ease the terror that still clung to her. But even as she closed her eyes, she couldn't shake the feeling that the shadow was out there, hidden, waiting.

Her mother's expression didn't change, her face set in a calm, unreadable mask. "Now, darling," she said quietly, "I don't know what you saw out there, I'm just glad you're safe now."

"It was real, Mom!" Holly's voice wavered, the terror in it unmistakable. "I saw it! It was a monster—a huge, awful thing, covered in black mud. It looked right at me, and I know it killed the dog! The dog bit my book bag, and then the next time I looked…" Her voice faltered. "It was just lying there, dead!" She held up her bag, the bite marks deep in the fabric, as if they held all the proof she needed.

Her mother took a long, thoughtful look at the torn bag. Her hand rested on her cheek, her gaze cool and assessing. "Darling, I'm sure something frightened you dearly. You've got such a vivid imagination, Holly—you're always reading scary stories." She paused, her tone softening. "Sometimes, when our minds are stirred up, they can play tricks on us."

Holly shook her head, her face growing red. "This wasn't a trick. The monster looked at me, Mom. I didn't imagine it!"

After a moment, her mother continued, her tone calm and steady, "Alright, darling. You're safe now, no matter what happened. If one of the farmer's dogs attacked you, that must have been awful—just frightening. But you are, indeed, very safe. Thank the stars—you are very precious and protected."

She gave Holly's hand a reassuring squeeze. "And if you saw a shadow in the middle of the day, then perhaps... well, you might have just imagined this 'monster'. Try to forget the whole thing. I can't have you thinking about that...it's just not suitable for you to worry over."

Holly stared at her mother, dejected, her disbelief growing. How could she dismiss it so easily?

Her mother's voice softened, becoming almost a lullaby, "I know that dog seemed dangerous, terrifying... but trust me, you were never truly in harm's way." She knelt down, her arms circling around Holly, pulling her close in a gentle embrace. Her hand moved in slow, soothing strokes along Holly's back, each patting rhythm as steady as her heartbeat. "Forget whatever you saw. You're safe now, completely safe, darling. Your brother and I will always protect you and make sure you grow up *just* as you should. You don't need to worry about anything—not about what you saw, or *anything* else in the world, for that matter."

She leaned back slightly, looking down at Holly with a gentle, steady gaze, her hands still resting on Holly's shoulders. Then she straightened and helped her daughter to her feet, brushing a stray lock of hair from Holly's forehead. "Now, go upstairs, run yourself a nice warm bath, and clean up," she said, her voice as soft as ever, though there was an odd, quiet firmness beneath it. "Maybe do a little drawing before dinner, try to calm down and rest. How about you don't read any of your scary stories tonight, okay? I know you love them, but stick to drawing or watching TV tonight."

Holly nodded slowly, her trembling beginning to ease

16

under her mother's reassuring touch, and she turned to head upstairs. Her mother watched her go, her face composed, her expression calm yet stern. When Holly disappeared around the corner, her mother lingered for a moment, her eyes fixed on the empty staircase. After a quiet breath, she muttered to herself, "Farmers and their dogs, such an unnecessary danger. Unacceptable.", and shook her head. She then turned and glided back into the kitchen with a confident, purposeful calm.

Chapter 4

14 Years Later

Gaeldritch glided through the forest as the evening light bled into dusk, her form a fleeting shadow of black against the deepening night. She moved with an eerie swiftness, a shade slipping between the towering pines, barely stirring the underbrush beneath her feet. The air was thick with the scent of damp earth and resin, the trees standing like solemn sentinels as she made her way toward a sacred enclave—an old circle of stones, untouched by time, veiled in secrecy.

At the heart of the circle lay a weathered altar, its surface smoothed by decades of ritual, crowned with a hollowed stone basin. The wind murmured through the clearing, rustling the needles and swaying the branches. Gaeldritch moved with purpose, gathering a bundle of dry twigs and brittle branches from the forest floor. With a flick of her wrist, she cast them into a fire pit near the altar.

From within the folds of her flowing robe, she retrieved a small, blood-red vial, its contents thick and shimmering like liquid garnet. As she uncorked it, the scent of iron and something pungent rose into the night air. She poured the dark liquid over the kindling, the droplets sticking to the wood.

Then, with a sharp strike of flint against steel, sparks leaped forth from her pale hands, igniting the wood in a sudden bloom of flame. Firelight flared to life, licking at the night, casting writhing shadows upon the stones. The clearing pulsed with warmth and orange light, the flames cracking and snapping.

Gaeldritch settled upon a boulder, its surface worn smooth by time and shaped by hands many years ago. She sat in silence, her gaze fixed on the night sky as the moon ascended, a silver guardian in the abyssal black. Embedded quartz crystals within the stone circle caught its luminescence, refracting the pale glow in a dance of reflections. Their cold radiance shimmered in her gleaming eyes.

When the moment ripened—when the moon stood directly above, a celestial eye gazing down upon her—she rose and began her incantations.

"Elementa creationis, facite iussa mea..."

Her voice wove through the air, an arcane whisper threading the fabric of the unseen. One by one, she uncorked vials of colored liquids—some viscous, others thin as mist—and poured them into the stone basin.

"...datva me durstim, sudarsanam!"

The substances coiled together like living entities, some merging without disturbance, others hissing, bubbling and spitting as if recoiling from each other's touch. The mingling fluids shimmered unnaturally, their hues shifting in the firelight—deep crimson, ghostly blue, jade green.

Gaeldritch's voice rose, commanding, resonant with power.

"Bayani ye sudha balam..."

With deliberate precision, she plucked a branch with a

19

glowing ember from the fire and touched it to the concoction. A single breath of stillness—then an eruption of flame.

"Pariva rayanti!"

Fire roared from the basin, twisting and writhing like a spectral beast unleashed. It flared upward in tongues of green and orange, snapping and crackling, its shadows leaping across the altar, contorting into shapes both wondrous and terrible. The moonlight poured down upon it, silver beams mingling with the spectral fire, their interplay painting the clearing in a haunting spectacle of shifting light and darkness.

Gaeldritch leaned forward, her face hovering just above the flickering flames, the heat licking at her skin. Her breaths grew deep and measured, each inhale drawing the fire closer, feeding her essence into the ritual. The thick, scented smoke coiled around her like serpents, slithering into her lungs. She welcomed it, consuming the fire's vitality as if it were a sacrament, pulling vast amounts of the smoke into her lungs with each inhalation.

Then, with a voice like steel wrapped in silk, she uttered the final command:

"Ostende mihi visionem!"

The air quivered.

A ripple passed through the fabric of reality. The world blurred at the edges, tilting into a void where time and space became fluid. And then—

A vision struck her, sharp and undeniable.

First, the crown of a head, brown hair gleaming under unseen light, the face veiled in shadow.

Then—a silver cross, suspended in midair, glinting coldly in the moonlight.

Next, numbers drifted into focus, ancient bronze against

the darkness: *7... 3... 0,* hovering like an omen.

And finally—a small white house, its paint peeling, its frame hunched against the night, standing alone in an ocean of darkness.

Each image seared into her mind, vivid and unrelenting, leaving its mark as though carved into stone.

Gaeldritch lingered in the moment, her breathing turned shallow, her body taut with the weight of the revelation. She let the vision settle, imprinting itself upon her soul. Then, with the reverence of one who understood the gravity of such powers, she bowed her head to the unseen forces, a silent offering of thanks.

She did not move until the flames in the basin had burned themselves out, until the moon had shifted its watchful gaze further across the heavens.

Only then did she rise, her silhouette a shadow against the dimming firelight. Without a word, without a sound, she turned and melted into the trees, her form swallowed by the consuming dark.

She walked unseen, untouched, a phantom retreating into the heart of the forest.

Into the mountain's embrace, deep into the labyrinthine caverns where her hidden hovel was nestled.

Chapter 5

Holly, 22 years old, sat at her mother's dining table, across from her as they ate supper. The atmosphere was formal, as it often was when her mother insisted on "good manners" during meals.

Her mother looked at her daughter with a mix of concern and curiosity. "Tell me, darling," she said, her voice soft but probing. "You seem disturbed these past few weeks. Something's bothering you. What's going on?"

Holly put her fork down, a little too forcefully, and took a deep breath before answering, her voice light at first. "I'm just tired, Mom. I don't need more sleep. I'm just tired of the day-to-day routine. Tired of the tedious, repetitive life I'm living."

She paused, and then, once the words started to flow, she couldn't stop. "I thought once I got a decent job and a house, life would just magically be awesome. Like, finally, I'd be happy. But it's all just a hassle, it's very annoying and boring. Is this it?"

Her mother's brow lifted at Holly's bluntness. She set her fork down, giving her daughter her full attention.

Holly leaned back, rubbing her forehead. "Every day it's the same thing. Deal with customer complaints, go home, clean the house, do my laundry, wash the dishes. That's my life. Is that what it's supposed to be about? I should be grateful, I know, but…" She let out a frustrated sigh. "I thought this was supposed to be more fun, more exhilarating. Like, I thought I'd feel more… alive, you know what I mean?"

Her mother stared at her for a long moment, then spoke, her voice calm but weighted with conviction. "Darling, the sooner you realize you don't truly know what the future holds, the better. Trust in the plan—the plan life has for you."

Holly's eyes widened in frustration, and she quickly shook her head. "Mom, please. Don't go off on some religious rant about destiny and plans—that doesn't actually help in the real world."

Her mother didn't flinch. "Trust in the plan…it's exactly what you need, darling. The sooner you stop trying to control the outcome and start trusting the future, the better." She paused, her tone steady and resolute. "This is what will bring you peace. And try not to doubt that you are very special, very safe, and that everything will work out."

Holly rolled her eyes, a little exasperated. "Yeah, okay, Mom. I really don't want to get into some crazy discussion right now. I'm just frustrated right now. I can't see the point to all of this…all of this trouble if it's all…well, pointless."

Her mother nodded thoughtfully. "Okay, I'll let it go for now. But listen—I need you to trust in the future, in your future. And if you can do that—trust in my words, I guarantee you'll find what moves your spirit before long."

Holly's shoulders slumped, a deep sense of defeat creeping into her. "I don't know. I just know I don't fit in. I feel like I'm the black sheep or something. I'm not like everyone else. My whole childhood I was different than everybody else. And

I feel a bit… empty. Like, what's the point of all this?" She gestured vaguely, the weight of her frustration too much to explain in words. "Nine-to-five, clean the house, pay the bills, rinse, repeat. It's not what I thought it would be."

Her mother nodded slowly, her gaze softening. "Yes, darling. I understand. I really do."

Holly wiped her mouth with her napkin, then set her silverware down on her plate. "Okay, Mom. I'm gonna go. I'm just gonna curl up in bed tonight, watch something classic—a 1930s black-and-white, I think. One of the old classics, they've been calling me lately."

Her mother smiled, though there was something wistful in her eyes. "Okay. Enjoy your show, darling. Remember, try to relax and don't worry so much—fear and frustration do not help. You are stronger than you think—trust me. I'm sure good things are coming your way."

Holly nodded, "Okay, Mom", standing up from the table. She didn't look back as she left the room, and left the house, her footsteps heavy.

She drove away from her mother's house, passing the old farms as she headed into the newer part of town. Her home was nestled in a five-year-old neighborhood of closely built houses, each one echoing the sameness of the development. It was nice, but she preferred the more spacious area where her mother's house stood—the place where she had grown up.

After Holly left, her mother walked into the back office, closing the door softly behind her, moving with quiet purpose. Lowering herself into her dark leather chair, she sat at the desk, her gaze locking onto an open book before her.

At the center of the page, a meticulously drawn Christian cross stood stark against the parchment. Beneath it, written in perfect, flowing cursive, were the words:

"730 White."

Holly's mother traced her finger beneath the drawing, her touch slow, deliberate. When she reached the words, she tapped the page gently—once, twice—before exhaling through her nose, as if coming to some unspoken decision.

She reached for the main desk drawer, sliding it open with practiced ease. From within, she pulled out a small silver chain, the cool metal glinting under the soft glow of the desk lamp.

At the end of the chain hung a silver crucifix.

For a moment, she simply held it there, suspended in the dim light, her fingers wrapped lightly around the delicate chain. Then, ever so slightly, she lifted it higher, bringing it before her eyes.

The crucifix swayed gently, back and forth, back and forth, catching the light with each slow arc.

Her breath steadied. Her lips parted as if to speak, but no words came.

Chapter 6

Anthony Scolati sat at his desk, the soft glow of the green-glass lamp casting a warm circle of light over his open book. His fingers traced the pages with precision as he read, his lips silently repeating each cherished word. This time alone with his religious books was his sanctuary—a moment when the world faded away, leaving only the comforting embrace of his faith.

To Anthony, nothing compared to those hours spent at his desk in the front room of his small house. His love for God and his devotion to his church were woven through every fiber of his being; these passages were more than words—they were life itself. With each sentence, he felt as if he were speaking directly with the holy spirit—a quiet conversation that stirred his heart and filled him with peace. There was no better way, he believed, to spend his free time than in communion with these spiritual texts, the timeless wisdom drawing him ever closer to the presence he adored.

Anthony was deep in his training to become a priest, immersing himself in all things religious—in everything pertaining to the spirit of the the Divine. From a young age, he had been a devout Catholic, his faith unwavering regardless of how exotic or obscure the texts he encountered might be. His religious fervor deepened with his coming of age, and his studies were driven by a singular purpose: he sought to be a vessel for the healing light of God—a force to exorcise demonic spirits and save wandering souls. Anthony saw himself as an agent of the Divine's will, a future exorcist perhaps nearly as important as the Right Hand of God—one who could push back the darkness, though he tried to dismiss that thought as pride. He dared to imagine that someday he would wield the power to confront and defeat evil itself.

His current study focused on an old Catholic text from the 1600s, *Of Exorcisms and Certain Supplications*—a tome he devoured with both reverence and urgency. He traced his finger beneath each sentence as he read, letting each word settle into his mind. Every line felt weighty, brimming with wisdom and purpose. He studied with intense, determined focus, taking each word to heart. This was more than theology; this was his path—the most serious and solemn teachings he had ever encountered.

The previous night, as sleep began to overtake him, Anthony experienced something extraordinary: a waking vision, vivid and unmistakable. A figure of golden light appeared before him, parting the shadows in his bedroom, and urged him to exorcise a dark spirit from a certain woman's body. He saw her clearly—her brown hair disheveled, her eyes wild with torment, blood smeared across her mouth and chin, and a look of horror etched on her face. He knew that when he encountered her, he would recognize her immediately. And he would be ready. He felt certain that God's light would be his weapon to drive out the darkness and banish whatever unholy spirit resided within her.

The vision ignited something powerful in Anthony—a sense

of urgency unlike any he had felt before. He had been handed a sacred charge, a message delivered directly from an angel. This divine calling filled him with an electric excitement, imbuing his mind with purpose and energizing his studies in a way he had never experienced. He understood that all his years of training, devotion, and prayer had been leading him to this moment, this new stage in his life. This was his heritage coming to fruition. This was his purpose.

The room was hushed, the lamp's gentle light casting shadows across the desk. He was nearly finished reading—just one final paragraph remained—when a sudden distraction stole his attention.

Tap, tap... tap, tap.

The sound drifted from the back of his modest home, emanating near the back door just beyond the kitchen. Visitors were a rarity, and they never knocked at the back door. Besides, this was no insistent knock but a delicate tapping—more like the tiptoe of a small creature or the faint touch of wind-tossed debris along the siding.

Anthony set his bookmark with care beneath the paragraph he had just read and rose to investigate. Silently, he left the front room, gliding through the kitchen and into the laundry room, where the back door waited. Flicking on the back porch light, he peered through the door's small window. Outside, everything appeared undisturbed and still; the tapping had ceased as mysteriously as it had begun. Perhaps a bird or a small animal had paused at his door, only to move on when it found no invitation. He listened for another moment but heard nothing more than his own measured breathing.

Returning to the kitchen, he paused on the pristine white

tiles. His stomach reminded him it was time to eat. Although his thoughts lingered on the ancient text he had been studying, he decided to begin dinner—a comforting routine that promised solace amid the night's subtle unease.

He filled a saucepan with water and set it on the stove, turning the burner to high. As he retrieved a bag of pasta and his salt container from the cupboards, he considered his plan for the evening. After dinner, he would perform his nightly ritual: methodically tidying his space as if consecrating it. Clearing his desk, putting away his books, and straightening every surface brought him a quiet focus, a fitting prelude to the deeper work of prayer and reflection that would follow.

Leaving the kitchen, he flicked on the hallway light and made his way toward the bathroom, his hand caressing the chain of his silver necklace, which held his most cherished trinket—a small, silver crucifix he polished with devout care.

He suddenly stopped midway down the hall. A small smudge of mud on the white-tiled floor had caught his eye. Frowning, he bent down to examine the faint streak of dirt, puzzled by its presence in his meticulously kept home. Stepping into the bathroom, he gathered a few squares of tissue and carefully wiped away the unexpected blemish.

How did that get here? he wondered. His home, with its white walls and floors, was his sanctuary—a pristine haven, a personal little heaven, always kept meticulously clean.

After ensuring the corridor was spotless, he began a rhythmic murmuring of the Lord's Prayer as he entered the bathroom and shut the door behind him.

"Pater noster, qui es in caelis..."

The familiar cadence of the prayer in Latin soothed him, each syllable rolling off his tongue, a soothing incantation.

As he emerged from the bathroom, he continued softly,

"...*sanctificetur nomen tuum*"

The ancient words resonated in the quiet, their comforting rhythm a bulwark against the unease of worldly life.

Yet, as he stepped back into the kitchen and gazed at the water in the saucepan, a chill of inexplicable dread prickled at his awareness. Something was off. His eyes darted over the countertops and the stovetop, and then his nostrils caught a rich, loamy scent—a fragrance of fresh soil that did not belong indoors.

He stood frozen in disbelief, his breath caught in his throat. The scent of damp earth clung to the air—thick, loamy, unnatural. It did not belong here. His home was a sanctuary of order, a place where the scent of freshness and cleaning supplies should have lingered, not this unsettling, earthen aroma.

His eyes flicked across the room, scanning every detail with methodical precision. Then—there. A single, dark smudge of mud marred the otherwise pristine white tiles near his feet, stark against the spotless floor.

A shiver crept down his spine as he knelt, reaching out with tentative fingers. His fingertips brushed against the smear, the damp residue cool against his skin. His stomach tightened. *Impossible.* His home was immaculate. His shoes had been left neatly at the door, as always. He had walked these floors in nothing but dress socks—there was no way he had tracked this in.

"*Adveniat regnum tuum...*"

Slowly, he straightened, his heartbeat a dull thunder in his ears. The tiny hairs along his arms and the back of his neck bristled as an almost imperceptible draft of cool air touched his skin.

"...fiat voluntas...", he continued his prayer

His gaze drifted toward the front room. At first, everything seemed as it should be—the lamp on his desk still glowed softly, his book lay exactly where he had left it, undisturbed. But something felt wrong. The unease slithered deeper into his gut as his eyes focused.

Then, he saw it.

The front door wasn't fully shut. It stood open—just a few inches—but enough for a thin ribbon of night air to coil its way into the house. Enough to explain the draft.

His throat tightened. His lips barely moved as he began whispering his prayer once more, the words spilling from him with a newfound urgency—

"...sicut in caelo et in terra..."

His fingers fumbled in his pocket, grasping for his cell phone. The cool surface of the device met his palm, and he clutched it as if it were a lifeline. His thumb hovered over the emergency call button, sweat dampening his grip.

Was he overreacting? The rational part of his mind fought to assert itself. *Had he left the door open earlier and simply not clicked it shut?*

Yet his body told a different story. His hand trembled. His breath came shallow and rapid, each inhale laced with the sharp tang of adrenaline. His instincts screamed at him— something was wrong—call the police. But he hesitated, breathing, wondering...

The silence pressed in around him, thick and stifling.

Then, without warning—

In a blur of motion, a gigantic, mud-caked hand slammed into his own, sending his phone crashing to the floor with a shattering crack.

Anthony gasped, eyes wide with horror.

A searing pain exploded in his hand—the bones shattering—sending shockwaves of agony up his arm. Instinctively, he clutched his injured hand, but before he could cry out, the same filthy hand reached from behind and clamped over his mouth, silencing his scream. Another massive hand, black as night, wrapped around the back of his neck, pinning him with inhuman strength.

He struggled desperately, twisting his shoulders in vain, but the relentless grip held him like iron.

A nauseating chemical stench filled the air—a sharp, acrid odor of decay and earth that seeped into his senses, poisoning his mind, his lungs. His vision blurred. His strength ebbed.

He was helpless.

Suspended in midair by one of the colossal hands, Anthony felt a cold, crushing pressure around his neck, and then—

Crunch.

His vertebrae gave way.

His body instantly turned numb.

His limbs dangled helplessly like a marionette. His eyes caught sight of the other hand—slick with black sludge—reaching slowly for the light switch.

With a deliberate, unsettling motion, the hand flipped the switch off, plunging the room into darkness.

In the faint afterglow of the lamp in the next room, he saw the huge hands release him, setting him down on the cold kitchen floor.

Just as a spark of hope flared within him—maybe the beast would leave him alone now— a heavy, woven black sack was forced over his head, muffling his weak whimpering cry. The air inside was stale and dank, saturated with the musty scent of earth and decay.

The ghastly hands folded him entirely into the sack, tucking every limb with eerie precision—as if he were a paper doll.

Inside the oppressive darkness of the black bag, his heart pounded furiously, yet his body lay heavy and immobile, paralyzed and trapped within the woven confines.

Overhead, the shadowed figure crouched low, its face hidden beneath layers of dark, viscous muck. With slow, deliberate movements, it pulled the sack's drawstrings tight, cinching the fabric around Anthony's body until it molded like a second skin, each tug squeezing the air from his lungs.

As the sack closed in, any lingering traces of consciousness were swallowed by the overwhelming blackness.

Anthony's final breaths dissipated into silence.

He sank beyond sleep—into a profound stillness amid the suffocating embrace.

Anthony's life slipped away.

"Tum-Grissell," the creature rumbled.

Its voice was deep and resonant as the ancient earth, imbued with a solemn, final authority. The name hung in the air like a decree.

In one fluid motion, the mud creature hoisted the sack over its shoulder, Anthony's lifeless form dangling within like a grim relic.

It moved through the house with silent precision, as if intimately acquainted with every shadow.

Pausing at Anthony's desk, it extinguished the green-glass reading lamp, plunging the room into absolute darkness.

Then, without another sound, it glided through the front door and disappeared into the waiting night—leaving behind only the faint, lingering scent of damp earth, a silent witness to the horror that had unfolded.

Chapter 7

H olly sat at her desk in the dimly lit insurance office—
just another day on the job. The main room was
eerily silent, save for the soft hum of the fluorescent
lights above. She was alone, surrounded by filing cabinets and
the towering stacks of paperwork that seemed to multiply
overnight. Bundles of untouched documents littered her
desk, a testament to the never-ending workload that only
she seemed to work through.

But instead of tackling the mountain of forms, Holly's
attention was fixed elsewhere.

Through the glass walls of his office, her boss, Mr. Warren,
lounged comfortably in his chair, feet propped up on his desk,
grinning like a man without a single care in the world. His
laughter burst through the stillness of the office, sharp and
grating.

Holly hunched over her desk, scowling as she glared at the
paperwork before her.

"Mr. Warren—Mr. Annoying," she grumbled under her
breath, voice dripping with irritation. "He never does anything. Meanwhile, I get to drown in all this mind-numbing
paperwork while he spends the entire day yapping on the
phone with his obnoxious friends—lucky me." She let out

an exaggerated sigh, flicking a stray paper aside as if simply moving it could make the pile smaller.

She worked at Bryndelle Insurance, which was the town's lifeline, the premier provider that no one in town dared stray from. It had a monopoly on the town's financial security, and with that came an unrelenting flood of work. The paperwork never stopped. It flowed in like a relentless tide, an ocean of forms, policies, and claims that Holly alone seemed to be responsible for. Meanwhile, Warren contributed nothing but background noise.

Her eyes flicked back to his office, where he sat reclined, phone still pressed to his ear. Another chuckle, another easygoing smirk. Her fingers curled into fists. Oh, to be so blissfully useless and still collect the lion's share of the profits—he owned the business, after all—inherited just a decade ago.

She forced herself to focus back on the work, grinding her teeth as she sighed. If she didn't do it, no one would.

"Okay, Dave, yeah… I'm heading to get it now. Yeah, it's faster than the last one, so, you know, it's gonna be good. Okay, I'll talk to you later."

Holly could hear every word of his conversation, his booming voice effortlessly cutting through the glass walls whenever he got excited.

With a final laugh, Mr. Warren ended the call, stood, and strolled out of his office. He stopped beside Holly's desk, waiting for her to acknowledge him. She plastered on a polite expression, masking her irritation as she looked up.

"Hey, I'm gonna be gone for a few hours—probably the rest of the day," he announced, flashing his signature self-satisfied grin. "I need you to lock up tonight. I'm picking up my new car. Take care of everything while I'm gone."

He paused, as if suddenly struck by a thought. "Oh, almost forgot… I need you to handle the cleaning around here for a while. The cleaning lady quit last week, so it's up to you until I find a replacement. Cleaning stuff's in the utility closet—you know where everything is. Make sure the bathroom sparkles, too. Don't be afraid to get your hands dirty."

He didn't wait for a response.

He turned on his heel and strode toward the front door, then suddenly stopped, glancing back. "Oh, and make sure you finish cleaning up before you head out tonight. Don't want the mess to linger overnight."

With that, he walked out, hopped into his SUV, and sped off, leaving Holly staring after him, speechless.

For a long moment, she just sat there, gazing out the window, her face unreadable.

Finally, she exhaled and muttered, "I really can't stand that guy… this job… and this whole stupid, boring town."

The words slipped out like a confession to the empty room.

Hours later, Holly found herself kneeling on the grimy tile of the office bathroom, scrubbing the toilet with a look of utter disgust. The sharp scent of disinfectant burned her nose as she scoured away stubborn stains, her frustration simmering just below the surface.

"Oh! This is so gross… a full week of customers and I'm stuck cleaning up after everyone."

She moved to the sink, wiping away water spots from the mirror, erasing careless smudges left by people who never thought twice about the effort it took to clean up after them. Finally, with a heavy sigh, she grabbed the mop, dipped it into the soapy bucket, and began dragging it across the floor, the faint squeak of the mop handle echoing in the confined space.

As she worked, she muttered sarcastically, "Wow, look at me—living my dream life, cleaning up after Mr. Warren and a bunch of disgusting people."

She rolled her eyes and glanced at her reflection in the now-spotless mirror, almost daring it to talk back.

Chapter 8

The mountains cradling Hidden Lake were a study in contrasts—jagged and rugged in some places, yet softened elsewhere by dense clusters of ancient trees, tangled underbrush, and small, swampy pools. At the loftier elevations, the landscape was dominated by crumbly white limestone, its surface intermittently broken by scattered meadows and venerable pines that clung stubbornly to the stony earth. Below, in the valleys and gorges, open clearings rimmed with marshy patches yielded to dense forests where towering pines and the leaves of quaking aspens rustled secrets into the wind.

Not far from a slender inlet stream that meandered gracefully toward Hidden Lake lay a secret realm—a labyrinth of abandoned mine shafts, natural caves, and deep grottos. These secluded enclaves, concealed from prying eyes and accessible only by a handful of winding, narrow paths, had become the domain of the few small creatures that wandered too far—and of the watchful stewards of the forest—the coven. Among them, none were more respected than the Grand-Witch herself—the ancient and enigmatic Gaeldritch.

As evening descended and the sun dipped low, painting the sky in hues of fire, Gaeldritch embarked on a crucial task. With measured urgency, she navigated the twisting main trail, scurrying from her underground hovel toward the small stream she called *Mikadom*, where the cool waters of the inlet spilled into Hidden Lake—*Makodom* is the word she used to refer to the large lake. Ever faithful to her heritage, Gaeldritch had bestowed these landmarks with names in the tongue of her childhood, the ancient Latin of the old country, each syllable a link to her world that had long since faded into history.

Excitement flickered within her as she hurried along the path, her ornate staff held as a scepter of dominion. Climbing from the rocky trails into the dense embrace of underbrush, she found herself beneath towering pines that arched overhead, their dark boughs forming a cathedral of shadows. The evening light, filtering through the swaying branches, cast an amber tapestry upon the forest floor, a shifting mosaic of dusk and fire.

A short distance from the path Gaeldritch glided through, a young woman in a black robe stood in silence. Her jet-black hair framed a face marked by a curious and unsettling tattoo-like painting on her face—a series of black lines drawn at awkward angles across her face, back-and-forth, a strange sigil with some hidden meaning. With delicate precision, the young woman tied a tangle of black thread around a pine branch—perhaps a snare for a small creature, or a cryptic warning to those who might dare encroach upon the coven's sacred grounds.

As Gaeldritch passed the young witch, she cast a sharp, piercing glance in her direction. At once, the girl lowered her eyes in silent deference, acknowledging the presence of her superior. The exchange was brief, wordless, yet heavy with meaning. Satisfied, Gaeldritch turned her attention back to the path ahead, her mind fixed on the long-awaited task before her.

After several hundred more feet, the trail abruptly ended in a barrier of dense tangled brush and thick pine boughs. Without breaking stride, Gaeldritch raised her staff before her, and the surrounding vegetation parted at her silent command, revealing a narrow passage twisting through the thick forest. As she moved through the dense brush and bramble, her staff held aloft, the green sea of foliage parted before her, while in her wake, the brush and pine boughs collapsed back into place, sealing off all trace of the hidden trail.

She would reach her destination and wait patiently until sunrise, when the ritual would commence. As she continued along the winding trail beneath the ancient trees, she repeatedly whispered softly to herself,

"Tang laskrow, ting laskroy,
Dread, flood the blood,
Sacred thread, never dead."

Chapter 9

Holly woke up in the early dawn of the morning, sat up in bed, and stretched, ready to start her Sunday. She yawned, hopped out of bed, and headed into the bathroom to freshen up and brush her teeth. She then went to her walk-in closet and dressed for jogging—she was planning an endurance run today and was longing to be immersed in nature.

In the kitchen, she made herself a hearty breakfast of bacon, eggs, toast, and a nice cup of black coffee. As she ate, she browsed a bird-watching website on her laptop, contemplating how birds are so free-spirited with such elegance.

Picking up her phone, she dialed her mother. "Hi, Mom. Yeah, I'm heading to the lake today to run laps. The mountains have been calling me. I need to get out into nature and away from my soul-sucking office."

Her mother replied, "Yes, you need to go to the lake today. Next Sunday, you will go up there again, perhaps? Being in nature does your spirit well. The lake is such a special place, it's just beautiful and full of wonder...and life."

"Yeah, I've been thinking about it all week, Mom." Holly agreed. "I so want to get out of town. I need to get away from the suburbs and I'm looking forward to some alone time today, anyway. Ryan's been so condescending the last few times we've talked—I've been avoiding him the last few weeks, it's just not doing it for me. He thinks because he's rich he's better than everyone else. He keeps suggesting we take our relationship to the next level, blah, blah, blah—that's a hard no from me. Yeah, I'm just not into him. Anyway, I'm heading out now. I'll take pictures of any birds I see up there and send them to you."

"That's perfect, darling, I look forward to hearing all about it." her mother replied warmly. "Oh, and Wednesday, Thomas is coming to dinner with his new acquaintance, Julie. I need you to join us."

"Oh, a new girlfriend, eh? Okay, I'll try to make it. Love you, mom. Talk to you later."

"Love you, darling. Have a wonderful day."

Holly ended the call, grabbed her backpack with a few snacks, and jumped into her car. The drive to the lake was perfect: beautiful, never any traffic heading to the lake, and she felt great. She pulled into the parking lot, got out, and stretched, glad to see she was the only person there. "All by my lonesome—heaven," she murmured to herself. She set off on a fast-paced jog on the dirt trail along the lake edge.

After completing the first lap, she muttered, "Six miles down—not bad, about an hour," then began her second lap at a steady pace. A quarter of the way through her next lap, she felt a need deep down in her core to stop for a minute and take in the scene. She paused to soak in the sounds and sights of the lake.

She was standing beside a small stream, its gentle song echoing in her ears as it poured over the rock falls and tumbled into the lake below. Sunlight danced on the rippling water, turning it into a ribbon of silver winding through the forest. She looked up-stream toward the source of the crystalline water, listening to the chatter as it coursed away from moss-covered rocks.

Where does that begin? she wondered, gazing into the shaded creek beyond. It seemed to vanish into mystery, from a hidden source deep in the cover of the foliage, like a secret tucked away in the heart of the forest, just waiting to be discovered.

A bird called to her from somewhere above the stream, its song sharp and strange—a melody she'd never heard before. *What kind of bird is that? That's a new one*, she thought, tilting her head and squinting toward the direction of the sound. As her gaze followed the stream upward, she noticed a narrow, nearly hidden trail alongside it, a faint path of impacted earth and green-colored rocks woven into the underbrush.

Just then, something farther upstream caught her eye—a glint of light flickering through the trees, shimmering on the water's surface. *What was that?* she wondered, *a piece of quartz in the stream?*

Curiosity sparked, and without a second thought, Holly began following the faint trail upward, stepping carefully over roots and stones, her eyes fixed on the hidden glimmer ahead. The forest grew quieter as she ventured up a steep incline, deeper and deeper into the forest. The mystery seemed to pull her forward, as if the stream itself was leading her toward some secret paradise to be discovered.

The sound of water rushing over rocks reminded her of crystal chimes banging together in the wind, filling the air with a soft, enchanting music. Holly smiled to herself. "It's so beautiful here—like I'm in a green tunnel with a sparkling crystal floor," she muttered to herself, marveling at how the sunlight filtered through the trees, casting dappled patterns on the mossy ground.

The strange bird called again from somewhere above, its song rising like a beckoning note. Her interest deepened, and she thought, *Mom would know what bird that is. If I could just get a glimpse of it - a photo, it'd be a real treasure.*

She continued upward along the stream, stepping carefully over damp stones, her attention shifting between the glinting water and the dense canopy above. The glimmer she had seen below had disappeared but she didn't care, she was loving the sense of discovery as she stepped forward.

Eventually, the narrow trail began to disappear, swallowed by thick clusters of bushes and tangled vines. She scanned the stream's bed but saw no sign of the mysterious quartz she was hoping to find scattered on the stream bed under the running clear water. Yet, the setting was so beautiful, so serene, she didn't mind at all. The untouched wildness around her felt like its own hidden treasure, urging her onward, deeper into the green world ahead.

Holly stepped onto the rocks in the stream bed, gracefully hopping from one to the next, the thrill of the wilderness filling her with energy. She must have gone nearly a mile before she stopped to catch her breath, taking in the wild scenery around her. Quaking aspens and pine trees arched overhead, their leaves and branches creating a cathedral of green, while the stream babbled over the stones beneath her feet.

Just then, something unusual caught her eye—small, dark bundles hanging from the branches of a nearby tree. She squinted, stepping closer. "What the hell are those?" she muttered under her breath.

Her heart quickened as she moved in for a better look. Her eyes widened as she realized what they were: small, lifeless animals hanging upside down, each wrapped tightly in what looked like strands of black fishing line. They swayed gently with the breeze, almost as though they were watching her in silent greeting.

A chill crept over her, breaking the spell of the peaceful forest.

In her peripheral vision she saw a slight movement. As she turned to see it's source, her heart seized—standing before her was a black-robed figure cloaked in shadows and silence. Her breath caught as the figure drew back its hood, revealing slick, pitch-black hair framing a face touched by the forest itself: skin pale-gray and rough, as though brushed by death, deeply lined with the ages. It was the old witch.

Holly stood frozen in shock as Gaeldritch lifted a gnarled, bony hand, her fingers twisted like ancient branches, and pointed directly at her. Her cold, fathomless eyes glinted with purpose, locking onto Holly with a gaze that seemed to pierce her soul. Then, in a voice like crackling leaves, she hissed a single word.

"*Gou-zistrica!*", the ancient and potent word of power resonated.

The air seemed to vibrate, carrying the weight of the spell as it washed over Holly, rippling the air around her with constriction. Before she could react, her vision blurred, and her body suddenly felt impossibly heavy. She staggered, her knees buckling under the word's weight, and within moments, the world around her faded to black as she fell into a deep, unyielding sleep.

Gaeldritch deftly approached within reach of Holly in a split second as her body went slack, her head falling back, and with a gentleness that was oddly unnerving, Gaeldritch caught hold of her mid-fall and eased her to the ground, the spidery grasp of her ancient hand cradling Holly's head. The old witch paused, gazing at the young girl's face, then ran her fingers slowly across Holly's head in a series of circular, rhythmic motions, Holly's breathing now deep and steady under the witch's spell.

A dark glint flickered in Gaeldritch's eyes as she pressed her fingertips to Holly's scalp, feeling the girl's pulse beneath. Her gnarled fingers began to shift, and from beneath her blackened nails, thin black threads, thicker than strands of hair, snaked outward. The worm-like threads wriggled along Holly's skin, moving with unnatural purpose. They traced her hairline, slithering across her temples and around her ears, then burrowed one by one beneath her scalp, each thread vanishing as it disappeared under her skin.

Gaeldritch's eyes rolled up into her head, her face creasing in joy, as she exhaled and let out a soft moan of ecstasy.

The last of the threads sank in, leaving no mark, yet something seemed different about Holly's face—an odd stillness settled over her features, her expression almost tranquil. The old witch whispered an incantation: "*Sit metamorphosin fieri cursim utcumque sumptus hiktilda!*" ending with another short moan of joy.

Gaeldritch then removed her hand from Holly's scalp, staring down at her unconscious body, standing above her. She then clenched her bony hand into a fist, then slowly unfurled it, her fingers coiling and extending with a deliberate rhythm. She repeated the motion a few times—clenching her hand into a fist, and extending her long fingers—before leaning back, a satisfied smile curling her thin lips. Her gaze, heavy with a sense of finality, fixed on Holly as she muttered, "*Factum est.* It is done!", and then smacked her palms together with a sharp clap.

Chapter 10

Holly stirred groggily, gradually coming to her senses. She lay on the dirt, on the small side-stream trail, not fifty feet away from the main lake-edge trail. She felt disoriented and saw that the sun was low on the horizon. *What happened?*, she thought. "Oh, damn," she murmured. "I've got to get out of here—it'll be dark soon." Bewildered, she stood and brushed herself off and began walking back to the main lake trail, eventually reaching her car just as the sun started to set. "Oh no, I feel so dizzy and sick," she muttered, rubbing her head, "I think I slipped and hit my head or something."

I can't remember what the hell I've been doing, she worriedly realized. She could only remember arriving at the lake and beginning her run, but everything else up to when she just woke up was just drawing a blank.

Driving home in a daze, Holly barely registered the familiar streets passing by. She gripped the steering wheel tightly, her mind feeling slow and foggy. She eventually pulled into her garage in a daze and closed it behind her, stepped out of the car, and, without bothering to turn on any house lights, walked into the house and straight to her bedroom.

Sitting on the edge of her bed, she felt the weight of

exhaustion settle over her. She pulled her cell phone out and dialed her mother's number, needing to hear a familiar voice.

When her mother answered, Holly tried to keep her tone light. "Hey, Mom. I'm back. The hike was... nice, but something strange happened. I think I might have passed out on the trail and hit my head—it's all a bit fuzzy. I think I'll...I think I need to go to the doctor tomorrow, just to make sure everything's okay. I'm so tired."

Her mother's warm voice was like a balm. "I'm sure you're fine, darling. You're stronger and healthier than you know. A little bump on the head won't keep you down. The lake was good for you—trust me."

Holly smiled, feeling some of the tension leave her shoulders. "Thanks, Mom. I think so too. But... I'll get checked out just to be safe." She hesitated, feeling very tired. "Okay...I need to go. Goodnight, Mom."

"Goodnight, darling," her mother replied softly, her voice full of love.

As Holly hung up, she glanced toward her bedroom window—all was still. The only sound was the hum of the house settling around her, grounding her in its warmth and safety. She lay back for a few minutes before realizing she needed a hot shower to clean up.

The hot water running over her tired body felt like a healing salve. Some of the confusion from earlier washed away with the dirt and grime. As she was close to finishing her shower and washing her hair, she brought her hand down from her head and noticed something clinging to her hand—a nickle sized, glossy black spider gripped across the top of her hand. She screamed, flailing her hand in a frenzy, flinging

50

the spider into the bottom of the tub next to the drain. The spider scurried against the flow of water rushing to the drain, fighting to escape, it's legs moving in a blur.

Holly jumped out of the shower, wrapped herself in a towel, and turned the water as hot as it would go, letting it run, watching the spider eventually get washed down the small space under the drain seal. She watched the water swirl down the drain for a few seconds longer before closing it, muttering, "Not climbing back up here, you creepy bug." She pondered for a moment, *I wonder if that disgusting thing has been in my hair since the lake?,* then muttered in disgust as that possibility sunk in, "Ugh, I can't even.., that's so gross!"

She gazed at her reflection in the mirror and let out a weary sigh. "What a day. First, I hit my head, and then I get attacked by a massive spider. Just nasty."

Exhausted after the ordeals of the day, she put on her pajamas, crawled into bed, and turned on a classic horror movie to fall asleep to. Within minutes, Holly's eyelids shut, pulling her into a deep sleep.

Chapter 11

Julie Winthrop sat alone in her cozy house, a sanctuary she had lovingly claimed as her own just a year ago. Modest and square, it stood with quiet resilience, its white-painted bricks lending it an air of pristine simplicity. It was not grand, nor imposing, but something about its sturdy structure gave her comfort, as if the very walls had been fashioned to guard against unseen evils.

Nestled in the older part of town, the house sat just seven blocks East from the quaint city center, where old-fashioned street lamps bathed sidewalks in pools of warm, flickering light. Small, timeworn shops lined the streets, their wooden signs swaying gently in the night breeze. She had always loved the serenity of this place, the way life moved at an unhurried pace, untouched by the chaos of the outside world.

Yet tonight, there was an unease in the stillness.

A devout Catholic, Julie found solace in her daily prayers, the ritual grounding her in something larger than herself. As bedtime approached, she prepared for her final prayer of the day—her prayer before going to sleep. She knelt beside her bed, crossing herself with reverence before pressing her palms together, fingers pointed toward heaven. With bowed head, she whispered the familiar words, her lips moving in silent devotion, each syllable a tether to her faith in the divine.

After she finished, she lingered in the stillness, as she often did, drawing comfort from the tranquility of the quiet. But as she moved to stand, a strange weakness settled in her limbs. A sudden wave of dizziness overtook her, and she sank back down, hands bracing against the floor.

The air around her thickened, warm and strangely dense, pressing against her skin with an almost sentient presence. It wasn't just fatigue—no, this was something else entirely. A hush fell over the room, deeper than silence, as though the very fabric of reality had shifted.

Then it came.

A tremor passed through her body as her vision blurred, consciousness flickering like a candle caught in the wind. And then—light.

Golden and radiant, it consumed everything, flooding her mind with a brilliance that was neither blinding nor harsh, but warm and all-encompassing. It wrapped around her like a celestial embrace, telling of something vast and ineffable.

From somewhere beyond the light, she heard it—the rhythmic, ceaseless crashing of ocean waves. She forced herself to breath in and out, and not panic, an attempt to accept the experience without resistance. The sound of the waves in her mind rolled and crashed, a lullaby of the deep, powerful forces moving through her. But soon, the tide of sound began to shift. The waves faded, transforming into something new.

Trumpets. And then more.

A great symphony of brass, their voices rich and sonorous, swelling in perfect harmony. The notes resonated not just in her ears but within her very soul, vibrating through her, a chorus of the heavens.

She felt herself being lifted, drawn toward something luminous, something sacred just beyond the edge of understanding. Peace washed over her like water gliding in a rush, unlike anything she had ever known.

Then—darkness.

The golden light flickered.

A picture unfurled before her inner-vision.

A woman's mouth, lips parted, crimson blood trickling down in slow, viscous streams.

A silver crucifix, gleaming in the dimness, held aloft as though warding off an encroaching force.

A shadow—shapeless yet sentient, writhing, waiting, breathing.

And then—letters.

Brilliant, burning letters, each one flashing across her mind in searing golden light, flames extending from their edges. Over and over, they pulsed, unwavering against the consuming dark.

H... O... L... Y...

H... O... L... Y...

And then—darkness and silence.

The visions vanished in an instant. The golden light was gone. The music had muted. The warmth had dissipated.

She opened her eyes.

She was back in her bedroom.

Julie gasped, her body shuddering from the force of the experience. She clutched at the bedsheets, her breath coming in slow, measured inhales. But the memories lingered—haunting and immutable, etched into the very fibers of her being.

And then—

A voice in her mind.

Deep. Clear. Unyielding. Startling.

Have courage.

Be alert.

It rang through her like a bell struck in the hollow of her mind. Not a question, not an echo, but a command. A call to vigilance. A warning.

Her heart pounded as she sat motionless, absorbing the enormity of what had just transpired. Slowly, she reached up and traced the sign of the cross over herself, her fingers ghosting over her forehead, heart, and shoulders, as if to seal in the sacred energy still crackling in the air.

With unsteady hands, she reached for her crucifix that dangled around her neck, clutching it tightly in her palm. The cool metal pressed against her skin, anchoring her back to reality.

She crawled into her bed and lay back against her pillow, staring at the ceiling, her mind racing.

This was no ordinary dream.

She had been called. She was excited to have a received a vision from the divine, or perhaps an angel had visited her— she wasn't sure exactly what or how it happened but it had happened—it was real. She felt gifted and was excited to have been chosen.

The meaning was not yet clear, but one thing was certain— her path had been set in motion. She did not know what she would face in the coming days, nor what purpose had been placed upon her shoulders.

But she knew this:

She had a calling, a mission.

Chapter 12

Holly awoke shrouded in a haze of exhaustion, as if sleep had been nothing more than a fleeting illusion. Her limbs felt weighed down by an invisible force, and every small movement—each attempt to lift her head from the pillow—required monumental effort. As the soft, intrusive light of dawn crept through her window, a thought bubbled up: she needed to schedule a doctor's appointment. The unsettling feeling of what had happened at the lake still lingered, a feeling that something was amiss.

With a tired hand, she reached for her phone and dialed the doctor's office. In mere moments, an appointment was secured for 8:30 the following morning. Arriving late to work was a minor inconvenience she was happy to accept, especially amid the relentless frustrations that had lately punctuated her work days.

While dressing in the muted early light, an unusual, prickling sensation began to spread across her scalp. It was delicate and fleeting at first, reminiscent of the softest contact of a mosquito's touch. Yet, as she ran a brush through her hair, the sensation escalated—transforming into a sharp, maddening itch that demanded attention.

Instinctively, she began to scratch, her fingers digging

fervently into her scalp as if attempting to uproot the source of her irritation. Her nails scraped back and forth, an incredible feeling of relief washing over her, much like the feeling had from the peeling away of parched, flaky skin a few days after a sunburn. Back and forth, she began releasing a soft moan of relief that mingled with the sound of her anxious breathing.

When she finally withdrew her hand, she was met with a small but unexpected sight: a small bundle of the delicate strands of her soft, brown hair were tangled in her fingers and caught in her nails. For a moment, time seemed to slow as she stared at them, her breath catching in her throat. Although it was only a small handful—not enough to cause alarm—it was still unsettling. She didn't like the idea that in a few frantic seconds of scratching, she had unwittingly pulled out a small handful of her hair without a touch of pain.

Determined not to dwell on the small loss, she rolled the errant strands into a tiny ball in her palms and tossed them into the trash with a shake of her head. "Maybe that damn spider bit me on the head," she muttered under her breath, the words tinged with both disbelief and revulsion. "So gross."

At work, the day passed in its usual monotonous rhythm— endless paperwork, ringing phones, and customers with the same routine questions. By lunchtime, she had managed to push aside her unease, focusing instead on the familiar, tedious tasks of the office.

Then a man arrived.

He was older, dressed in a worn tweed suit that smelled faintly of mothballs, his demeanor unremarkable. He approached her desk, withdrawing a check from his pocket.

"Here's my premium.", he said dryly.

As he extended his hand to pass it to her, Holly's breath hitched.

His hand.

It was bony, almost skeletal, its pallor a sickly shade of gray. Long, black fingernails curled from his fingertips, thick and unnatural. A shudder ran down her spine. It was a sight dredged from a nightmare, something inhuman and wrong.

A strangled gasp escaped her lips before she could stop it. Then—she screamed.

The man recoiled, his expression twisting with confusion and alarm. His wide eyes locked onto hers, searching for an explanation.

Holly blinked, her heart hammering in her chest. The sight before her shifted like a mirage.

His hand was normal.

Just an ordinary, aging hand. No gray skin. No blackened nails.

She swallowed hard, her breath unsteady.

Before she could fully process what had just happened, the sharp click of a door opening drew her attention. Mr. Warren emerged from his office, his gaze flicking between Holly and the shaken customer. His expression was unreadable, but the firm edge to his voice made it clear he was not pleased.

"What's going on?" he asked, his tone even but expectant. "Are you alright, sir?"

The older man, still rattled, grumbled as he pressed the check into Warren's hand. "She scared the life out of me!"

Without another word, the man turned and stormed out of the office, leaving a tense silence in his wake.

Holly, mortified, felt heat rise to her cheeks.

"I—I thought I saw a ha—" She caught herself. "A spider,"

she stammered instead, her voice brittle. "I'm so sorry, sir. I'm sorry, Mr. Warren."

Mr. Warren's frown deepened.

Holly rushed to explain, her words tumbling over each other. "I—I fell while jogging on Sunday and hit my head, and I think I hurt my head real bad, I'm dizzy. I think it messed me up. I've been... seeing things."

Her boss folded his arms, his gaze narrowing slightly.

"I have a doctor's appointment in the morning," she added, grasping for anything that might smooth over the situation. "Maybe I have a concussion or something."

For a moment, he said nothing, his eyes piercing.

Then, with a sigh, he shook his head. "Look, I can't afford for you to be having issues at work. If this happens again, we'll need to have a serious talk." His voice was flat, matter-of-fact. With that, he turned and walked back to his office, leaving Holly standing there, her skin still prickling from the encounter.

By the time she finally arrived home, exhaustion weighed on her like a leaden shroud. She moved on autopilot, too drained to do much more than fix herself a quick dinner. The food did little to revive her, and by the time she set down her fork, her body ached for sleep.

She changed into her pajamas and made her way to the bathroom, her movements sluggish. As she reached for her toothbrush, her gaze flicked to the mirror—and she froze.

A small black spot marred the skin of her right cheek, just near her nose.

She frowned, leaning in closer. Ink? It looked like a tiny smudge from a pen, probably from work, an absent-minded touch she hadn't noticed before.

She reached up to scratch at it.

It didn't budge.

A strange unease curled in her stomach. She grabbed a damp towel, pressing it to the mark, rubbing harder—but no matter how much she scrubbed, it wouldn't come off.

Her reflection stared back, unmoved. The mark remained.

"Strange," she murmured, her voice thin in the quiet. But she was too tired to think about it now.

As she turned away from the mirror, something else caught her eye.

A single black thread, about three inches long, clung to the fabric of her pajama top near her shoulder.

She plucked it off without a second thought, rolling it into a tiny ball between her fingers before flicking it into the small bathroom trash can.

With a sigh, she turned off the light and climbed into bed, pulling the covers up to her chin. The TV flickered on, filling the room with a low hum of voices, a familiar comfort against the silence.

Within minutes, she was asleep.

Chapter 13

H olly woke with more energy this morning, though her jaw felt a bit sore. Maybe *I was grinding my teeth last night*, she thought, *or maybe it's a cavity*. She sighed, gently massaging her jaw. "Just what I need—a tooth ache." she muttered.

Holly jumped out of bed and started to get ready for her doctor's appointment and then another day of work at the office.

While brushing her hair, she noticed something unusual: a short, thick black hair poking out of her scalp, standing out among her soft brown strands. It looked like glossy black fishing line. Dropping her brush, she hurriedly examined the strange hair with her fingers. She tugged, but it wouldn't budge. Her stomach turned. Grabbing a pair of scissors from her vanity drawer, she snipped the thick black hair, studying it between her fingers for a few twists before tossing it in the trash.

"Gross… I'm turning into the fly," she muttered, shuddering. Shaking it off, she left the house for her doctor's appointment, trying not to dwell on the disturbing little find.

At the doctor's office, Holly explained everything that had been happening—her fall at the lake, her itching scalp, and the odd black mark that had recently appeared near her nose. The doctor examined her closely, all the usual checks along with examining her eyes and ears, and listening to her heart, and then gave her a reassuring smile.

"Physically, everything looks fine, you are a healthy young woman." the doctor said. "Have you been under any extra stress recently?"

"No, not really under more stress than usual," Holly replied. "Well, I did have a huge spider scare me in the shower on Sunday, but that's about it."

"And what about work? How's work going, Holly?"

"Work is always a bit of a slog-fest. I really don't like it but what are you gonna do?"

The doctor nodded and continued.

"Okay, Holly, you seem healthy. You say you hit your head but I can't see any evidence of that. It seems you may have blacked out but, thankfully, your head doesn't seem to have been hurt. There's no sign of concussion, though we could get you in for a brain scan."

Holly nodded, "Yeah, okay. I don't know. Maybe I did just black out in the bushes."

"As for this black mark…" The doctor leaned in, inspecting the spot on Holly's cheek. "It looks like a beauty mark, just a common mole. You could see a dermatologist if it bothers you, but I think it looks quite nice." The doctor gave Holly a comforting pat on the shoulder. "Sometimes, with fainting—an episode of blacking out—it can leave you with gaps in your memory surrounding the event—it's just the way your brain works. Physically, I think you're fine. You just had a small incident and that's it."

Relieved, Holly thanked her doctor and left to go to work,

pushing the odd details of her morning aside.

The day at the office had been long and monotonous, each passing hour dragging into the next. By the time Holly finally got home, she felt utterly drained. She slipped into her favorite sweat pants and sweater top, relishing the softness against her skin, and decided to channel her lingering frustration into something productive.

Grabbing her cleaning supplies, she headed to the bathroom and set to work. The memory of the spider that had clung to her hand still sent an involuntary shiver down her spine. Determined to banish every trace of it, she scrubbed the bathtub with meticulous care, the rhythmic motion of her hands oddly soothing.

When she was done, the tiles gleamed, and the scent of lemon cleaner filled the air. Satisfied, she washed her hands and collapsed onto the couch. Reaching for her favorite book on birds, she thumbed through its worn pages, savoring the familiar illustrations and facts about her beloved corvid family—crows, ravens, rooks, jackdaws, jays, nutcrackers, and her favorite of all, the magpie.

The magpie's iridescent plumage and mischievous nature always fascinated her, and as she read, she felt a small flicker of peace settle over her—a welcome reprieve from the strange unease that had been lingering in the back of her mind.

She was only half-paying attention when her phone buzzed, its shrill ringtone pulling her out of her reverie. Glancing at the screen, she sighed. It was Ryan—the guy she was dating. If she could even call it that. Their relationship was casual at best, though lately, it felt more like a slow, inevitable fade. Yet Ryan seemed oblivious, clinging to the idea that it was something more, it seemed he couldn't understand why she wasn't infatuated with him—he *was* handsome and his family had plenty of money.

"Hi, Ryan," she answered, keeping her tone deliberately neutral.

The conversation started politely enough, but it dragged on, the seconds ticking by like hours. She offered a few half-hearted responses, nodding out of habit even though he couldn't see her. All the while, her mind wandered back to her bird book, still lying open on the couch.

Finally, she decided to cut it short. "Hey, I need to get going. I'm tired," she said firmly, interrupting him. "I took a fall while running on Sunday, so I'm going to rest tonight. My head hurts so I'll talk to you later, okay?"

Her excuse wasn't true, but it worked. Her head felt fine, she just felt a bit disturbed—a touch *off*. After a brief pause, he relented, and she hung up with Ryan as he gave a 'goodbye' in a condescending and irritated tone of voice.

Leaning back, she let out a long, relieved sigh, her shoulders sinking into the cushions. For now, she had reclaimed her evening from a relationship she knew deep-down she didn't even want.

Holly's stomach rumbled, so she headed to the kitchen and heated some leftovers. She sat down to eat, flipping through her book absently, when she felt a sudden prick against her tongue. She swallowed her bite, running her tongue along her teeth, and felt it again—something sharp, wedged between her molars. Frowning, she went to the bathroom to investigate.

Standing in front of the mirror, she grabbed some floss, but as she leaned in, she saw something dark between her teeth—another glossy black hair sticking out of her gums.

She grabbed tweezers, pinched down on it and tried to pull it out. It slipped at first, but she clenched down tightly and pulled again. An inch of the shiny black thread stretched out of her gums—then another, and another. Her heart raced as she kept pulling, horror and disbelief flooding her mind.

Three inches, then four. What is this? She pulled and kept pulling, a small trickle of red blood and a dark oily liquid oozed from her mouth, over her bottom lip, as the thread continued to be drawn from her gums, painless to her as she yanked. It coiled and clung to her fingers and then dangled into the sink basin. She cried out in horror as it stretched on and on, a few feet of it extending out of her open mouth.

Then—snap! Her back molar popped out, clinging to the black line. She moaned in horror, even though she felt no pain whatsoever from the surprise extraction. She was unable to stop pulling as inch after inch of the dark line emerged from her mouth—pop—another tooth released from her gums, every few inches marked by another tooth—snap—more teeth clinging to it, like red and white beads on a terrible necklace. Blood and a strange black oil dripped from her lips, down her chin and splattered into the sink. Her wide-eyed face was a mess of gore, yet she felt no pain—only a strange compulsion to keep pulling.

She felt her mind spiraling as she continued to draw out the thread, feet of it, each tooth popping out one by one until only a single top front tooth and bottom front tooth remained in her gums, the rest of her teeth pulled from her gums and connected by the thin black line. She looked down at the sink—a sickening spiral of shiny thread dotted with her teeth, glistening with red and black liquid. Her hands were soaked in red and black mixed with saliva, her mouth felt hollow, and, strangely, she started to laugh—to cackle—to maniacally roar with laughter. There was no pain, only surprise at the unexpected horror.

She jolted awake on the couch, her chest heaving and her heart pounding like a drum. Her hands were clutching her jaw, and for a moment, panic consumed her. Frantically, she ran her tongue along her teeth. All there. Everything was fine. But it felt so real.

Still trembling, she stumbled into the bathroom, flipping on the light with unsteady fingers. Leaning close to the mirror, she inspected her teeth, turning her head this way and that, searching for any sign of damage. Nothing. Relief washed over her, and she let out a shaky sigh.

"This is so messed up! Get a grip, Holly," she muttered, wiping the sweat from her brow.

She lingered for a moment, staring into her reflection. Her hair was disheveled, her face pale, and her eyes carried a restless energy she didn't quite recognize. She smirked, attempting to dismiss her unease.

"I guess it's true," she said, her voice lighter now, "we all go a bit crazy sometimes."

She went back to the kitchen, reheated her leftovers, and ate in silence, trying to shake the horrific image from her mind. After dinner, she got into the shower, letting the warm water wash away the tension. When she finally climbed into bed, she put on an old movie for comfort—a good, old black-and-white classic. She smiled as the familiar scenes played, charmed by the film's old-school grit as she drifted to into sleep.

Chapter 14

The next morning, Holly awoke feeling remarkably refreshed, her body humming with vitality. The fatigue of yesterday had evaporated, replaced by a buoyant energy that pulsed through her limbs with the promise of a new day. With an almost childlike exuberance, she sprang from bed, the covers fluttering behind her like cast-off burdens. She slipped into her work clothes with practiced ease, then stood before the mirror, fingers dancing through her hair in swift, fluid motions—taming fly-aways with the grace of someone who had done it a thousand times.

In the kitchen, the morning sunlight streamed through the blinds in golden shafts, illuminating the quiet space as she prepared a modest yet comforting breakfast of eggs and bacon. The sizzle of the pan, the warmth of the rising steam, the scent of salt and butter—it all wove together and pleased her heart and soul. It was a simple meal, but it nourished more than her body; it was familiar, warm, and grounding—the kind of breakfast that sent the message—you're home, life is good.

Once she had savored every bite and meticulously washed her dishes, she slid behind the wheel of her car and pulled out of the driveway, ready to take on whatever the day had in store.

Her morning zeal, however, didn't last long.

The workday settled over her like a dull gray fog. It unfolded with a numbing sameness, a quiet monotony where one moment bled into the next, each task echoing the last. Time dragged, languid and heavy, as if the very air in the office resisted movement. Seated at her desk, surrounded by the familiar drone of her computer and the heating system rumbling in the back closet, Holly's mind began to wander—drifting like a leaf on a breeze to the distant serenity of Hidden Lake. She could almost feel the cool touch of the wind on her skin, hear the rhythmic rustle of the trees and the soft lap of the lake's water against the shore. The mental image of jogging beneath an open sky, feet pounding along a forest trail, filled her with a sudden rush of yearning—a desperate need to move, to breathe, to escape the stale cycle of everyday office life.

That day, her boss, Mr. Warren, spent over an hour on the phone with a woman he seemed disturbingly thrilled to speak with. The conversation, intimate in tone and unrestrained in warmth, echoed through the glass walls of his office, which failed to muffle the whispered flirtations. Holly couldn't help but eavesdrop, listening discreetly, certain that the woman on the other end was not his wife, Susan, but rather a mysterious Anna.

"What a creep," she muttered under her breath, her inner voice tinged with both disapproval and disgust.

When the long day finally stumbled to a close, Holly retreated to her car like a soldier returning from battle. As she turned onto her street and rolled up toward her driveway, her gaze landed on her next-door neighbor—a tall man in his mid-seventies with a mane of thick gray hair and a walrus-like mustache. He was slowly moving through his work, wielding his hedge clippers with mechanical precision, steadily trimming the wild green borders of his yard.

As her car slowed near her driveway, his head turned—abrupt, deliberate—and his eyes locked onto hers. The intensity of his stare hit her like a jolt. It wasn't curiosity or recognition; it was a stern, evaluating gaze that made her stomach tighten. For a brief moment, she glanced down at the dashboard, half-expecting a warning light to be blinking. Was something wrong with her car? Or worse—something wrong with her?

In an effort to dispel the tension, Holly raised a hand in a small, awkward wave, pairing it with a hopeful smile. It lingered, tentative and sincere, but the old man didn't budge. He kept scowling, his face locked in an expression of irritable defiance.

Her smile dropped. She sighed, quiet and defeated.

"Fine! Don't wave, you grumpy old man," she muttered under her breath, her voice tinged with frustration.

She pulled into her garage, parked, and pressed the button to shut the door behind her. As it lowered with a slow mechanical groan, a sense of profound relief washed over her—like a veil drawn between her and the world. Finally, she was home. Safe. Alone. Enclosed within the walls of her sanctuary, where the hum of life outside could be silenced and forgotten.

With a final click of the engine, Holly sat still for a moment, letting the quiet settle around her like a warm blanket. She was ready to shed the irritations of the day, to embrace the soothing rhythms of her evening, to sink into peace.

But the illusion shattered with a single, unwelcome thought:

It's Wednesday.

She sighed.

Of course. Tonight was the planned dinner at her mother's house. She was expected to smile, to chat, to meet her brother Thomas's new girlfriend Julie and act like the picture of familial grace.

A groan escaped her lips as she went inside the house.

She sighed, long and weary, bracing herself for one more performance before the day could truly end. All she really wanted was to eat something simple, crawl into bed, and lose herself in a good movie. Instead, she had to keep her composure intact and her nerves steady just a little while longer.

Chapter 15

Holly was always happy to see her brother, but after the long, draining day at work, she felt mentally exhausted. She thought about canceling, craving nothing more than a quiet night at home, but she knew how much this dinner meant to her mother. It seemed important to her mother that she meet Julie, and Holly didn't want to disappoint her mother.

She took a deep breath, brushing off the lingering frustration from her day, and told herself to rally. Family mattered, and she knew that once she got there, being around them might even lift her exhausted spirits.

Holly stepped into her walk-in closet, carefully selecting an outfit that struck the perfect balance between stylish and understated. She wanted to look polished but not overly formal—after all, it was just a family dinner, albeit an important one. Slipping into a flattering blue dress, she took a moment to assess her reflection. Her long, light-brown hair cascaded in soft, effortless curls, and her makeup was subtle yet enhancing. Satisfied with her appearance, she grabbed her purse and hurried out the door, mindful that she was already running a few minutes late.

Her mother had made it clear—this was a semi-formal

dinner. No sweatpants, no T-shirts. Holly had no intention of making a poor first impression on Thomas's new girlfriend.

When she arrived at her mother's house, she was greeted with warm smiles from her mother, her brother, and Julie. As expected, they were ready to eat, and she was the last to arrive.

Holly's mother, Hannah, always the epitome of grace and sophistication, looked effortlessly elegant. Even in her early fifties, she turned heads wherever she went. Her impeccable style, perfectly coiffed hair, and flawless makeup gave her an air of timeless beauty. She carried herself with a refined charm—poised yet inviting, a woman who knew the power of a well-placed smile.

Thomas, ever the picture of confidence, looked sharp in a well-tailored blazer that accentuated his striking blue eyes. His dark brown hair was neatly styled, a deliberate effort for his date with Julie. Meeting women had never been a challenge for him—he was self-assured, engaging, and kept himself in peak physical condition. His charismatic smile had always been his secret weapon.

Julie, poised and radiant, exuded an effortless elegance. She wore a fitted white dress that complemented her figure beautifully, accentuated by delicate silver jewelry that shimmered under the soft dining room lights, her brown hair radiant and curled perfectly around her neck and shoulders. Every detail of her ensemble, from her polished accessories to her graceful posture, highlighted her femininity. But it was her smile—warm, genuine, and luminous—that truly completed the look.

As they settled in, Holly couldn't help but observe the scene before her. It was a dinner of first impressions and subtle assessments.

Her mother said a quick prayer before they began, "Lord God, we thank You for this bountiful meal before us, and we thank You for this chance to gather and visit with each other, especially for the opportunity to meet and get to know Thomas's new friend, Julie. Amen." Afterward, they all started eating without much conversation.

Holly wondered if the prayer was heartfelt or if her mother was putting on a big show for the sake of Julie. In fact, Holly's mother usually said no prayer before a meal, and when she did, it is was always very short and generic.

Julie looked to be religious—she was wearing a rather large silver crucifix around her neck, and Holly guessed her mother's prayer might have been an effort to make a good impression.

The food was delicious: steak with mashed potatoes and a side of green beans. The calmness of the scene was interrupted when Holly surprised herself. She was cutting a bite of her steak when she had willfully raised the shiny blade of the steak knife up to her mouth and slashed her tongue. She had done it without realizing what she was doing, and now she was pouring blood out of her mouth.

"Ow! Oh, no. I bit my tongue!" she yelped, banging her fist on the table, gripping the steak knife tightly.

"Oh my God! Are you okay? You... you're bleeding pretty seriously!" Julie exclaimed, her face pale as she fell silent in shock as she gazed at the blood spilling down Holly's lips and chin onto her plate.

Both Thomas and Holly's mother, however, sat there calmly, not a word or expression crossing their faces. They simply looked at Holly with blank stares, as though they weren't surprised in the least bit at the blood running down Holly's face.

Holly stood up to go to the bathroom and cleanup the blood, but as she got to her feet, she surprised herself and changed direction, rushing toward Julie in a frenzy, plunging the steak-knife straight into the center of her chest.

Julie fell off her chair and collapsed onto the floor. Thomas and Holly's mother didn't budge. Holly quickly leaned down over her and moved her head close enough to bite Julie on the scalp. Holly opened her bloody mouth wide, revealing that her teeth had become long and sharp like a piranha's teeth, the irises of her eyes had turned a bright red. She bit down, sinking her teeth into Julie's scalp. She then released her bite, and let go of Julie's head, letting it flop to the floor. With Julie's blood now dripping off her chin, mingled with her own blood, Holly gazed at Thomas who was looking directly in her eyes, still expressionless. Holly glanced at her mother to see that she had continued to hold a blank, expressionless stare as well, both of them completely unphased by the sudden violence.

Holly snapped awake with a jolt, realizing she was sitting in her car at home in her garage still, dressed and ready for dinner, a deep panic rolled through her. Another nightmare—one that felt disturbingly real. It seemed she had fallen into a deep sleep with a horrible nightmare just as she was preparing to leave to her mother's for dinner.

"Holy shit! What is going on? I've got some crazy dream disease or something... I didn't sign up for this disaster of a life!" she yelled at the world, trying to shake off the lingering dread. She took a few deep breaths.

"Go to dinner, eat, come home. Hold it together, Holly. You

are fine." she affirmed to herself, with a deep sigh.

She opened the garage, started the car and made her way to her mother's for dinner, trying to stay calm, trying to forget the crazy dream she had just endured.

When she arrived at her mother's house, the scene was eerily similar to her nightmare. The real Julie looked a bit different than in her dream, but much about her was very similar, and shockingly, Julie wore a silver crucifix which was identical to the one from Holly's dream. Holly's mother was also wearing a necklace that held a silver crucifix which was strange since she'd never seen her mom wear a cross as jewelry, or even known she owned one.

When they sat down for dinner, Holly felt a wave of relief when her mother brought out roasted chicken with rosemary and rice for dinner, accompanied by a nice red wine. *No steak, so no steak knives*, Holly thought, easing up a bit.

"Holly, you mentioned you appreciated a good red wine with dinner, so I bought you a nice Chianti," Holly's mother added with a smile.

"Julie, I really like your cross—it's such a lovely silver—just like mine," Holly's mother said with a polite smile.

Julie unconsciously grasped the silver cross in her hand as she spoke. "Thank you! I've had it since I was a kid—I really never take it off." Then she added with a smile, "I like yours as well."

Holly's mother responded to Julie with a polite smile.

"Yeah, it fits you, Julie. Silver looks really nice on you," Thomas added with a flirtatious grin.

As they ate, however, Holly caught herself spacing out—not eating, but simply looking at Julie. And not just looking—staring—at the side of Julie's head, exactly where she had bitten her in the nightmare she'd had earlier that evening. Realizing her gaze had turned sharp, almost threatening, Holly quickly looked away, attempting to appear innocent, and glanced at Thomas—who was watching her intently, unblinking. Feeling uneasy and unsure of what to do, Holly looked away again and took a sip of wine.

Suddenly, Holly let out a loud sneeze, startling herself and catching the attention of everyone in the room. Julie looked up from her plate and offered a warm smile. "Bless you, Holly!"

Holly mumbled a quick thanks, raising a napkin to her face. But when she pulled it away, she noticed that Julie's expression had shifted from kind to curious. Holly followed her gaze, her fingers brushing her chin where a few drops of red wine had escaped, trailing downward like streaks of spilled red ink.

She raised her napkin to dab at her mouth, but before she could finish, her brother, Thomas, gave her a strange look— peering into her soul with his ocean-blue eyes.

"Holly, wipe your mouth and chin," he said in an assertive tone, the way an older brother might.

Holly dabbed at her chin a few more times with the napkin, her cheeks flushing as embarrassment settled over her like a heavy blanket. She felt small, almost childish, in a room full of composed adults. Thomas flashed her a peculiar smile, then looked away, leaving Holly unsettled and wondering just how much of her dream was going to echo into reality—or, even worse, if this was another dream.

"How's your job going, Holly?" Thomas changed the subject.

"It's good, you know, it pays the bills… but it's… well, it's just a job…feels pretty meaningless, like what's the point?" Holly replied with a shrug. "How's your work going, Thomas?" she asked in return.

"I can't complain," he replied with that same smile. "I'm doing a lot of work out of town these days. There's a big need for intellectual property loss mitigation and corresponding litigation. Yeah, sorry—boring even to mention, let alone go into detail. As you said, it pays the bills."

Holly's mother interjected, "Both of you are so very talented and incredible beings—that's a fact. Holly, rest assured you'll find that special 'it,' that *je ne sais quoi* that will make you truly fulfilled."

Holly smiled, appreciating her mother's encouragement, though a part of her wondered what that elusive "it" might be.

Thomas then asked Holly, "Are you still watching a lot of horror movies these days, Holly?"

Holly's mother interjected, speaking directly to Julie, "You know, Julie, since Holly was a small child she's enjoyed scary movies. She's a confirmed ghost story and horror film addict."

"It's true," Holly added with a small laugh, "I fall asleep to horror movies every night. They're my comfort genre."

Julie nodded in acknowledgment, looking at Holly, her polite expression fading into a look of wonder and confusion.

After dinner, Holly was the first to excuse herself. She offered an apologetic smile as she gathered her things. "I'll visit more next time we get together, but tonight I'm really tired, so I think I'm gonna head home," she said, saying goodbye to her mother and Thomas.

After hugging her mother and Thomas, Holly turned to Julie and wrapped her in a polite embrace. "It was nice to meet you," she said warmly.

Julie hesitated, her gaze lingering on Holly's face a moment too long—like someone trying to place a half-remembered dream. "It was nice to meet you too, Holly," she replied slowly, her voice soft but deliberate. "I look forward to seeing you again."

Julie continued to study her, eyes fixed on Holly's face with quiet intensity. Feeling the weight of the stare, Holly's own gaze began to drift around the room, avoiding direct eye contact. A flicker of discomfort passed through her.

Julie tilted her head slightly. "Are you feeling alright, Holly?"

Holly's mother interjected, "She's fine."

Without missing a beat, Holly replied, "Yeah, I'm fine, just a little tired." She offered a quick glance and a curt smile to the group. "Take care and have a good night, everyone."

As she walked to her car, a sense of unease tugged at her. The odd moments from dinner echoed in her mind— Thomas's strange smile, Julie's lingering gaze. It all seemed to ripple with some hidden meaning just out of reach.

As she drove, she started muttering to herself, "Okay, that's over with. Maybe I've got narcolepsy mixed with psychosis or something. I don't know. This seems like a movie, but this is real life…it's not a movie."

Back at her mother's house, Thomas and Julie were wrapping up the evening, helping clear the table and finish the last of the dishes.

"Thank you for dinner. We had a nice time visiting, and I'm so glad you got to meet Julie. The food was excellent," Thomas said warmly, his smile reaching his eyes.

"Yes, it was lovely to meet you. God bless you," Julie added, giving Holly's mother a small hug.

As they headed toward the door, Thomas stepped away

from Julie and leaned in for a goodbye hug. In a quiet murmur, he whispered, "Is it her?"

Holly's mother gave a slight nod, her face serene, though her eyes hinted at something deeper. "It is certain. Very good," she replied just as quietly, then added in a normal tone with a cordial smile, "Have a good night, you two."

After watching them drive off, Holly's mother locked the front door. Her expression shifted to one of steely determination. She moved down the hallway, her footsteps deliberate, and entered her back office, closing the door softly behind her.

When Holly got home, she took a shower, put on her pajamas, and climbed into bed. She was exhausted. Once settled, she turned on her favorite classic horror movie, and smiled. There was something so comforting about the familiar black-and-white scenes and eerie soundtrack.

It was always good to be back at home in bed, where everything felt normal and safe.

Chapter 16

Thomas and Julie drove through the empty city streets, the soft hum of the engine the only sound between them. The night was quiet, yet a strange tension lingered in the air, unseen but palpable.

"Would you like a little more wine at my place or yours? Or do you want to call it a night?" Thomas asked, his voice light, almost coaxing.

Julie sat rigid in her seat, her gaze fixed on the road ahead but unfocused. Her fingers twitched in her lap. Thoughts churned in her mind, too heavy, too consuming to let anything else in. She hadn't even heard him speak.

"Hello? Julie? Are you there?"

She jolted, as if pulled from the depths of a dream.

"Yes. Sorry. I was... What did you say?" she murmured, shaking off the haze.

"I asked if you wanted to come back to my place for a glass of wine before I take you home. What's on your mind?" His voice was patient but tinged with curiosity.

Julie hesitated, the weight of unspoken words pressing against her chest. Then, after a deep breath, she answered.

"This is going to sound really strange, you are Christian right?", she asked

"Yes, I already told you that when we first met, remember?", he answered

"Yeah, I do. Okay, it's just that, well, I don't know how to say it, so I need you to trust me like one God-fearing Christian should trust another...I need you to take me to your sister's house."

Thomas's hands tightened on the steering wheel. He turned his head slightly, eyebrows raised in skepticism.

"What, right now? We're not going to Holly's," he said flatly.

Julie met his gaze with determination, her voice firm now. "Thomas, I need you to trust me. Your sister is in danger. I know this for fact and I need you to have faith in me."

Thomas let out a short, dry laugh, shaking his head. "Holly's fine. What are you talking about?" He exhaled, exasperated. "Let's just go to my place and talk about this, okay? You can explain whatever is on your mind—"

"You have to listen to me," Julie interrupted, her voice rising with urgency. "Something is wrong. Something... dark. And it needs to be stopped."

Thomas sighed, eyes flicking back to the road as he continued toward his home. "You're not making any sense, Julie. What exactly are you saying?"

Julie's hands balled into fists. "You'll think I'm crazy, but I don't care. I need you to trust me." Her voice softened, trembling. "There is something evil threatening Holly. Not just her life—but her soul, Thomas. Her eternal soul is in danger, and I can't ignore it."

A muscle in Thomas's jaw twitched. He kept his expression neutral, but his fingers drummed against the steering wheel in quiet agitation. The streetlights outside flickered past, casting fleeting shadows over his face.

"This is just the wine talking," he muttered. "You've had too much. We're almost to my place, and we'll talk about it there. And then I'm taking you home—you need to rest."

The car turned onto his street, the familiar sight of his home approaching. The garage door rumbled open as Thomas pulled into the driveway.

Julie, her heart pounding, leaned toward him. "You won't believe me, but I have to tell you because it's your sister, and I truly believe she needs my help. Right now. Tonight."

Thomas parked the car and cut the engine. Silence fell like a heavy curtain.

"Alright, Julie," he said, turning to face her. His tone was calm, but his eyes were sharp, scrutinizing. "Tell me what you think the problem is."

Julie inhaled deeply, searching for the right words.

"If I can protect your sister from something you don't even realize is threatening her, is that worth trusting me?" she asked. "Can you trust me? Will you trust me?"

Thomas held her gaze, his expression unreadable. Then, after a long pause, he spoke.

"You have no idea how important Holly's safety is to me. There is nothing—nothing—more important to me than her safety."

Julie exhaled in relief, her posture relaxing slightly. "Then please, listen. We don't have time to waste. I know I have to help her. It's more than just instinct—it's a calling. A mission I was given, and I can't fail."

Thomas tilted his head slightly. "A mission?"

Julie hesitated before answering. "I had a vision."

His reaction was unexpected. He didn't laugh or scoff. Instead, his expression intensified, his gaze more focused.

"A vision?"

Julie swallowed hard. "Yes. A vision... from God or an angel. It showed me that I was meant to save a girl from an evil spirit. But until tonight, I didn't know who that girl was. Then at dinner, I saw things—things that made it all clear. It's Holly. I have to protect her. I'm supposed to save her!"

Thomas didn't blink. He sat in still silence for a long, weighted moment.

"Julie," he said softly, almost kindly. "You might be surprised to hear this, but I believe you. I believe you completely. I know you had a vision."

Julie furrowed her brows. Something in his voice had changed.

Then, she noticed it.

A scent.

Faint but growing stronger, creeping in through her senses. A sharp, chemical tang.

She wrinkled her nose. "What's that smell? It's like... turpentine or something."

Before she could react, Thomas's hand clamped over her mouth.

A massive, suffocating force.

Her head slammed back against the headrest as he pinned her down.

Julie thrashed, her muffled screams lost in the tight seal of his palm. But only for a second.

A thick, acrid vapor invaded her lungs. A damp, earthy, almost decayed scent filled the car—a stench that did not belong to any known chemical but something older, something unnatural.

Her limbs weakened. The fight drained from her muscles.

83

Her eyes fluttered, rolling back.

Then, stillness.

Thomas calmly removed his hand from her face, watching as her body slumped against the seat, her breath now slow and shallow.

Reaching down, he grasped the silver crucifix that had rested against her chest, the delicate chain glinting in the dim light. With a quick tug, he snapped it off.

For a moment, he stared at it in his palm, then let it slip it into his shirt pocket.

His lips parted, and in a low, resonant voice, he uttered with finality:

"Tum-Grissell."

Chapter 17

Holly sat at the kitchen table, twirling her fork through a plate of pasta drenched in a creamy white cheese sauce, half-watching a nature documentary about the African savanna. Steam curled from her plate, mingling with the dim kitchen light as her gaze flickered between her meal and the small TV in her kitchen. On the screen, a wake of vultures tore into a sun-scorched carcass, their hooked beaks plunging into rotting flesh.

She swallowed her last bite, momentarily mesmerized by the slow, deliberate feast unfolding before her. Nature had no remorse.

After rinsing her plate, she retreated to her bedroom, eager to unwind and go to sleep. Just as she was about to slip beneath the covers, the doorbell rang.

A sharp, unwelcome sound.

She glanced at the clock—nearly midnight.

Her stomach tightened.

"Who in the hell is at my door this late?" she muttered, irritation prickling at the edges of her exhaustion. She hesitated before moving, hoping—praying—the visitor would lose patience and leave.

But the doorbell rang again. And now a series of knocks.

Gritting her teeth, she padded back into the kitchen and yanked open a drawer, pulling out her chef's knife. The cool steel felt reassuring in her grip as she crept toward the front door.

She peered through the peephole.

Her grouchy old man neighbor stood there. But something was… off. His usual scowl was replaced with an unnatural, almost serene smile.

"Oh no. What does he want now?" she whispered, gripping the knife tighter.

Then came the voice. Soft. Measured. Polite.

"I'm so sorry to disturb you so late. I'm your neighbor. I just need to ask a quick favor. I have a small emergency and I really need your help."

Holly exhaled sharply. It was late, but not dealing with him might lead to bigger problems, and maybe she could really help an old man in need. With a sigh, she unlatched the door and pulled it open.

Her breath caught in her throat.

Her neighbor was gone.

And in his place stood a stranger.

He was tall and gaunt, with gray, greasy long hair, dressed in a long black robe, the fabric thick and heavy, embroidered with deep red stitching that ran along the sleeves. Around his throat sat a stiff, white pleated collar, and atop his head rested a wide-brimmed black felt hat.

The man's dark, piercing eyes bore into her, and as the porch light illuminated his features, she took in the details—a large wooden crucifix dangling from a chain around his neck, and a small, leather-bound book hanging at his waist in an open-top case.

He looked like he had stepped out of the Middle Ages.

A wave of unease slithered through her, tightening its grip around her ribs.

Before she could react, the man's face contorted with rage. "Ketzer! Ketzer! Zauberer! Gottloses, du Hexe!"

His voice was a thunderclap, filled with venomous fury.

Then, without warning—he lunged.

Holly staggered back, barely processing the movement before his hands clamped around her throat, cold, relentless. His breath was hot as he bellowed at her, his voice raw with conviction.

"Du wirst verbrennen! Das feuer wird dich reinigen!"

Her vision blurred. Her lungs screamed.

Then, instinct—something ancient, something buried—took over.

Her fingers tightened around her knife. With a sharp, fluid motion, she drove the blade upward, slicing through his heavy woolen covering, feeling the blade sink into his flesh.

A strangled gasp tore from his lips.

But she didn't stop.

A force unlike anything she had ever known surged through her.

Her heartbeat thundered in her ears, her breath no longer frantic, but controlled—powerful. Her irises flared, shifting to an unnatural, feral red, and a sharp pain shot through her gums. She felt it—her teeth elongating, curving into razor-sharp fangs.

The old man reeled, blood sputtering from his lips. But Holly didn't hesitate—she didn't want to.

With a growl, she ripped the knife free and plunged it into him again. And again. And again.

Each thrust sent a jolt of dark, intoxicating pleasure through her—a primal, vindictive ecstasy, as if righting a great wrong. The man stumbled backward, gasping, his horrified eyes staring at her with fear and surprise.

He collapsed, blood quickly pooling around his body, covering the wooden floorboards of her main room in deep crimson. His body twitched once, then fell still with a final exhalation.

Holly stood over him, chest heaving, hands slick with blood.

But she wasn't horrified.

She was empowered.

Her breathing slowed. A strange, satisfied warmth settled in her chest, a sense of absolute, undeniable superiority.

And then—

The old bloody corpse on the floor inexplicably began to smolder, thick black smoke rising in twists and curls.

Orange embers sparked from his skin, tiny at first, then growing, spreading like fire licking dry parchment. Within seconds, he crumbled into ashen remains, collapsing into gray and black dust at her feet.

Holly took a slow, steady breath, staring at the remnants of the man she had just destroyed.

She remained standing above the ashen remains, her heart pounding, her chest heaving with each breath.

Her eyes scanned the living room and peered out the front door, wondering if anyone had seen or heard the struggle. With a shaky step, she retreated further inside, swinging the door shut, a maelstrom of confusion and awe swirling within her as she relished the intoxicating, newfound power surging through her veins.

Holly woke up in her bed, breathing heavily. "Holy shit! I'm losing my mind—these dreams are so messed up!" she gasped, feeling her heart still pounding in her chest.

It was another horrid vision, a very livid nightmare, a waking torment.

"This wasn't real. It isn't real. This isn't real," she repeatedly told herself.

She took a sip of water from the glass on her nightstand, then rolled over, pulling the covers up, so tired. Soon, she drifted off again with a gentle smile on her face.

Chapter 18

Another morning, and Holly felt awake, alive, and ready to tackle the day. Yesterday had worn her out, but she'd had a good, fitful sleep and felt refreshed now. She went to her closet, put on her work clothes, and headed to the bathroom to brush her hair.

As she looked in the mirror, Holly's stomach dropped—there it was again: the same thick, black hair she'd snipped off on Tuesday morning had somehow regrown, now sticking out about an inch from her scalp. She quickly grabbed her scissors and cut it away, tossing the wiry, fishing-line-like strand into the trash.

"Oh no, this can't be happening! A gnarly, thick, black hair! So gross," she muttered with frustration. Then she noticed her new so-called beauty mark looked slightly larger than before. She scratched at it a few times, testing again if it was just a spot of ink, but it wouldn't come off.

"Great, now I need to see a dermatologist, too," she groaned, feeling a wave of irritation.

After gathering her things, she got into her car and pulled away from the house. As she drove away, her neighbor—the grouchy old man—was outside trimming his bushes again, and she gave him a quick wave. True to form, he didn't wave back, but just scowled at her as she passed.

"Morning, Mr. Annoying. You cranky old loser," Holly muttered to herself with a smile as she drove off toward the office, hoping the rest of the day would be smoother. As she drove away, she decided she didn't care about pleasantries anymore—feeling bold, she lifted her hand and extended her middle-finger in the slight hope that the grouchy old man would see her rude gesture as she drove away.

Yet another boring day of work dragged on for Holly, filled with the usual routine: answering phone calls, responding to emails, and filing paperwork. The hours dragged on and on. By the end of the day, she was eager to head straight home.

As Holly pulled into her driveway, her eyes caught sight of the same neighbor in his front yard again, methodically raking his lawn that appeared to have only a few leaves lying there. She decided instead of the usual polite smile and wave, she'd do something different—she'd scowl back at him. She glared at him, her eyes burning with anger, lips curled into a sharp frown, and her expression hardened with disdain.

When he saw her expression, he quickly turned away, his posture stiff.

"What an idiot," Holly muttered under her breath, rolling her eyes as she grabbed her bag. "He doesn't even know the basics of being a decent human being. Stupid scumbag."

Still miffed by his permanent lack of manners, she brushed it off as she headed inside, feeling amused at giving him a taste of his own medicine.

"You'd think someone that old would have a clue by that time in their life, but not that moron," she muttered to herself.

Letting someone like him ruin her night wasn't worth the energy. Her home welcomed her with its familiar warmth, and she quickly let the tension and amusement of the encounter fade into the background.

Holly went to the kitchen and flipped the light on. The sun was already setting, and with late fall upon her, the daylight seemed to vanish almost as soon as she returned home from work.

She went for a glass of orange juice. As she sipped it, she felt a lingering unease from the strange, vivid dreams that had haunted her nights lately. She decided to grab her chef's knife from the drawer, feeling a little more secure with it close by as she enjoyed her drink. To pass the time, she began flipping through her bird book, trying to keep her nerves calm, spending a few minutes to decompress from the pressure of the day.

Tick!

A small noise emanated from the main room and snapped her attention away from her book. Holly glanced into the darkening main room—and her heart skipped a beat. She couldn't believe her eyes!

Out of the darkness, in the dim light of the kitchen light's radiance, an old woman's wrinkled, pale face stared back at her from the shadows, eyes fixed intently on her. Holly yelped, stumbling backward as the face quickly drew back, fading into the blackness.

Her hand tightened around her knife. "Whoever you are in there, I'm going to defend myself unless you turn the light on and give yourself up! Lay down on the floor now or I'm gonna stab the hell out of you!" she called out, her voice trembling but firm. She stood up in a posture of power, wielding the knife just as she had in her nightmare the night before.

Silence hung heavy in the air, broken only by the sound of

her breathing. She waited, straining to catch any sound or movement. Gathering her courage, she took a step toward the main room. Just then, the face reappeared, emerging slowly from the shadows, and spoke in a raspy hiss: *"Hiktilda..."*

Then it vanished into the darkness once more.

Holly screeched in surprise and almost dropped the knife but steadied herself, clutching it tighter. In one swift motion, she darted around the corner, reaching for the main room's light switch. The room flooded with light, revealing... nothing. Just her empty couch, TV, and sitting chair.

"Oh my God... I've completely lost it. I've lost my mind. That's it—I'm completely goddamn insane," she burst out, stepping back into the kitchen and slumping down into a chair at the kitchen table, trying to calm her heart—trying not to scream in frustration.

The tension barely had a chance to settle before the living room light flickered, then went dark with a sudden pop behind her. Heart pounding again, Holly swiveled her head to stare into the main room and froze as the same raspy voice hissed from the shadows of the main room, *"Nothing to fear."*

A chill ran down her spine. Every nerve told her to run, but an unexpected surge of courage compelled her to stay. She forced herself to breathe, glancing nervously into the inky blackness of the main room.

"Who...who are you?" Holly's voice was barely more than a whisper.

Silence followed, thick and unnerving, as though the very air had grown heavy around her.

Holly bolted into the main room, flipping the wall switch up and down, but it was no use—the light bulb had indeed burst. Determined, she darted across the room, knife in hand, to the lamp by the couch and flicked it on, flooding the room with soft light.

She scanned the area, heart pounding, when suddenly movement caught her eye—a large spider—one that looked identical in color and shape, but much larger in size, to the same one from her shower encounter—scurried out from beneath the sitting chair and darted for cover under the couch.

Holly shrieked, jumping back and dashing into the kitchen. "Holy shit! It's huge! It's that damn spider's mother! What in the world?! That thing is freaky big!" she gasped, catching her breath.

Without another thought, she ran back into the kitchen and grabbed her cell phone. She dialed Ryan, impatiently tapping her knife against the table as the phone rang, keeping an eye on the couch in the main room.

"Hi, Ryan, I need your help! I need you to come over and get rid of a spider in my house…" she blurted as soon as he picked up. "No, it's not *just* a spider. It's huge and ran under my couch. I'm not joking—it's really big… No, it's not like an inch long; it's as big as my goddamn hand! Yes, come over now; I don't care if it's late. There's no way I can sleep with this thing in my house!"

Her voice was desperate. She knew how ridiculous it sounded, but this spider felt like more than just a pest—it felt like a curse—like a demon haunting her.

She ended the call and stood in the kitchen, keeping a diligent watch on the living room couch by peering out from behind the kitchen wall separating the two rooms.

As the minutes crawled by, Holly fidgeted, tapping her fingers and the chef's knife against the wall, never taking her eyes off the dark gap beneath the couch where the monstrous spider had disappeared.

The sudden knock on the front door made her jump. She took a deep breath and dashed across the main room to the front door and flung it open, relief flooding her as Ryan stepped inside, holding a small baseball bat in one hand and a flashlight in the other.

"So, where's this *huge* spider?" he asked, his tone clearly exasperated and in disbelief that she was so frightened by a spider.

"It's under the couch," she said, pointing anxiously with the knife. "I'm telling you, it's huge. I'm glad you brought the bat."

"You think that knife is big enough to kill a spider?" he sarcastically asked her.

Keeping a safe distance, she glided back to the kitchen and hovered by the kitchen wall as Ryan crouched down next to the couch, clicked on his flashlight, and peered under the it. The narrow beam swept back and forth, illuminating only shadows.

But then, the lights flashed out again, the bulb in the lamp had now burst just as the main light's bulb had moments earlier. The room plunged into darkness. She peered at Ryan's hunched form before the couch, his head turned to look at her, flashlight illuminating his face—and Holly froze. It wasn't Ryan's face anymore. The pale, wrinkled visage of the same old woman's face was staring at her, twisted into a wicked, wrinkled grin. The mouth opened, and a cackling laugh exploded out, chilling and inhuman.

Holly's scream echoed through the house as she stumbled backward, her heart pounding with terror in a rush of panic as the old hag's cackling grew louder and louder with each second.

95

Holly awoke sitting at the kitchen table with the knife in her hand and the glass of orange juice standing in front of her. "Holy...what the hell?! Oh, my...I must really have narcolepsy. I'm falling asleep while drinking a damn glass of orange...", she paused in surprise.

She noticed her right thumb nail was a bruised black and green color. She gazed at it for a moment and then said to herself, "This is just not real. This is not reality. I need to sleep like a normal person. I can't, I can't... I need to get over these messed up fever-dreams."

She went to grab her glass of orange juice for a drink but noticed behind the glass something black. She recoiled her hand in a flash. It was the same shiny, black spider that had been under the couch a few moments ago, in her dream. It was standing calmly on the kitchen table. It didn't budge but instead just stared at her with it's glossy black eyes, motionless.

Holly tightened her grip on the knife handle, and slowly used the blade to push the glass of orange juice to the side, away from the critter. The spider didn't budge. In an instant, her irises turned bright red, and in a flash she swung the knife down and smashed it into the center of the large arachnid, pinning it against the kitchen table with the blade. To her amazement, the spider's trapped body instantly started to smolder and billow out black smoke, just as the old gray-haired man had in her previous nightmare.

Holly sat there, heart racing as the spider's remains crumbled into ash, the faint scent of burnt paper lingering in the air. She watched as the last tendrils of black smoke twisted upwards and dissipated, leaving only a faint, dark smear and a small pile of ash where the spider had been.

She stood up and took a step back, breathing heavily, feeling both a strange satisfaction and an eerie unease. She glanced down at her bruised thumb nail, the black-green color seeming even darker than before. Holly's mind raced. *What did this mean? Am I losing it? Was any of this real?*

She took a steadying breath, grabbing a paper towel to wipe away the ashes on the table. "Enough of this," she muttered, trying to calm herself. "No more dreams, no more spiders, no more freaky faces, no more... whatever this is."

Holly snapped awake, sitting at the kitchen table with a knife in her hand and her glass of orange juice in front of her. "Killed that nasty thing! That little bastard can go to hell!" she yelled in triumph..

Then she calmed down, coming to her senses and said to herself, "I'm having a damn nervous breakdown. I just had a damn dream within a dream. I can't even tell what's real anymore!"

She went to the freezer and pulled out a frozen turkey dinner and microwaved it and went to her bed room. She climbed into bed and ate her TV dinner on her lap while watching her go-to classics again. She finished her dinner and paused the movie to go to the bathroom and brush her teeth. After brushing her teeth, she made a few vampiric smiles in the mirror to herself and said "Perturbant teeth" to herself in a mock, over-the-top vampire voice.

Holly chuckled to herself as she finished her dramatic impression, flashing herself a shot of her teeth, imitating the classic vampire 'open mouth with fangs, ready to bite', in the mirror. "Goodnight, mortals," she said, shaking her head at her own silliness. She made her way back to bed, where the familiar comfort of her blankets and her movie awaited her.

She crawled under the covers, watching her movie, feeling strangely comforted by the black-and-white scenes flickering across the screen. Tonight, after everything, she was ready to get a good night's sleep. She took a deep breath, grounding herself, letting her mind settle as she drifted off.

But just as she was falling asleep, she thought she heard a faint, raspy whisper echoing from somewhere in her room. Her eyes snapped open, and she sat up, glancing around her dim room. Everything looked as it should, nothing seemed out of place. Her heart beat faster, but she told herself it was only her imagination.

"Enough with these goddamn dreams," she whispered, pulling the blankets up higher.

As the night wore on, she finally drifted into a quiet, deep sleep, the echo of "It's alive... alive!" from her TV lingered in her mind, weaving itself into her sleep.

She found herself wandering through a fog-drenched landscape, surrounded by towering pine trees and ominous shadows. In the distance, a faint glow illuminated a hulking solitary figure, slowly approaching, its gaze filled with a haunting mixture of familiarity and ferocity.

The world around her felt unreal, a place caught somewhere between nightmare and memory, where eerie voices floated on the wind. But rather than fear, Holly felt an odd calm as she watched the creature, her subconscious replaying the timeless themes of humanity, horror, and acceptance.

Chapter 19

Holly's brother, Thomas, sat in his bedroom with the lights off and his screenless window open to the outside air. Behind him, on a small couch, lay Julie, with a black bag wrapped over her head. Her ankles were tightly bound with a black cord, and her arms were tied behind her back.

Without turning his head toward her, Thomas spoke to Julie on the couch, "You thought you were close, your plans for banishment...but you never had a chance. We see more than you can imagine."

Julie tensed when she heard his voice. She had suspected she had been in danger, her vision had warned it, but to hear it admitted in such a casual tone from Thomas, her new boyfriend, whom she'd only met two weeks earlier, unsettled her deeply.

Thomas tilted his head slightly, his expression both condescending and amused. "We see everything." He leaned back, crossing his arms. "You think you had a chance, but you never did."

Julie clenched her fists, feeling both anger and fear rise within her. "Why are you telling me this? What are you going to do to me?" she mumbled, the bag over her head muffling her speech as she tried to steady her voice.

Thomas chuckled softly. "It doesn't matter. She's beyond your reach. She has returned, and there's nothing you, or anyone, can do to stop it now."

In a low, quiet voice, Thomas murmured to himself, "She is protected. The transformation flows, no matter the cost." He bowed his head and grumbled a last phrase in an extremely low tone of voice, with finality, "Tum-Grissell."

As he stood, he undressed, and by his will, his skin began to secrete a black, muddy ooze, covering him until he was nearly invisible in the darkness. His ocean blue irises filled with small flecks of orange until the blue was supplanted entirely by the mud from within. He moved to the closet, pulled out a much larger black bag, and, in one fluid motion, deftly pushed Julie's body inside, cinching the bag shut. Her body flailed, but as the bag tightened all movement stopped. Hoisting it over his shoulder, he left the room in silence.

Chapter 20

"Another day of nervous breakdown nightmares.", Holly said as she opened her eyes and woke to the new day. She got out of bed, got dressed and went to have coffee for breakfast, just good black coffee.

As she left the house to head to work she saw her old man neighbor and returned his scowl with her own scowl. As she drove off, she laughed to herself, "How'd you like your own medicine, you grumpy old stick-in-the-mud!" She once again, raised her hand with the middle-finger extended and added a curt, "See this, loser?"

Work was the usual day again, nothing but the same phone calls and the same paper work, insurance, insurance, insurance, she'd had enough insurance for a life time. As she finished up work she started to wipe down her desk and went to the closet to get the vacuum and clean the office up. Mr. Warren had left the office a few hours earlier and had ordered her to "sparkle the place up" before she left for the night.

Holly grabbed the vacuum and paused for a moment to reflect. She threw the vacuum handle down to the floor, "I'm not doing this shit. Not tonight. He can fire me if he wants, I don't care."

She had had enough. She walked out and locked the door

behind her and jumped in her car to drive home.

Holly was barely a block from her office sitting at a stop-light when she was aghast at what she saw. Her so-called boyfriend Ryan was walking down the street, facing away from her, and was holding the hand of girl, they then stopped and hugged for a few seconds and were laughing and kissing each other.

"What the hell? That jerk is cheating on me... He's cheating on me, and I don't even like him! Well, good! I'm done with that clingy loser! I can't stand dishonest scumbags like him!" she exclaimed, gripping the wheel. "Stupid liar!" She smacked her steering wheel with her palms a few times and then pressed the accelerator hard as she drove past, but Ryan didn't notice her pass.

As Holly pulled into her garage, a strange feeling washed over her—like someone, or something, was in the backseat behind her. She felt a chill of unease, so she quickly stepped out of the car and went straight into the kitchen and pulled the chef's knife out, and instantly felt a bit of relief. It felt solid in her hand, and that made her feel dangerous.

Holly headed to her bedroom to change out of her work clothes and into comfortable sweats. She set the knife down while she dressed, then picked it up again as she stepped out of the closet. Exhausted from a long day of tedious work, she was glad to sink into the couch.

After zoning out for a few seconds, she remembered the dream about the spider lurking underneath the couch. Summoning her courage, she decided to check under it. Grabbing the couch with one hand, knife gripped tightly in the other hand, she leaned and effortlessly lifted the couch a few inches off of the floor, tilting it back as she scanned the underside, looking for anything that might be clinging in the dark corners. It was clear.

Satisfied, she set the couch down and headed to the kitchen and put her knife back in the drawer, and then straight to her bedroom, looking forward to a good night's rest. As soon as she lay down, the TV murmuring softly in the background, she drifted off to sleep within minutes.

Holly snapped awake in the darkness of her bedroom. *It must be the middle of the night*, she thought and confirmed that her clock said 12:02 am. She rolled to her side and groaned, reflecting on what a strange week it had been. As she shifted onto her other side, she noticed a large, sprawling, pitch-black shape in the upper corner of her dark room. It didn't make sense.

Propping herself up on one elbow, she squinted, focusing on the shadow. It looked like an abnormally large shadow of a spider, probably four feet across, with long, multi-jointed legs sprawled out another four feet from the center, clinging to the walls in the corner of her room where the walls met the ceiling. She leaned in closer, trying to make sense of it, her pulse quickening. Suddenly, a rapid *tick, tick, tick* came from the shadow.

Heart pounding, Holly reached over and switched on her nightstand lamp. The room flooded with light, and the corner was empty—nothing there. Just another strange waking dream—a horrid vision.

Holly calmly climbed out of bed, went to the kitchen, and grabbed her flashlight from the junk drawer, along with her knife, before returning to her bedroom. Settling back into bed, she gripped the flashlight and knife tightly, eyes wide and alert. "Okay, I'm ready for it...let's go..." she whispered to herself.

Tick, tick, tick!

The sound echoed again, and she flicked the flashlight on, scanning the room—nothing. But as the beam crossed her hands, she noticed something surprising: two more of her fingernails, along with her other thumbnail, had turned a bruised black and green color. "What the hell is going on? How did I hurt my fingers?" she muttered, staring at them in disbelief.

Tick, tick!

The sound cut through the silence once more. "And what the hell is making that noise?!" she burst out, her pulse racing, scanning the room with the flashlight beam.

Holly sat in the dark for a few more seconds, then abruptly turned the lamp on flooding the room with light. *Well, I'm awake now; I might as well take a hot bath*, she thought, hopping out of bed and heading to the bathroom. She turned the water on hot, adding a generous amount of bubble bath for a soothing touch.

Setting her flashlight and her knife on the vanity counter-top, she closed the bathroom door and locked it. Even though she was alone in the house, the thought of a shadow lurking nearby left her uneasy. Holly undressed and slipped into the filling tub, letting the hot water rise around her. After a few moments, she turned off the tap and relaxed, savoring the sauna-like warmth.

Just as she started to feel calm, her nerves jumped and her stomach rolled in fear at a sound of wooden heels clicked on the hard floor of her bedroom just outside the bathroom door.

It wasn't the same ticking as before—it was a footstep. Holly's eyes darted to the slot at the bottom of the bathroom door, her heart pounding as she spotted two columns of shadow, two feet blocking the lamplight from her bedroom.

She scrambled out of the tub, dripping wet, and grabbed her knife. "Whoever is there, I'm holding a knife—and if I catch you, you're going to regret it! Old lady, you hear me?" She strained to hear any response, then leaned closer to the door, hoping to glimpse the feet again. As she focused on the bottom of the doorway, the lamp light in her room clicked off, the light in her bedroom had flickered out, the slot under the door was swallowed by darkness.

"Okay, you got it! I'm calling the cops!" she yelled, grabbing her phone and dialing 9...1...1. But as she pressed the numbers, the screen filled with random letters and symbols. *Oh great, now my phone doesn't work. Maybe the steam is making it go haywire,* she thought in frustration.

Feeling a mix of fear and disbelief, she turned to the mirror, taking a moment to compose herself. She dressed quickly, then caught her reflection again, inspecting her teeth as if to ground herself, grappling with the strange blur of dream and reality her life had become—a series of short, relentless nightmares.

"Enough!" she cried, and suddenly, she jolted awake. She was back in her bed. Midnight, still. Rolling over, she repeated in a hoarse whisper, "I have had it," hoping to shake off the lingering chill of the dream.

"It's just a dream. They are just dreams," she muttered, her hands trembling as she tucked herself deeper under the blankets. "Chill out, Holly. It's not even real. And even if it were... it's just a shadow anyway." She forced herself to take

105

a deep, calming breath, letting her mind settle. Gradually, the tension eased, and she drifted back into a deep sleep.

Chapter 21

At the break of dawn, Holly's mother stood in her quiet office, scanning the well-worn bookshelf in search of a treasured volume. When she finally found it, she carefully removed the book and settled at her desk. The cover was a masterpiece of intricate design, adorned with Moorish-inspired patterns interwoven in a myriad of vivid hues that seemed to dance in the soft light. A subtle smile played on her lips as she opened the tome and methodically flipped through its delicate pages until she reached the passage she had been seeking.

With deliberate grace, she raised her right hand, fingers splayed like the branches of an ancient tree, and in a steady, commanding voice, she recited, *"Uchtred vanki... When the heart weeps for what it has lost, the spirit laughs for what it has found."*

Holly awoke and lay in bed for a few quiet moments, relishing the fact that it was nearly afternoon—she had slept in and felt remarkably well rested.

"Saturday—yard work, laundry, and cleaning... a bunch of pointless work that means nothing in the long run. Oh, yeah, exciting," she muttered sarcastically. With a resigned sigh, she pulled on her worn-in sweats—the ones she reserved exclusively for yard work—and made her way to the bathroom to brush her hair.

As she gazed into the mirror, her stomach plummeted. Her soft brown hair was no longer alone; thick, black strands were scattered among her natural locks, and the skin beneath the hair began to itch with an intensity she'd never felt before. With rising frustration, she began scratching her scalp, but each desperate motion only intensified the maddening itch.

She felt absolutely terrified seeing her body changing before her eyes, each day this week something horrible and new, and all of this on top of the horrible nightmare episodes.

As she clawed her scalp with her nails, each scratch sent clumps of her familiar brown hair tumbling away, gathering between her trembling fingers. Despite her shock at watching her hair fall in handfuls into the sink, the act of scratching brought an odd, almost addictive relief that overwhelmed her thoughts. Tears welled in her eyes as she continued the relentless back-and-forth motion, unable to break free from the compulsion.

"I must be dying! I don't care anymore—I'm ready to just let go! I don't care if I'm falling apart!" she cried, her voice cracking as she confronted her disheveled reflection. The bathroom light seemed to mock her, highlighting every black strand. At last, she ceased clawing at her skin, her fingers frozen mid-scratch as the maddening itch subsided.

Her breath hitched when she ran her hand over her scalp. Every last one of her soft, brown hairs had fallen out, replaced entirely by the two and three inch long black strands that glinted under the light. "Fine!" she cried, her voice trembling with a mixture of anger and resignation. "I'll just wear a hat—

who cares anymore? I'm just a freak of nature now! My life is ruined!"

Fueled by her frustration, she stomped across the room and flung open her closet door with such ferocity that its hinges rattled. There, a faded but familiar winter beanie caught her eye. With shaking hands, she snatched it up and pulled it tightly over her scalp, indifferent to how its texture clashed with her strange new hair.

When she returned to the mirror to adjust the beanie, another unsettling change caught her attention—the beauty mark on her cheek, once a delicate speck only days ago, had grown larger and darker. She hesitated, her fingers hovering uncertainly near her cheek, then slowly traced the edge of the mark, half-hoping it was merely an illusion.

Her reflection loomed in the glass, nearly unrecognizable. The beanie slipped slightly, but she didn't bother to fix it. Instead, she exhaled a defeated sigh and pressed her head against the surface of the mirror. "What's happening to me?" she whispered, her voice barely audible over the pounding of her heart. "I hope this is a damn nightmare…I need to wake up!", she screamed in the mirror. She longed to cry, yet found herself unable to shed a tear—something inside had shifted, leaving her unsure if any trace of her former self still remained.

In a daze, Holly slowly drifted into the kitchen and sank heavily into a chair at the table, her mind swirling with despair and confusion over the loss of her familiar brown hair and the sudden emergence of strange black strands. As she stared down in silent desolation, her eyes eventually wandered upward to the surface of the table. There, in the center, stood the glossy black spider—the very creature from her nightmare the night before—seemingly waiting for her. Her pulse quickened as she looked into its many shining eyes. She drew back, taking several deep, steadying breaths as her gaze remained fixed on the silent creature.

She stared at it, wondering how this spider could possibly make things worse than they already were. Her physical transformation—her body seeming to fall apart before her eyes, becoming something unrecognizable—made the horror of seeing the spider pale in comparison.

"It's just a spider, and it isn't real. It's only my fear...it's only my fear, looking back at me," she murmured softly, "My fear...my fear looking back at me."

With measured calm, she extended her hand and placed her palm on the table. The spider remained motionless, watching her with an unnerving intensity. "It's okay," Holly whispered, the cadence of her voice both reassuring and tentative. "I'm not in danger, and neither are you."

After a slight adjustment with one of its forelegs, the spider began inching closer—leg by leg—its tiny, gleaming eyes never leaving hers. Holly was captivated by the creature's unrelenting focus on her. "It's okay," she repeated, more to herself than to the spider. "There is nothing to fear. It's only fear." When it finally reached her hand, she inhaled slowly and allowed it to climb delicately onto her fingers, its body methodically pulling upward until it settled on the back of her hand. Lifting her hand slightly off the table, the arachnid clinging to the top of it, she marveled at the dark creature contrasted against her skin.

With a sense of wonder, Holly brought her hand closer to her face. "See?" she said in a fragile whisper. "There is nothing to fear." In a subtle, almost eerie gesture of acknowledgment, the spider lifted its two front legs before lowering them again. A surprising warmth spread through her—a strange, inexplicable connection with this creature. Slowly, she set her hand back down on the table. The spider deliberately stepped off her skin and back onto the table, crawling to the center, resuming its original position, and then, before Holly's astonished eyes, it vanished into thin air. A gasp escaped her as the air caught in her throat, leaving her to silently replay the encounter and ponder its mysterious significance.

After several long minutes, Holly exhaled a deep, steady breath and rose from the chair. She wandered back to her bedroom and collapsed onto her bed, her thoughts a turbulent mix of unanswered questions. An overwhelming urge to seek comfort and guidance pulsed within her—she needed to speak with her mother. Without hesitation, she picked up her phone to call her, but paused when she noticed two new missed calls and accompanying voicemails—both from her mother. She decided to listen to the messages first.

Her mother's warm voice filled her ear:

"Good morning, darling. I know you've had a rough week— the roughest in your entire life—and I've been thinking about you constantly. Something very important is happening to you, and you must trust me—it is the best thing that could happen to you—the most blessed moment of your life. I need you to forget everything about your old life and head up to Hidden Lake today—now. This isn't a suggestion—this is a command— an order. Go to the lake and do forget everything else. I'm going to leave you another message that you must listen to immediately."

Holly was astounded but felt comforted at hearing her mother's words. She queued up the next voicemail and listened intently:

"Now, I have one more thing to tell you, and it's the most important message I'll ever give. Listen closely—press your ear to the phone... *Hiktilda uchtred vanki tayeef exuldi*! Go to the lake now!"

Her mother's commanding tone, more authoritative than anything Holly had ever heard, left her thunderstruck.

Astonished, Holly felt the words resonate deep within her, shattering the chains of ignorance and confusion—her mind became free in that instant. A flame of life—a fire of raw energy—swelled in her heart, illuminating a newfound awareness of who she truly was. The plan was now unmistakably clear: everything she had once clung to—her house, her car, her job—was to be abandoned, discarded like the remnants of a bygone life. She was meant to be reborn.

Taking a deep, liberating breath, Holly felt a weight lift from her shoulders. Her mother was right—nothing else mattered now. "I'm not the same person anymore," she whispered to herself. "The old Holly is nothing but an old apparition, just a past memory, a dream."

With newfound purpose surging through her veins, she hurried to her closet, slipped into her running clothes and shoes, and made her way to the garage without delay. Sitting in her car for a few moments, she pondered the gravity of the changes unfolding within her. She didn't understand what was happening, but she didn't need to—she felt driven beyond any need of thinking. Then, with a sudden burst of determination, she stepped out of the car—instead of driving, a crystal-clear urge compelled her to run to the lake—leaving her car behind as if it were merely a relic of her past.

A renewed sense of hope had ignited in her heart; her

mother's message had sunk deeply into her soul, promising something far greater than the troubles of her recent days.

Hidden Lake lay about twenty miles away, yet she felt that no distance could halt her—she was a force of nature, unstoppable and alive like never before. With an authentic, radiant smile lighting her face, she sprinted out the front door—leaving it unlocked as if her old life no longer mattered—and charged down the road, faster than she had ever run, never wanting to look back, as she raced toward the canyon leading to the lake.

Chapter 22

As Holly neared the canyon road leading to the lake, she realized she was passing by Ryan's neighborhood—closer to the canyon's mouth, where an exclusive development of the town's most opulent houses had sprung up. On impulse, she veered off course and sprinted toward his home. The route wound along steep, curving asphalt roads that snaked upward until she reached his house.

Rather than run up the driveway, she stopped near the seven-foot-tall stone fence and leaped up the side of it, grasping the top with her hands and effortlessly pulling her body over. In one smooth motion, she jumped down to the other side, into the bushes that thickly covered the yard. She darted from bush to bush, from tree trunk to tree trunk, swift as a deer, then jumped over a small fence surrounding the porch and knocked on his front door.

She paused only briefly to consider her actions before casting aside all hesitation—trusting her impulses and embracing spontaneity. There was no time to plan what she might say; simmering rage boiled within her, her heart burning with anger toward him.

Without further hesitation, she pressed the doorbell. Ryan

opened the door, dressed in pajama bottoms and a T-shirt, his surprise evident as he scanned the driveway.

"Hi, Holly. How's it going? Did you... run here? That's weird," he remarked with a puzzled smirk, glancing around for her car.

"Yeah, I ran all the way here," she replied coolly. "I wanted to bring you a gift. May I come in for a minute?"

"A gift, huh? Well, I suppose you can come in, but you can't stay long—I have an important meeting and need to be somewhere soon," he said, stepping aside with a curious smile.

As she entered, his eyes widened in puzzlement. "What the hell did you do to your hair? It's all dyed black. You look like a crazy person!"

Holly stepped past him into the spacious room and swung the door closed behind her, ignoring his question. Eyeing Ryan with an intense, almost unnerving gaze, she inquired, "A meeting, huh? What's your meeting about?"

Taken aback, Ryan curtly replied, "It's none of your business. Stay in your own lane, Holly. What the hell happened to you—and your hair? Where were you, Childs? You look like hell."

The condescension in his use of her last name stung like a blow—reminiscent of a coach barking orders at his players. Though pure rage simmered inside her, Holly maintained a calm composure.

"Look, I wanted to give you something...something meaningful..." she murmured as she stepped closer. Lifting her hand, she gently caressed his cheek with her fingertips. Ryan visibly relaxed, perhaps anticipating the promise of a tender kiss—or something more.

Suddenly, her fingernails curled into his skin, and his body

115

stiffened. He drew a strained breath before freezing in place. Holly's fingertips lingered on his cheek—pressing in—as she met his gaze with an unreadable expression.

"Ryan, you've been keeping secrets from me," she said softly, her voice chillingly cold.

Ryan's eyes narrowed as his initial surprise gave way to fear and repulsion. He attempted to pull away, yet something about her touch held him—as if he were ensnared in an invisible web he had only just noticed.

"I know about your meetings," she whispered, her tone low and laced with menace. Leaning in, her face hovered just inches from his, her warm breath caressing his cheek.

"This game you think you're playing," she continued, her eyes narrowing with a predatory gleam, "it's over now. It's no game—it's very real. No longer will you treat me like a lesser creature. You are the one who is nothing—you are absolutely worthless."

His jaw clenched tight, his eyes flickering with fear. And then, without warning, black, gleaming threads—identical to the hairs on Holly's head—erupted from beneath her fingernails, darting across his cheeks and face. They wriggled and undulated before plunging into his skin, twisting and swaying as they anchored themselves into his flesh.

Holly stared in disbelief and wonder at the surreal spectacle. To her great surprise, an overwhelming wave of euphoria surged through her, filling her with a primal pleasure that left her breathless and yearning for more.

"It feels so good!" she blurted, caught between shock and exhilaration. She gazed at Ryan's face as his eyes rolled back and his skin turned an ashen, ghostly hue. Maintaining her hold on his face, the black threads pulsed and writhed beneath his skin as they siphoned his life force. An electrifying rush coursed through her veins—deep and primal—and a smile curled on her lips as she let out a soft moan of pleasure.

Simultaneously, the black threads atop her head—seemingly attuned to her euphoria—began to sway and coil in a frenzied dance, toppling her beanie onto the floor.

"They're feeding..." she moaned. "I am feeding!"

The realization struck her like a bolt of lightning. A surge of understanding washed over her—her hunger was intertwined with the black thread, an insatiable craving shared through an unseen connection. They were all part of her, and she, an inseparable part of them. In mere seconds, the threads stretched several inches longer, and Holly was overwhelmed by an ecstasy she had never before imagined, her moans of pleasure growing louder with each passing moment.

And then, after a few more seconds...

The black threads slowly stilled, retracting from Ryan's skin and sliding seamlessly back beneath her fingernails. She allowed her hand to fall, exhaling deeply as Ryan's body crumpled lifelessly to the floor. Gazing down at his motionless form, what had happened dawned on her—she had stolen his life force. She had consumed him. His body lay in a heap, marred by bruises in shades of purple and blue, like rivers etched across his face and neck.

Retrieving her beanie from the floor, Holly slipped it back onto her head, her fingers lightly brushing the black, thread-like hair on her scalp with newfound reverence. Stepping outside, she gently closed the door behind her.

She felt nothing for the corpse inside.

She looked forward and resumed her run toward the canyon without looking back. Her mind raced as swiftly as her feet.

"I can't believe it... It felt so good. I feel so good!" she exclaimed in excitement, quickening her pace to a full sprint.

She pressed on relentlessly, even as she navigated the steep, winding ascent of the canyon. Mile after mile blurred past, and by the time she reached the lake—twenty miles from her house—only two hours had elapsed. Yet Holly felt incredible: her pulse barely above normal, her lungs steady—not even gasping for breath.

At the lake, her gaze fixed on the secluded side-stream she had explored just a week earlier. Instinctively, she knew somewhere up there, in the mountains, was her true destination. Her mother's message earlier that day had awakened something deep within her. She had shed her former life entirely, like it was empty—meaningless.

The Holly she had been for twenty-two years—fearful, striving to be something she was not—had been replaced by someone powerful, free, and divine. She felt renewed. Embracing her transformation completely, she laughed as she leaped up the trail.

Ryan's fate troubled her not in the slightest—it felt utterly justified. In her mind, he had earned every ounce of what had befallen him. He had manipulated her—probably many others—and even if he hadn't earned it, she simply didn't care. No rationalization was needed; she felt no remorse for him. She knew the truth: he was inferior to who she truly was. Along with everyone else in town, they were all nothing compared to her. They were lesser creatures, while she had ascended to a divine plane.

She had given him his due, plain and simple. To her, they were all nothing more than scum—unworthy creatures who deserved the fate they received. There was not even a trace of remorse left—only a cold, unyielding satisfaction in her own surging power.

Freed from the stifling obligations and expectations that had once dictated her every move, Holly no longer felt tethered to the mundane—a house to clean, yard work to endure, or a dead-end job to survive. She had transcended the confines of her former life, rising above the world's constraints like smoke slipping through a cage.

As she raced up the small stream-side trail, her thoughts intensified, fueling the wild burst of energy coursing through her veins. She felt unstoppable—a true force of nature, ruthless and untamed. No longer anyone's pawn, she had become her own woman—a true goddess—standing on the precipice of a world she would bend, shape, and claim as her own.

Chapter 23

Holly moved swiftly and without hesitation up the rugged trail. This place no longer felt like a quiet retreat—it pulsed with a deep, mysterious energy, a secret sanctuary that felt sacred, as though it had always been meant for her. Each step stirred a sense of destiny, the very ground beneath her feet seeming consecrated, waiting patiently for her return.

With effortless grace, she leapt from rock to rock along the narrow stream. Each stride heightened her awareness of every sound, every scent that drifted through the air. A raspy, ethereal voice echoed in her mind: *Good, darling, keep coming... come to me.* The cadence was urgent and intimate, reverberating in the depths of her soul.

After what felt like both a fleeting moment and an eternity, Holly arrived at a clearing that stirred memories of a darker past. This was the place—where, just a week ago, she had seen dead animals hanging from trees, their bodies wrapped in eerie bundles of thread. The vivid recollection of that fateful day washed over her: the moment she first encountered the presence that would alter her life forever.

Her eyes scanned the clearing and landed on a shadowed figure, partly obscured by dense brush—cloaked in dark, flowing robes. She recognized the face immediately: ancient, familiar, and haunting. It was the Grand-Witch from her nightmares. Their eyes met. In that silent, charged instant, they exchanged a small, knowing smile. A homecoming. An unspoken understanding. Holly had returned to where she truly belonged.

"Hello, darling. Do you remember me?"

Holly nodded.

"My name is Gaeldritch."

Gaeldritch's presence was electric and comforting all at once—a fusion of the past and the powerful new self Holly had become. Words were unnecessary; both understood the purpose of her journey and what was to come.

Gaeldritch stepped forward and stood before Holly. In a low, deliberate voice, she said, "I will place my hand on your head for the final words of power, darling."

Holly removed her beanie, letting the cool forest air touch her new black hair. As she bowed her head, Gaeldritch raised her arm and gently laid her hand on the crown of Holly's head. A charge rippled through her body. Excitement surged as Gaeldritch bellowed the ancient words:

"Aplak ivrin namta marpa!"

A wave of warmth radiated from Gaeldritch's palm, flowing down through Holly's body. She felt the black threads unfurl—sprouting not only from her scalp but weaving through her veins, strengthening her limbs, sharpening her senses. A primal, ancient energy filled her—a force of creation reborn.

Gaeldritch's voice became a melodic whisper, sharp and soft like wind threading through trees. "Remove the clothing of mortals," she instructed, eyes glowing with otherworldly light. "They are no longer suitable."

Holly nodded. She reached down and untied her worn running shoes and discarded them. Piece by piece, she shed her past, each garment falling to the earth, swallowed by the forest floor—the final remnants of her old life removed.

Bare beside Gaeldritch, Holly welcomed the breeze that kissed her skin and the pulse of the earth beneath her soles. A gentle rhythm from the forest floor thrummed upward, embracing her.

Gaeldritch stepped back, her eyes gleaming with approval. "You've shed the last vestiges of your short, profane life," she said. "Now you stand as you truly are. You accepted the black thread, and it accepted you. Your long awaited renewal is here!"

Holly flexed her fingers, feeling the raw power rising within her. Her fear, doubt, and weakness were gone—left behind with her clothes. She had risen.

The transformation took hold. Holly stood transfixed as her body reshaped before her eyes. Her black-thread hair writhed and grew, extending from her head to her waist within seconds, alive with purpose. Her skin turned pale and cool, yet throbbed with strength. Her fingers stretched an inch longer, the sinews inside shifting painlessly but powerfully. Her features sharpened—nose, chin, teeth—all becoming more defined. Her fingernails darkened to a bruised green-black, thickening into claw-like tips. Within seconds, she was reborn—a chrysalis cracked open, revealing something beautiful and terrifying.

Gaeldritch watched her, pride burning in her eyes. "You are whole again," she said, reverently. "Fully renewed. The world is yours to shape, to command. And soon, you'll remember the full extent of your power. This body is our sacred gift—the vessel of the great soul we have long awaited. *Your* soul."

Holly ran her tongue over her teeth, marveling at their new strength. Her long, spidery fingers flexed with precision and force. Her hair—now animate—curled around her like loyal sentries, responding to her unspoken thoughts. In that moment, she felt as if she could stretch her will to the mountains and draw their power into her bones.

"Oh, Gaeldritch," she said, her voice transformed—raspier, deeper, more resonant. "I never imagined it would feel like this. I'd forgotten... I feel alive. Words can't describe it."

A silence fell as she absorbed the magnitude of her change. Then, softly, she asked, "Why did I have so many nightmares and visions these past few days?"

Gaeldritch reached for her hand and gently clasped it. "Our benefactor, Vizier Julian—you'll remember him soon— he explained it to me long ago. After you were gifted the black thread, you began your sublimation process. Your fears were purified. Your mind, tempered. You were flooded with memories—yours and others', recent and ancient. The process forced you to the edge. Only then could the thread judge your worthiness. And you, darling, were found more than worthy."

She continued, "The black thread is our companion, our strength. It lives within us, pooling beneath our fingernails, tinting them green-black. It moves through our spinal column. It winds through our arteries and veins, protecting us—and in return, we nourish it and give it a home. Our weak human hair has been replaced by our sacred thread, which grows at will. We clip it, weave it into sacks for Tum-Grissell, ropes and twines for our robes, and adornments for our staffs. It stores the light of sun, moon, and stars—gathering power.

It is alive, and it loves us, as we love it."

Holly listened in silence, the mysteries unfolding.

Gaeldritch paused, then added, "You're exceptional. The black thread destroys most who touch it. But you and I, and a few others, are chosen. Julian calls us the *Maha-Devi*—the great, shining few."

And at last, Holly understood. The nightmares. The visions. They were not curses—they were rites of passage. Sacred steps in her rebirth.

A sudden joy bloomed in her chest. She laughed—bright, wild, and uncontrollable. The black threads within her seemed to dance in joy with her.

Gaeldritch, watching her old friend laugh for the first time in ages, joined her. Their laughter rose together, ringing through the trees like a hymn of defiance and triumph.

Their shared joy echoed through the forest, brimming with ancient power and promise. Even the air seemed to hum with electricity, as if the woods themselves quivered in awe of what had returned.

Chapter 24

Gaeldritch's face broke into a delighted grin, her ancient eyes gleaming with pride. She whispered reverently. "My dear, your real name is Hiktilda Uchtred. Though the world may have known you as Holly Childs for a brief time, in the spirals of fate you have always been Hiktilda—Master of Corvids and Arachnids, the Grand-Weaver of our sacred black thread."

The name stirred within Holly—no, Hiktilda—like a long-forgotten melody, and memories began to surface in the depths of her mind: visions of ancient forests, darkened skies, and hallowed rituals. She recalled herself, centuries past, robed in black and standing beside Gaeldritch, drawing strength from elemental forces as she bent the very threads of life.

Taking Hiktilda's hands in her own bony ones, they allowed the black threads beneath their nails to dance and intertwine at their touch. "You remember," she said in awe. "Your essence lay hidden, waiting for you to shed the mask of Holly—a protective cocoon—until the time was right. And now, behold: you rise, beautiful and whole once more! Now we may continue what we began centuries ago, my darling—woven into the very fabric of the world is our will."

Hiktilda's heart pounded with exhilaration. Her fingers tightened around Gaeldritch's as a familiar, profound smile graced her lips. She was ready to reclaim her true path, to feel the commanding power of the threads that now coursed through her, and to reshape the world in ways she had long forgotten.

"What will be done first, Gaeldritch?" she asked, her voice brimming with excitement and confidence, her eyes alight with wonder.

Gaeldritch's eyes twinkled. "First, my dear, allow me to return your raiment and staff, and then we shall celebrate your return tonight, with your coven—your family. And then... we will weave as we once did, creating a tapestry of our will in the world."

Reaching into her bag, Gaeldritch produced a heavy black robe and a pair of leather boots with one-inch heels—almost identical to her own—and handed them to Hiktilda. Slipping into the dark robe that fit her perfectly, Hiktilda then pulled on the boots as the laces of black thread tightened at the command of her will, without even her touch.

Their laughter mingled with the rustling of the forest, carrying a promise of arcane knowledge and ancient power reborn. Together, they walked through the brush toward a towering pine tree, where, leaning against its trunk, stood a formidable staff.

Gaeldritch hoisted the staff toward Hiktilda, drawing attention to its intricate carvings and the bundle of braided black threads lashed securely at its tip—a wicked, black broom-like emblem of authority. "This is yours, Hiktilda," she declared, handing over the staff. "I have safeguarded it for you for centuries, along with your robe, and many other possessions now secured in the coven's chambers."

As Hiktilda grasped the staff, a cascade of memories flooded back—each carved symbol pulsing under her fingers, unlocking fragments of her past. She recalled wandering through shadowed woods, casting spells under midnight skies, and wielding this very staff with mastery. It was a conduit—a connection to the forces that had once flowed through her and were now reawakening.

Looking up at Gaeldritch with steady determination, Hiktilda said, "Thank you for preserving it for me. I feel whole with it in my hand; with each passing moment, more of my past returns."

Gaeldritch nodded approvingly. "Good, darling. Soon, very soon, all will return—our rituals, our sacred words, our purpose. Your mother and Thomas are eager to see you in your true form again."

The two witches ventured deeper into the woods, each step drawing Hiktilda closer to the life she had once lived in the forgotten past. She felt her power unfurl—a dark, potent force that had long lain dormant, now embraced fully.

They approached a cluster of smooth boulders beneath the expansive boughs of an ancient pine. Gaeldritch gestured gracefully toward the stones. "Let us sit and talk for a few minutes, darling."

Hiktilda settled onto the cool stone, gazing out over the dark forest where tall trees swayed as if in acknowledgment of her return. The quiet hum of the woods was both familiar and soothing, like an old melody stirring in the depths of her memory.

Gaeldritch's voice dropped to a near-whisper as she said, "The power of the nature remembers you, just as you are beginning to remember it. The power within you is not new, Hiktilda—it has merely been sleeping, waiting to awaken."

Running her fingers over the intricate carvings of her staff, Hiktilda felt more memories stirring. "Why did I forget all this? What happened to me?" she asked, her curiosity raised.

Gaeldritch sighed, a slow, heavy sound that seemed to echo ancient sorrow. "You were brutally murdered, dear one. Long ago, far away from here, a band of zealots destroyed your body with fire. Yet, in your wisdom, you spoke the proper words of power when it mattered most. While the flames consumed your flesh, your words shielded your soul, saving you from oblivion. It was an incredible display of will power to keep the presence of mind to speak the words of protection while flames consumed your flesh. It was the saddest day in my life. And I could do nothing to save you."

Hiktilda absorbed the revelation with a mix of sorrow, relief, and a growing resolve for vengeance. "Yes, Hiktilda," Gaeldritch murmured, resting a gentle hand on her shoulder. "Now, you are ready to reclaim all that was once yours. Our coven awaits, and soon the ancestors of those zealots will pay for the misdeeds of their predecessors."

A profound silence fell between them, the ancient forest cradling their shared understanding. Then, Gaeldritch spoke again with a more up-beat tone, "Do you remember the man you saw once covered in mud? You may have deduced that he is your brother Thomas—though not your brother by blood, of course."

Hiktilda listened intently.

"He has watched over and protected you for the past 22 years, Hiktilda. Remember the dog that once attacked you as a small child? Thomas defended you then, and he has shielded you from far greater dangers since then. In your home, your mother was your protector, and whenever you left your home, Thomas was always nearby."

As fragments of memory coalesced, Gaeldritch continued, "His self-given name is spoken with reverence, it is Tum-Grissell. He was created by our coven's master—our great benefactor, Vizier Julian—and is among his most cherished creations: an earthen being of the highest order, endowed with wisdom and immense strength, he is a golem, an *Abominatio*. You have been blessed by the coven with a protector dedicated to protecting you for all these years. You have been cherished and well guarded, my dear."

Hiktilda's eyes widened as vague recollections of Thomas— or Tum-Grissell—flashed in her mind, a quiet presence that had always been there, now coming into sharp focus. "An *Abominatio*…" she murmured, awe and understanding mingling in her tone.

"Yes," Gaeldritch affirmed softly, "he is far more than he appears. Molded from the very earth, he was fashioned to endure and to watch, bound eternally by loyalty to our coven, an incredible creation."

Hiktilda nodded slowly, deeply moved by the depth of care bestowed upon her. Gaeldritch's expression softened further. "Tum-Grissell has been steadfast, knowing that this day would come—that you would awaken to your true self. You will see him soon. And your mother, too—though she is not your first mother. Her true name is Hazel, and she has been as essential to you as Tum-Grissell. Both have sacrificed much to protect your body, the holy child, for your safe return."

A warm, ancient bond stirred within Hiktilda as she looked up at Gaeldritch. "Thank you for telling me this. I am eager to see them both. Thank you, Gaeldritch."

Gaeldritch smiled with pride. "Then let us now return to the coven, where your family awaits."

Chapter 25

As moonlight filtered through the trees, casting silvery patterns upon the forest floor, Hiktilda rose to her feet with her staff in hand—her mind and body brimming with renewed strength, her spirit soaring. The weight of her former human life—small, constrained, and unknowing—melted away like a distant dream. In that moment, she was fully alive.

Gaeldritch led her deeper into the woods along hidden paths known only to the coven. The winding trail, set among ancient trees and gnarled roots, grew cooler with each step, carrying whispers of the earth and echoes of past rituals. With every footfall, Hiktilda's senses sharpened; memories of her once-hidden power and purpose stirred, awakening the spirit she had long forgotten.

Eventually, the path opened onto a low rock face shrouded in dense foliage. Gaeldritch motioned toward a narrow opening in the hillside. "Our sacred dwelling," she said softly, pride glowing in her eyes. "Once you pass through this portal, you will be home."

Without hesitation, Gaeldritch stepped through the opening, and Hiktilda followed. Together, they descended a long passage carved into the stone—a journey into the depths where the coven awaited, ready to welcome her back into the heart of their family.

As Hiktilda advanced through the rocky corridor, she felt a profound sense of belonging settle into her very bones, filling the void where doubt and restlessness had once resided. When the passage finally opened into a vast chamber, dimly lit by the red-orange glow of firelight, a quiet warmth spread through her, embracing her like an old friend.

From across the chamber, Hiktilda heard her mother's voice sound with authority, "Grand-Witch Hiktilda returns!"

The cavern erupted in a resounding chant: "All Hail Grand-Witch Hiktilda!" The voices echoed off every surface, weaving into her very being. Her black hair cascaded in undulating waves, moving with a life of its own as the proclamation wrapped around her like a shroud of belonging, anchoring her spirit to this ancient sanctuary.

As her eyes adjusted to the dim light, Hiktilda beheld many familiar faces—some etched with the wisdom of centuries, others vibrant with youthful fervor. These were her kin, her family, bound by a connection deeper than blood. In the center of the gathering, she saw her mother, Hazel, standing beside Thomas. Gratitude swelled within her at the sight of their warm, welcoming smiles.

Thomas, his blue eyes filled with quiet reverence, wearing only a black short breech-clout, stepped forward. When he reached her, he knelt on one knee, bowed his head and spoke to her, "By your will, I do your bidding, Grand-Witch."

Hiktilda extended her pale hand, her long fingers caressing his head gently as she spoke with firm authority, "Thomas, you have fulfilled your duty and protected me. I am forever in your debt for a task well done, my faithful brother. You are truly magnificent. Please, rise and stand by my side, Tum-Grissell."

With an expression of gratitude and awe, he rose and moved to her side.

Then, Hazel stepped away from the others and walked toward Hiktilda. Though her mother of the past twenty-two years appeared much as she remembered, subtle differences marked her transformation. Her hair now cascaded freely over her shoulders in a darker brown than she had before.

"My daughter, my most cherished!" Hazel exclaimed in the tender, familiar tone of a loving mother.

Hiktilda enveloped her in a heartfelt embrace. "Mother, Hazel, I can never repay you for all you have done for me."

Hazel laughed gently. "Quite the contrary, Grand-Witch! You cannot yet recall the countless times you have aided me, back when I was a young woman. It is time you call me by my true name, Hazel—Hannah Childs was only the name I used for your upbringing, now to be cast away just as Holly Childs is no longer to be used by you," and with a slight pause, exclaimed, "For you are whole again, Grand-Witch!"

They smiled, gazing into each other's eyes as they clutched each other by the shoulders.

Hazel continued, her voice filled with joy, "It fills my heart with immense pride to see you restored to your true form, Hiktilda—just as I remember our first meeting in the old forest of Bavaria, but that was a long time ago, and we are here now. I will always cherish the memories of being your mother and guardian for that short time—such an honor to be so close to our holy child."

Hiktilda replied, "Hazel, my dear mother, thank you for your commitment and sacrifice. I will forever be strongly

133

bonded to you, darling."

Noticing the quiet murmur among the gathered witches, Gaeldritch raised her arms to hush the crowd. Then, with commanding reverence, she proclaimed, "The return of Hiktilda Uchtred, our once-lost sister, is complete! She is with us again! The Grand-Weaver of the Elbynelem Clan stands renewed, in full strength and glory, as she did centuries ago."

Her eyes turned to Hiktilda, gleaming, "Welcome home, Grand-Witch."

Hiktilda gazed out at the assembled coven, each face reflecting respect and admiration. With a nod and a serene smile, she raised her staff and declared, "We will make new strides into the future, and we will finish what we began centuries ago. I am home. I am returned, and I am whole again!" her voice, strong and resonant.

Gaeldritch then proclaimed with authority, "She has returned!" as the entire coven then echoed through the cavern with the final chorus resounding:

"All Hail Grand-Witch Hiktilda!"

II

IMPLICATIONS

Chapter 26

Grand-Witch Hiktilda sat beside her closest confidante, fellow Grand-Witch Gaeldritch, their aged yet strong forms rocking gently in time with their creaking chairs. The dim light spilling from iron lanterns clung to the cavern walls in flickering ribbons, casting elongated shadows that danced across the rough-hewn stone. Deep beneath the roots of Mons Tonitrus—Thunder Mountain, as the uninitiated called it—this chamber had long served as the heart of the coven's power, its influence sinking into the very bones of the mountain over the past century.

The distant drip of water echoed through the cavernous expanse, punctuated by the rustling of unseen creatures stirring in the dark. It was a sanctuary of silence, ancient and unbroken, save for the rhythmic creak of their chairs.

Gaeldritch turned her sharp gaze toward Hiktilda, her face carved with the wisdom of ages. Always enigmatic, her expression was a careful balance of calculation and amusement. Hiktilda met her gaze with an emotion far more tender—admiration, adoration, an unspoken understanding that spanned lifetimes.

At last, Gaeldritch broke the quiet.

"The town is in a state of shock," she began, her voice

a smooth, melodic murmur, layered with the weight of certainty. "I had some of our younger sisters erase the traces of your past—burned the evidence, the homes. Yours, your brother's, Hazel's... They are ash now. No trail remains of the lives you all left behind."

Hiktilda's head tilted slightly, her expression unreadable. When she spoke, her voice was calm but threaded with tension. "The old farmhouse is gone?" A pause. "And my mother—how does she feel about that?"

Gaeldritch waved a hand dismissively, her smile faint but knowing. "Hazel? Oh, darling, she does not trouble herself with such trivialities. She has seen many houses rise and fall, their walls nothing more than wooden cages to Hazel. Her true home is here with the coven, as it has always been. She understands that well."

Hiktilda's eyes flickered toward the lantern's pale bluish-white glow, her thoughts slipping into memories—ghosts of a past she could no longer fully grasp. But before she could speak, Gaeldritch continued, her tone dipping into something heavier.

"Law enforcement..." She let the words linger, darkening the air between them. "Not to worry, but they are involved now. And not just the local fools. They'll start pulling at threads, trying to weave explanations for what they cannot comprehend. We must be ready—give them a trail to follow."

Hiktilda did not react outwardly, though her rocking slowed ever so slightly. She let Gaeldritch speak.

Leaning forward, Gaeldritch allowed the firelight to catch the sharp planes of her face. "Yes, darling," she murmured, her words deliberate, her tone laced with something almost indulgent. "I understand that in the throes of your transformation, you were... overcome. A celestial rage, unleashed." Her lips curved, a whisper of wicked delight. "It was beautiful to see you spark to life again."

Hiktilda's own smile was slow, unrepentant. "I am alive again," she mused, voice dripping with satisfaction. "And my renewal... it still burns within me. A fire in my soul, a thing of pure delight, my darling Gaeldritch. I feel a sense of purpose again...it's been so long since it felt meaningful."

Gaeldritch's eyes narrowed slightly, pleased yet ever observant. "Ryan paid for it in a way that—shall we say—demands attention." She paused, weighing her next words. "...It was meaningful, yes, but lacked mystery. No veils to shroud his removal."

A heavy silence stretched between them, thick as the cavern's damp air. Gaeldritch drummed her long fingers against the wooden armrest, her gaze unyielding. Then, at last, her lips curled into a slow, mischievous smile. "But I must admit, darling, it was very satisfying to hear of your return, your vigor. To see you let go like that—it took me back to so many times we've shared."

Hiktilda's faint smile did not waver. "The pitiful maggot's death will lead to my family being presumed missing."

"Yes," Gaeldritch confirmed smoothly, her voice steady yet edged with meaning. "And you should know—Tum-Grissell protected you twice before your return. Two zealots of the cross... they came for you last week, reckless, determined, dangerous. But he saw to it they would not trouble you." She let out a small, knowing laugh. "Their absence, too, will be noted. Another thread to weave into the tale."

Hiktilda arched an eyebrow, intrigue flickering in her eyes. "Two zealots?" she murmured. "So now they will be searching for me, my mother, Thomas… and those two as well. Is that everyone?"

Gaeldritch's expression glimmered with secrets. "For now, yes. But you know as well as I do—Ryan's death is the keystone. They found him before we could burn the evidence. It will not be brushed aside like the others. His body demands answers. His family has pull."

Hiktilda's expression hardened, her serene poise now laced with quiet resolve. "Then let them search. Their curiosity will lead them nowhere."

Gaeldritch chuckled, a rich, dark sound that slithered through the cavern's stillness. "Of course, darling. We've faced worse than this. Still, there are loose ends. Vizier Julian is already aware. He remains untroubled." Her tone was almost amused. "He believes in us, as always, and he has already begun shrouding your family's finances—the wealth that allowed you all to live in such comfort for twenty-two years. He assures me it is handled, well-hidden. And he has the utmost faith in our ability to deal with the investigations that are surely coming."

Hiktilda's lips curled into a knowing smile. "Julian sees the clarity of our purpose. His faith is well-placed. This is a trifle. I have been reborn but a day, yet already my memories have flooded back. My incantations, my spells—they are mine once more." She exhaled, a slow, satisfied breath. "I am eager to see Vizier Julian again."

Gaeldritch leaned back in her chair, her sharp eyes gleaming with dark amusement. "Our benefactor," she mused. "For a man who is physically blind, he sees most clearly. His insights are unmatched, a true genius, though our enemies will never cease to underestimate him." Her smirk deepened. "He told me your power would return like a tide, that it would flood back into place where it belongs. I am charmed to see how right he was—to witness you take your rightful place by my side as Grand-Weaver of the coven."

Hiktilda let out a soft laugh, the sound a ripple in the cavern's stillness. "His blind eyes see the threads of fate as if they were woven before him."

"Then," Gaeldritch said, her voice silk over steel, "let us ensure his faith in us is not misplaced. We must resolve these matters quickly, before their curiosity turns into something more."

"Of course," Hiktilda replied smoothly, her confidence unshaken. Then, with a glimmer of dark amusement, she added, "And we'll find pleasure in the process."

Gaeldritch's laugh was quiet but rich with delight. "Oh, darling, I would expect nothing less from you. Now—let us speak of details. The game has begun, but it is we who will dictate how it plays."

Hiktilda gave a slow nod, her eyes alight with certainty.

Chapter 27

The town of East Bryndelle was a place where time seemed to hold its breath, a small settlement deep in the rugged forests of the Sierras. Founded in the late 1880s, it began as a modest mining town, its muddy main street flanked by flimsy wooden buildings thrown together to meet the rapid demands of prospectors. Yet as the mines dried up, the town transformed, reinventing itself as a hub for milling lumber from the dense Sierra forests and shipping it to the Sacramento Valley, 120 miles to the southwest. The western edges of the town, once wild with forest, were cleared for fertile farmlands, establishing East Bryndelle as a community rooted in industry and agriculture.

Over the next century, wealth began to seep into East Bryndelle like water filling a parched creek. The rickety structures were replaced with brick buildings and quarried stone from the rugged ridges nearby. The town's expansion blended its natural resources with a spirit of enterprise, turning it into a thriving community. Yet East Bryndelle bore a shadow: a now-defunct sister settlement to the west, separated by the churning Millfork River. West Bryndelle, once a mirror of its sibling, had withered after the mines closed. What remained were ghostly cabins and overgrown meadows, relics of a forgotten past. Rusted rails crisscrossed the forest floor, abandoned tools buried under moss and decay. The two towns were divided not only by the river but by the stark contrast between progress and ruin.

For most of its existence, East Bryndelle had been tranquil, its rhythm unbroken by the chaos that plagued larger cities. The population had grown steadily over the decades, reaching just over 3,000 souls. A recent surge of new residents—drawn by the town's charm and affordable housing—had breathed fresh life into its community. Remote workers from Redding, Sacramento, and beyond had arrived, mingling with families who had lived there for generations. Life in East Bryndelle was quiet. Predictable. Until this week.

Something had shifted, an undercurrent of unease rippling through the town. The local police, a modest ten-officer force, were more accustomed to handling lost pets and noise complaints than anything serious. Their chief investigator, Detective Andrew Sanders, bore the title of Chief Detective more as a formality than a necessity. In East Bryndelle, people left their doors unlocked and crime was rare. Or at least, it had been.

This Sunday morning, the air in the station was heavy, taut with tension. Sanders arrived early, his footsteps echoing against the linoleum floor of the modest brick building. The front desk officer, a steady man rarely perturbed by anything, handed him an Incident Report with trembling fingers.

"You're going to want to read this," the officer murmured.

Sanders scanned the first lines, his brow knitting tighter with each word. By the time he finished, he was seated at his desk, the report spread out in front of him like a harbinger of doom. Missing persons. Arson. A mysterious death. This wasn't just unusual—it was catastrophic.

The missing persons list had grown alarmingly fast over the past week. First, there was Anthony Scolati, a young Catholic priest in training who had vanished without a trace. Then came, Julie Winthrop, a beloved teacher at the local school, had also gone missing. Most recently Hannah Childs, her daughter Holly, and her son Thomas, each living at different addresses yet all disappearing within a day of one another. The family's homes had been set ablaze, reduced to charred ruins. Five missing. And then there was the body.

Ryan Danielson had been found dead in his home. No wounds, no signs of forced entry—yet his body was riddled with bruises so severe they suggested a brutal beating. The coroner's preliminary report was baffling, and whispers of something unsolvable had already begun to circulate among the townsfolk.

Sanders leaned back in his chair, the old wood groaning under his weight. He had seen his fair share of minor chaos— bar fights that got out of hand, a burglary here or there—but nothing like this. The implications of these cases bore down on him like an avalanche. This wasn't something his small team could handle.

He reached for the phone, his hand hesitating as if the action itself marked a point of no return. Dialing the number for the State Law Enforcement Deputy Commissioner in Redding, he listened to the line buzz. After a moment, a familiar voice answered.

"Watson here."

Sanders cleared his throat, forcing himself to sound steady. "Hello, Deputy Commissioner Watson—Richard, it's Detective Sanders from East Bryndelle." He paused, gripping the phone tighter. "I'm doing fine, thanks, but... I've got a situation here. A big one."

Watson's voice grew sharp. "What kind of situation?"

Sanders took a deep breath. "Missing persons. Five of them. And a homicide that doesn't make any sense. On top of that, multiple cases of arson....houses burned out. All in the span of a week." He hesitated before adding, "You know this isn't normal. Not for here."

The line went quiet, the silence stretching between them like the space before a thunderstorm.

"Do you have any leads?" Watson finally asked.

"Not yet," Sanders admitted, hating how hollow the words felt. "But I know I can't do this alone. I need your help. Fast."

Watson exhaled audibly. "Alright, Sanders. I'll see what resources we can spare. But if this is as serious as it sounds, you need to prepare for things to get worse before they get better."

"Will do, Richard. Thanks for everything."

Sanders hung up, the weight in his chest growing heavier. He stared out the window of his office, watching the early morning sunlight filter through the blinds. The peaceful streets of East Bryndelle felt like a cruel irony now, masking the chaos brewing just beneath the surface.

Something was coming for this town, something dark and unrelenting. Sanders could feel it in his gut. He didn't know what he was up against, but he knew one thing for certain—East Bryndelle would never be the same.

Chapter 28

H azel was dressed in a black robe, similar to those worn by Hiktilda and Gaeldritch, though hers was slightly thinner in places. She approached Hiktilda, who sat alone in her main chamber. As Hazel stepped closer, her head remained bowed, every movement laced with reverence and restraint. Her dark brown hair cascaded over her shoulders, framing a new and striking feature—an obsidian-black checkerboard grid painted across the center of her face, stretching from forehead to chin and from ear to ear.

It was a 7-by-7 square pattern, stark and deliberate, known among the upper echelon of the coven as the *Venus Quadrata*. This mark was no mere adornment—it was a blessing, one that granted immense power to its bearer. Hazel had earned it through centuries of service to the coven, culminating in her role as mother and protector to Hiktilda for the past twenty-two years.

On the night Hiktilda had finally shed the last vestige of the persona named Holly Childs and returned to the coven, Gaeldritch had bestowed the mark of the *Venus Quadrata* upon Hazel as her timely reward. With a concoction of a sacred black, oily pigment combined with other secret ingredients, she had painted the liquid onto Hazel's face. Every intersection of the grid pattern was meticulously applied, each square perfectly aligned with the next.

Hazel had accepted the mark eagerly, knowing that once the sacred black threads were woven into the design by a Grand-Witch's hand, it would unlock a rare illusion—a body and face of otherworldly beauty, capable of mesmerizing any man who dared meet her gaze.

The application had been painful. The black substance inflamed and burned the skin, forcing the glossy black ink deep beneath the surface—far more permanent than any tattoo. The result was a mark that would last for centuries, retaining its clarity and power without the slightest fading. Gaeldritch had completed the painting with uncanny speed, her long, agile fingers moving with supernatural precision. Then, using a potent salve, she healed Hazel's raw skin in under an hour—a process that would have otherwise taken days, if not weeks.

But the price of the *Venus Quadrata* was steep. Beyond the centuries of loyal service to the coven, for half the year, Hazel would wear the grid visibly across her natural face—a strange, unnerving look she considered a small price for the following six months in which she would have perfect beauty. It was a trade she had accepted without hesitation when Gaeldritch had offered it before Holly was born.

Hazel had waited twenty-two years—sacrificing every day, every hour, every moment—for the holy child, Holly. She had endured every trial without complaint, obeyed Gaeldritch's every command, and devoted herself wholly to the coven's cause and to protecting the new body of Hiktilda.

In return for her unwavering devotion, she had received

and savored other rewards she received along the way: euphoric visions Gaeldritch granted her from time to time, and occasional nights of unearthly ecstasy that left her aching for more. The coven was her life, her purpose, her sanctuary. For five hundred years, it had been her only priority and she cherished it.

The chamber Hazel now entered was dimly lit. Candles flickered in wrought-iron holders, casting dancing shadows across the cold stone walls. The air was heavy with the mingling scents of crushed herbs, warm wax, and something faintly metallic. Hiktilda sat waiting in her old rocking chair, her long fingers drumming rhythmically against the curved armrests. Her piercing gaze locked onto Hazel as she approached.

"Sweet Hazel, raise your head," Hiktilda said, her voice rich and commanding, laced with eerie warmth. "I'm so glad you're here. I look forward to getting to know you again— and to having your help with some troubling matters that need resolution. My memory is still returning, and I can't yet recall many details, my dear. Tell me, Hazel, what is your last name?"

Hazel lifted her head, her voice steady yet deferential. "My name is Hazel Kraus, Grand-Witch."

"And where were you raised before you found your true family?" Hiktilda asked, her voice probing.

"A small town called Friesing, north of München, where we met long ago… in Bavaria, Grand-Witch."

"When was that, Hazel?"

"We met in 1565, when I was thirty-five years old. You initiated me into the coven the following year, Grand-Witch," Hazel replied without hesitation.

Hiktilda smiled faintly, leaning back in her chair as it creaked beneath her. "Hazel," she repeated, savoring the name. "I'm glad to recall your mortal name… You have another name as well. We'll speak of it in time. But for now, I have a task for you—one that suits your talents and unique expertise."

Hazel straightened, eager to serve. "I am ready to follow your bidding, Grand-Witch. I will assist the coven however you see fit."

Hiktilda nodded, her approval a palpable force. "Good. You will now put your *Venus Quadrata* to use," she said, her tone sharpening with purpose. "Listen closely. You remember the man I worked for when I was Holly—Greg Warren. He owns Bryndelle Insurance, just off Main Street and Second East. He's married with children, yes, but he also keeps a mistress. Her name is Anna—I have heard him speak to her on the phone. I want you to follow him—very discreetly. He will meet with her, I'm sure of this, and then follow her to find out where she lives. Do not interact with either of them. These are my requirements. Do you understand?"

"I understand, Grand-Witch," Hazel replied with a nod.

"Perfect," Hiktilda said, flashing a sly grin. "That's just the first half. Once you've completed this, return to me. The second task will require you to use your powers of seduction."

"Yes, Grand-Witch," Hazel replied, her voice brimming with anticipation. "I understand completely."

Hiktilda's smile deepened. "Good. Then let's not waste any more time. Kneel before me, and we'll cast the spell of beauty now… *Nunc carmen pulchritudinis canemus!*"

Hazel smiled and knelt eagerly as Hiktilda rose from her chair, her movements fluid, serpentine. From a hidden pocket in her robe, she withdrew a small vial. Its clear glass shimmered in the dim light, filled with a blood-red liquid streaked with iridescent pink. The vial pulsed faintly, as though alive.

"Drink this, darling," Hiktilda instructed, her voice soft but insistent. "Drink it all... *bibe totum*. Yes, always continue learning the words—when spoken properly, they hold such power."

Hazel took the vial, her hands trembling slightly as she uncorked it. The scent was sharp and intoxicating—like crushed roses laced with iron. She raised it to her lips and drank deeply. The liquid burned sweetly as it slid down her throat, and her heart quickened as warmth spread through her core.

Hiktilda lifted her hands and began the incantation, her voice resounding with ancient power:

"Darifex prozeefus! Veneficium pulchritudinis, Hazel Wirgo feruzstisio!"

She pressed her fingers firmly against Hazel's face—her index on the right cheekbone, pinky on the left, and the others across the bridge of Hazel's nose. The checkerboard design beneath her touch pulsed with a rose-red glow.

"Taristti lilswar gribe! Black thread, scrawl and scribe!"

From beneath Hiktilda's blackened nails, fine tendrils of ink-black thread shot forth, writhing like living serpents. They burrowed into the painted grid, spiraling and twisting, weaving a sigil into the *Venus Quadrata*—a tangled form like a cursive S and V, looping over and over in chaotic beauty. The threads shimmered like liquid obsidian, radiating otherworldly power.

"Incantatio formosa finire! Sharadi me jala ja laya manan!"

With a sudden motion of Hiktilda's spidery fingers, the

threads recoiled, vanishing back into her nails. A brilliant flash of red light burst through the chamber. Hazel gasped softly as a wave of warmth surged through her, her entire body glowing crimson. A soft pink haze drifted from her form as the light faded, leaving her still and breathless.

When she opened her eyes, her transformation was complete. She appeared to be in her mid-twenties again. Her once dark brown hair was now a luminous golden blonde, cascading in flawless waves. Her eyes sparkled with a hypnotic fusion of emerald and sapphire. Her lips, full and sumptuous, were framed by flawless skin that seemed to glow from within. Green earrings, conjured from nothing, dangled from her ears, catching the flicker of candlelight.

Hiktilda pulled a small mirror from her pocket and held it up.

Hazel's hands flew to her face, trembling as she touched her cheeks and lips in awe. "Oh my... I can't believe it. I'm... I'm so beautiful. No—beyond beautiful! I'm the perfect woman!"

"Yes, dear," Hiktilda said, her smile curling with devious satisfaction. "This spell will last for half a year. And there is much more in store for you, as you continue to serve the coven, as you always do."

Hazel stood in silent wonder. She had been promised beauty for years, and now, at last, it had been granted—and it exceeded even her wildest dreams.

"Now, pay attention," Hiktilda continued, her voice adopting a lecturing tone. "We are no longer in München, Bavaria, five hundred years ago. We live in an age of technology, darling. Surveillance is everywhere. Cameras are everywhere. You might wonder how we manage."

She paused to ensure Hazel was listening.

"The elixir you drank, combined with the words I spoke— words of power—has infused your body with a unique vibration. In the old language we called this aura the shaya- lilla, the play of light, it bends and distorts it as it nears your body. To cameras, you'll appear as little more than a blur... a shadow... or sometimes even nothing at all. The light shimmer around you is something modern devices cannot capture. And with even more potent words and admixtures to our concoctions, we can extend that shimmer to affect human perception itself. The shaya-lilla is very powerful."

A slow smile crept across her lips. "An illusion bordering on true invisibility. You, my dear Hazel, are now what we call *shimmering*. Electronic devices can't capture your image clearly. People, however, will still see you."

Hazel's breath hitched. In all her years with the coven, she had never heard of such power.

Hiktilda's eyes sparkled with dark satisfaction. "Yes, darling. You're learning well. And this is only the beginning."

She threw her head back and began to cackle, the sound echoing through the chamber like a dark, melodic storm. Hazel, overwhelmed with excitement, joined her. Their laughter mingled, rising and swirling like a spell in motion— charged with promise, power, and the thrill of transforma- tion.

Chapter 29

Hazel emerged from a cluster of dense foliage— towering pines and wild, tangled underbrush that seemed impenetrable at first glance. She stepped out into the open from a faint, well-worn path, invisible to the untrained eye, that wound its way from the coven's hidden stronghold to a large house nestled quietly on the edge of the estate. Unlike the grand front entrance with its paved elegance, this side approach was discreet, designed for the members of the coven in their comings and goings.

Hazel wore a pair of faded gray sweats and running shoes— the kind of clothes that offered anonymity. The look was mundane, but the moment was anything but. Just as the sun crested the jagged treetops, golden light spilled across the land. It cast long, shifting shadows that danced across the curving driveway as she stepped onto its clean concrete. A large black SUV was parked there—a commanding presence, deliberately positioned.

Hazel moved with quiet confidence, each step deliberate, her presence unmistakable despite her modest attire. As she reached the vehicle, she opened the passenger door and found Michelle Simms waiting behind the wheel. A fellow sister of the coven, Michelle was no less formidable than she was beautiful. Her dark hair was swept back into a casual braid, but nothing about her demeanor was casual. Her features were sharp, effortlessly striking, and her eyes—keen, intelligent, and dangerously playful—glinted with untold secrets. A black diamond tattoo shimmered on her right index finger as she drummed her fingers against the leather steering wheel, the movement hypnotic and feline.

Michelle was more than just a coven member. She was one of the stewards of the Simms Family Trust—a centuries-old dynasty. The De Mantenero Vale Estate, under her family's name, spanned over six thousand acres of forested land. Thunder Mountain itself rose within its borders like a silent sentinel, and the house they now approached served as both a sanctuary and a front—blurring the line between the ordinary world and the coven's world. It was here that Michelle lived, alongside a select few of the coven's inner circle. The estate acted as a bridge between the coven and the profane, ensuring the witches had access to all the necessary trappings of modern life: food, technology, clothing and money.

Hazel slid into the passenger seat with practiced ease.

"Hello, Michelle," she said, her voice smooth and unhurried.

Michelle gave her a slow, appraising glance, lips curling into a smirk. "Wow," she murmured, shaking her head. "It's crazy how pretty you are. Absolute perfection." There was no mistaking the admiration in her voice—her gaze lingered on Hazel's flawless features.

Hazel smirked faintly but said nothing, closing the door with a satisfying click.

"I mean... wow. Unreal." Michelle let out a low chuckle before snapping back into business mode. "Alright—no time to waste."

With that, she pressed her foot to the gas. The SUV rumbled to life, tires rolling down the winding driveway and through a large automatic iron gate, surging onto the canyon road. The engine's low hum filled the cabin, broken only by the occasional gust of wind through the open windows.

Hazel leaned back, her gaze flicking over the verdant canyon scenery whipping past. The drive was quiet, but not comfortably so—something unspoken hung between them, thick as the morning mist clinging to the cliffs. A sense of urgency loomed, unspoken yet undeniable

As they pulled into town, the quiet of morning lingered, broken only by the low hum of the SUV's engine. Hazel, her eyes sharp and calculating, finally spoke.

"Let's park on Main Street and Fourth East."

"Sure thing," Michelle replied in an easy tone, her hands steady on the wheel. She smoothly parallel-parked the SUV, positioning it within clear view of Bryndelle Insurance—the office Hazel needed to watch.

Minutes stretched into over an hour as they watched from behind the tinted windows, the mundane rhythms of small-town life playing out around them. Hazel remained motionless, her gaze locked on the building's entrance, every sense attuned. Finally, the door to the insurance office opened, and Greg Warren stepped out. He moved quickly, striding toward his own SUV parked nearby, and drove off without hesitation.

"Let's go, Michelle. Follow him," Hazel said, her tone calm but insistent.

Michelle nodded, and the SUV slipped into motion, tailing

Greg with practiced subtlety. It didn't take long—he drove just three blocks west before pulling into the small parking lot of the City Park. Hazel and Michelle kept their distance but maintained a clear line of sight.

Moments later, a slender woman with long auburn hair, wearing a tan dress, stepped out of a small white crossover. She moved with quiet confidence as she climbed into Greg's SUV, her ease around him unmistakable.

"That's her," Hazel said, her voice low but certain. "H told me her name is Anna. This part of the job's halfway done. Now we just need to find out where she lives, then we head back."

They followed at a discreet distance as Greg's SUV exited the park and headed toward a small French-themed deli just a block away. Hazel and Michelle parked nearby, the black SUV blending easily into the background. From their vantage point, they watched Greg and the woman, Anna, settle at a table on the deli's patio, laughing, flirting, and sharing a leisurely meal. Sunlight danced off their wine glasses as they toasted, oblivious to the eyes watching them.

"Cheaters," Hazel murmured, a faint smirk tugging at her lips. "I don't think they'll be smiling for long."

Eventually, the couple finished their meal and returned to Greg's SUV and drove back to the City Park, Hazel and Michelle tailing them. After a few minutes of parting chatter and overly enthusiastic waves, Anna climbed into her own vehicle while Greg drove off.

"Okay, hopefully she heads home now," Hazel whispered, her tone steady but tinged with impatience. "Otherwise, we could be in for the long haul."

Michelle started the engine and followed the woman as she

navigated toward the newer suburban developments on the edge of town. Hazel's instincts were correct—Anna drove straight to a modest house, pulled into the driveway, opened the garage, and disappeared inside.

"That's her house," Michelle noted. "Should we go?"

Hazel paused, eyes fixed on the now-closed garage door, her mind working through possibilities.

"Not yet. Let's wait a little while. I want to see if she has a job. The way she walked in—it looked like she was on a schedule."

Time crawled by as they waited in the SUV, parked inconspicuously a few houses down. Over an hour later, Anna reappeared—now dressed in mauve scrubs. She jumped into her car, closed the garage behind her, and drove off with purpose.

"Okay, that's good," Hazel said, nodding in satisfaction. "Now we know a little more. Wearing scrubs makes it pretty obvious where she works."

"Head back then?" Michelle asked, her hand resting lightly on the gear shift.

"Yeah," Hazel replied, her voice carrying a quiet finality as the SUV turned and began the drive back toward the canyon.

They arrived back at the house on the De Mantenero Vale Estate within fifteen minutes. Hazel didn't wait for the vehicle to come to a full stop—before it had even settled, she flung the door open and sprinted toward the narrow trail that wound its way into the forest, leading back to the coven's hidden sanctuary.

Cool, pine-scented air filled her lungs as she moved with practiced speed, her steps light and sure upon the well-worn path. Towering trees whispered with the morning breeze, their shadows shifting in dappled patterns across the forest floor like living sigils.

She had barely covered a few hundred yards when Hiktilda materialized before her, staff in hand, as if summoned by the wind itself.

The Grand-Witch stood motionless, her dark robes flowing like liquid shadow. The morning light did little to soften the sharpness of her gaze—it cut through the air like a blade: measuring, knowing, impossible to evade.

"I knew you were returning," Hiktilda said, her voice calm but clipped, an unspoken command woven into every syllable. "So I spared you the trouble of the run. Time is not to be wasted."

Hazel skidded to a halt, breath quick but composed. Without hesitation, she reached into her purse and pulled out a folded scrap of paper.

"Yes, Grand-Witch," she said, extending the note. "We followed Warren's mistress Anna—I have her address. She was wearing scrubs when she left for work, so she likely works at the emergency clinic, or possibly a dental office near the center of town."

Hiktilda took the paper, her thin fingers folding it with meticulous care before tucking it into a hidden pocket within the folds of her robe.

"Good, Hazel. I will handle this Anna," she murmured, a thread of satisfaction weaving through her tone. "You were quick with this task. Things are aligning well today—a perfect beginning."

Hazel straightened slightly, the rare praise bolstering her confidence.

"Now, for your next task," Hiktilda continued, her voice rich with quiet expectation. She reached into another pocket and withdrew an unsealed envelope—deceptively light, yet heavy with purpose. With a fluid motion, she handed it to Hazel, who accepted it with steady hands.

"You must take this letter and place it inside Greg Warren's office before he closes tonight," Hiktilda instructed. "It must be hidden—visible enough to be found, but not immediately. Subtlety is essential. Do not fail me."

Her gaze lingered on Hazel, the intensity softening slightly as she appraised her transformed beauty with a knowing glint.

"Now," Hiktilda murmured, her lips curling into a faint, mischievous smile, "put that lovely face to work, darling. Michelle has everything prepared for you." A quiet laugh escaped her—a sound both playful and ominous—before she turned and glided up the trail, vanishing into the trees with the ease of a dream fading at dawn.

Hazel remained still for a moment, the envelope in her hand, the weight of her mission pressing into her thoughts.

Hazel returned to the estate house and climbed back into the SUV, her breath evening out as the last traces of adrenaline from her sprint began to fade. Michelle's quiet composure stood in stark contrast to the charged energy still pulsing through Hazel's veins. The world around them was calm, almost uneventful—deceptively ordinary. But within Hazel, every nerve hummed with purpose. Every step so far had been flawless.

"Ready to head back?" Michelle asked in a casual yet confident tone, her hands resting lightly on the wheel.

Hazel flashed a sly smile. "Yes, indeed. We're heading to

Main again—same place."

Without a word, Michelle reached into the back seat and pulled forward a sleek black bag, handing it over with a smirk.

"Here. You'll need this—nice dress, heels, some makeup, and an elegant red purse," she said, her voice tinged with amusement. "H had my mom put it together for you earlier today. Nothing turns a head like passionate red."

Hazel accepted the bag with a flicker of curiosity, peeking inside at the carefully curated ensemble. A wicked glint danced in her eyes.

"Let's get going, then."

Michelle nodded and shifted the SUV into drive. They glided out through the estate's towering gate, which closed automatically behind them, and descended the canyon road with swift precision. The SUV hugged the curves with ease as sunlight filtered through the trees in rhythmic bursts, flickering like a silent countdown. Hazel leaned into the seat, letting the steady motion center her thoughts.

This wasn't just another task—it was a performance. A role only she and a chosen few could understand. Every movement, every choice, was a deliberate thread in a grand tapestry, woven with intention and power.

As the outskirts of town came into view, Hazel unzipped the red purse. With careful, deliberate fingers, she slipped the envelope inside, tucking it securely in place.

Then, without hesitation, she got to work. She peeled off her sweats and running shoes, replacing them with the sleek, crimson dress that shimmered in the shifting light. The fabric molded to her body with elegant precision—provocative without being vulgar, striking without effort. She stepped into the heels, adjusted the straps, and checked her reflection in the visor mirror. Earrings—perfect. Lipstick—flawless. Hair—voluminous and intentional.

The woman staring back at her was poised, powerful, and dangerously magnetic.

Hazel's lips curled into a satisfied smile.

She looked like someone who could own the world.

The SUV slowed as they reached Main Street and Fourth East. Michelle parked with practiced ease, cutting the engine in a single fluid motion.

"All set?" she asked, her voice laced with subtle encouragement.

Hazel gave a slow, confident nod. She stepped out of the SUV with effortless grace, the door shutting behind her with a crisp, decisive snap.

The sound of her heels clicking against the pavement echoed through the quiet street, each step a statement. She approached the entrance of Bryndelle Insurance, the crimson of her dress and matching purse drawing the eye, commanding attention.

She belonged here. She *owned* this moment.

I was meant for this, she thought as she reached for the door handle, pulled it open, and stepped inside.

The insurance office interior was modest, with the faint hum of fluorescent lights overhead. Greg Warren sat at his desk, his tie loosened slightly, speaking with animation into the phone. His eyes flicked up as Hazel entered, and for a moment, he faltered. He quickly held up a hand, signaling for her to wait.

"Hey, one second," he said into the receiver before turning his attention back to Hazel with a quick, apologetic smile. "I'll be right with you, ma'am."

Hazel smiled demurely, her eyes sweeping over the office as she stood by the entrance. It was a simple, unassuming space—just a few desks, some filing cabinets, and stacks of neatly organized papers.

A minute later, Greg ended the call and approached her, extending his hand. "Hello," he said, his voice warm but tinged with curiosity. He was already captivated.

Hazel took his hand, her touch firm yet graceful. "Hello. I'm interested in your help, in getting some life insurance and was hoping you could be the one to help me out, to get it done."

Greg blinked, clearly taken aback by her beauty. His face flushed slightly as he stumbled to regain his composure. "Of course! I'd love to help. I'm all yours. We handle all kinds of insurance," he said, his words tumbling over each other.

"Great. Perhaps we could sit down in your office?" Hazel suggested, her lips curving into a subtle, inviting smile.

Greg nodded eagerly. "Absolutely. Sure. Right this way."

He led her to his office, gesturing to one of the chairs across from his desk. Hazel moved with fluid elegance, sitting down with the poise of someone who commanded attention wherever she went.

"So, you're interested in..uh.. you said life insurance…you know we provide all types of insurance here?" Greg began, folding his hands in an attempt to appear professional, though his gaze occasionally betrayed his distraction.

"Yes, life insurance, that's right." Hazel said, leaning forward slightly. Her voice was steady, melodic. "I have two younger sisters, and I want to ensure they're cared for if… anything unthinkable happens."

"That's a very thoughtful reason," Greg replied, his expression softening. "Life insurance is all about preparing for the unexpected. What size policy are you considering? That's usually the first question."

Hazel tilted her head, her eyes locking with his. "I think it depends on the cost of a $2–3 million policy versus $4–5 million. Do you have a quote that might explain my options? I'd like to take something home to review since I'm short on time today."

Greg nodded quickly, standing up. "Oh, absolutely. Let me grab a few options for you."

As he turned away and walked to a large filing cabinet, Hazel's movements became precise, almost mechanical. She slipped the letter from her purse and slid it under a thick stack of papers on his desk, ensuring just the corner was visible. It blended seamlessly with the surrounding documents, with a corner protruding. She exhaled silently, her confidence unshaken. The task was complete.

Greg returned to his desk moments later, setting a stack of price sheets in front of her. "These are great starting points," he said, sitting back down. Then, as if struck by sudden realization, he added, "Oh, I just realized—I didn't catch your name."

Hazel smiled, tilting her head slightly. "I didn't catch yours either."

Greg laughed nervously, extending his hand again. "I'm Greg. Greg Warren. I own this place. You can call me Greg."

"Nice to meet you, Greg," Hazel said, her voice smooth as silk. "My name is Chandra. Chandra Love."

Greg held her hand, his eyes lingering on her. Hazel tilted her head, her gaze steady and slightly teasing, leaving him momentarily speechless.

"I hate to cut this short," Hazel said, rising gracefully and pulling her hand free, "but I'm short on time today. Perhaps I could come back tomorrow when I have more time? You're very charming, and I'd love to continue this conversation."

"Tomorrow? Absolutely! Sure, we should meet tomorrow. I think we're, uh… hitting it off," Greg stammered, his nerves betraying his excitement.

Hazel picked up the brochures and flashed a playful smile. "Great, Greg. Then tomorrow… I'll see you then. Ciao," she said, adding a subtle wink before turning and walking out, her stride confident, her hips swaying just enough to leave a lasting impression.

Back in his office, Greg sank into his chair, a dazed grin spreading across his face. "Wow," he muttered, running a hand through his hair. "She really liked me. "

He laughed softly, feeling taller, stronger—invincible.

He took a deep breath and nodded to himself, muttering, "I mean, wow! She thought I was hot!"

Chapter 30

State Detective Smalls from Redding adjusted his grip on the steering wheel as the unmarked sedan rolled past the weathered sign welcoming him and his partner to East Bryndelle. The town was a small cluster of lights tucked away in the shadow of the Sierra foothills, surrounded by dense woods that seemed to press in on either side of the road. His partner, Detective Hastings, was in the passenger seat, tapping absently on his tablet as he scanned the details of the case they'd been assigned by Deputy Commissioner Watson.

"Missing persons and a homicide," Hastings muttered, scrolling through the email forwarded by East Bryndelle's Detective Sanders. "For a town like this, that's a major headline. Five people missing, one dead. Sanders must be pulling his hair out."

Smalls grunted in response, his eyes fixed on the road ahead. "For us, it's a normal Tuesday."

Hastings smirked but didn't look up. "You're not wrong. Still, small towns like this? Everyone knows everyone. Cases like these tend to mess with people. Paranoia. Rumors. Makes the locals harder to deal with, don't ya think?"

"Yeah, well, let's figure this out quick and get out of here,"

Smalls replied, his tone flat. "Places like this always feel like they're from another century. And the hotels? Always musty, with mattresses older than I am."

Hastings chuckled. "The joys of rural accommodations." He paused, scrolling further through the emails. "Alright, first stop: the homicide... Ryan Danielson's house. Sanders wants us to double-check the scene, see if his locals missed anything. His girlfriend probably caught him cheating, went ape on him."

"Can't wait," Smalls said dryly. "After that?"

"Danielson's body is still in their 'morgue.'" Hastings made air quotes with his fingers. "It's just a freezer in the basement of the PD, apparently. We'll give it a look before they ship it to Sac for a proper autopsy. Then we'll hit the other locations— the Scolati house, Winthrop house, and those burned-out homes that belonged to the three Childs family members. Neighbors said the Childs girl, Holly, was in a relationship with the homicide so there's that. Like I said, maybe she caught him cheating, went crazy on him."

Smalls nodded, mentally mapping out the day. "Sounds like a plan. Let's get it done and get out of here. I'm not a fan of small-town mysteries. They always come with too many ghosts and other weird spooky stuff."

Hastings glanced over at his partner, raising an eyebrow. "Since when are you the superstitious type?"

"I'm not," Smalls said, shaking his head. "But places like this have a way of digging up trouble. Old grudges, family secrets, the works. Add in missing people and a suspicious death, and you've got yourself a recipe for everyone in town to start pointing fingers. Bunch of witch-hunt type of nonsense that can boil over real quick."

"Sounds like you've been burned before," Hastings remarked.

"I spent a lot of time listening to plenty of wackos," Smalls admitted, his voice tinged with experience. "But that doesn't mean I like it."

The car fell silent for a moment, the hum of the engine and the asphalt highway under the tires filling the space. As they entered the town proper, the narrow streets gave way to a handful of businesses—a diner, a gas station, church, a small hardware store. The town felt frozen in time, its charm marred by the emptiness of the streets and the eerie stillness that seemed to hang in the air.

"You hungry?" Smalls asked abruptly, breaking the silence.

"Starving," Hastings replied. "I'm down to grab something before we start."

Smalls pulled the car into the parking lot of a small diner, its neon sign blinking unevenly in the encroaching darkness. "First order of business, then," he said. "Let's eat. Because I'm telling you right now, I'm not solving anything on an empty stomach."

Hastings chuckled, unbuckling his seatbelt. "If they've got coffee that doesn't taste like motor oil, I'll call it a win."

As the two detectives stepped out of the car and made their way into the diner, the weight of the case lingered in the back of their minds. East Bryndelle might have looked like just another sleepy mountain town, but they both knew better. Beneath its quiet surface, something was festering in this place.

Chapter 31

Cardinal Santino Tarvaldi was 77 years old, and he felt every one of those years pressing down on his weary body like an ancient cathedral roof, heavy with the weight of time. His bones creaked and popped each morning as he climbed out of bed—a laborious ritual that seemed to stretch longer with each passing dawn. The chill of early light seeped into his joints, an unspoken reminder that even the most devout servant of God could not escape the frailty of aging flesh. By evening, his energy would often ebb so completely that his prayers—once spoken with conviction—now came in hushed, faltering whispers. His once-ebony hair had faded to an unbroken silver, a mantle of age that caught the sunlight in ways he barely noticed anymore. Where he had once strode through sacred halls with the vigor of a man on a divine mission, he now moved with the careful precision of someone keenly aware of time's merciless toll.

His residence, an elegant yet modest apartment adjoining the Santa Monica Catholic Church, was his sanctuary in this season of his life. The polished wooden floors bore the echoes of his measured steps, and the walls, adorned with simple crucifixes and holy icons, reflected his life of humble service. This had been his home for the past year—a respite after decades of tireless work in Vatican City. For forty years, he had served the Holy See with an unyielding dedication, rising through the ranks to stand at the heart of the Church's global operations. But those days were behind him now. He had been reassigned, a quieter yet still vital role: an advisor, traveling to Catholic churches across the world, offering guidance and counsel to clergy and congregations alike. Santa Monica, California, was the first stop in this new chapter—a chapter he hadn't expected to unfold so late in his life.

This quiet Wednesday morning began much like any other. Santino stirred from slumber, the pale light of dawn filtering through the window. The air was still and cool, laden with a tranquility that seemed almost holy. He murmured a silent prayer of gratitude, a daily ritual to set his spirit right. The day ahead promised calm: a steady rhythm of sacred duties, opening and closing the house of God, punctuated by moments of reflection in the sanctuary. Yet, as he lingered in bed, savoring the stillness, he was struck with the most rare of happenings—a waking vision struck him with the force of a lightning bolt.

Visions were not unfamiliar to Santino. They had come to him sporadically over the years—mystical, vivid glimpses that hovered somewhere between dreams and divine revelation. Some were gentle, imbued with peace. Others, like this one, carried the weight of urgency, like the toll of a great bell echoing through his mind.

He shut his eyes and let the images play out upon his mind.

He saw a face: Father Peter Mallory, an old friend and Jesuit priest with whom he had shared many years of camaraderie and service. In the vision, they sat together in his car on a quiet suburban street. The silence between them was heavy, thick with anticipation, as though they were poised on the precipice of something monumental. Santino turned his head, his gaze falling on a small statue of a saint—a simple figure no more than two feet tall—standing in the yard of an unassuming house.

Peter broke the silence. His voice was calm but laced with urgency.

"Are you sure it's East Bryndelle?"

"I'm 100% sure," Santino replied, his tone resolute.

Suddenly, the world erupted in a cascade of blinding white light, followed by the deafening cracks of thunder. Once. Twice. Three times. Four. Each peal reverberated like a warning across the heavens.

The scene shifted. Now, Santino stood in the backyard next to a modest house. The air was charged, humming with an unnatural energy that prickled his skin. He saw Peter standing firm, holding a crucifix high in his right hand, as though wielding it against a towering shadow—a formless cloud of darkness that loomed with malevolent intent. Behind Peter, a figure lay crumpled on the ground, helpless and exposed. Peter's voice rose in a crescendo, shouting words Santino could not comprehend, his speech strained and desperate, each syllable like a battle cry against the advancing darkness.

His vision continued.

Santino's gaze narrowed, focusing on the crucifix in Peter's hand. It was no ordinary relic. It was the *Cross of Saint Paul*, a sacred artifact of immense power and history, known to only a few outside the College of Cardinals. Crafted of pure silver and gilded in gold, its centerpiece was a glimmering ruby that seemed almost alive, pulsing with an inner fire. Santino recognized it immediately. He himself had transported the relic from the Vatican to Santa Monica a year ago, believing at the time that the act would turn out to be purely ceremonial. Now, it was clear: the cross had a purpose far greater than he had previously imagined.

The vision shifted again, and this time Santino saw himself, standing in defiance against a being cloaked in darkness. He held his Bible aloft, its pages alive with a radiant, holy light. Words of power spilled from his lips—words he didn't yet know, yet in the vision, they came effortlessly, as if guided by a hand unseen. The dark shape recoiled, retreating into the shadows, its malevolence undone by the light.

Santino awoke with a jolt, his breath coming in sharp, shallow gasps. The clarity of the vision was undeniable. This was no idle dream, no fleeting fancy of an aging mind. It was a summons—a divine call to action. The urgency gripped him like a vice. He swung his legs over the side of the bed, every creak of his body drowned out by the roar of purpose in his heart. He had to act, and swiftly.

His thoughts turned to East Bryndelle, nestled in the mountains north of Sacramento, a few hours from Redding. He had recognized it instantly from the vision. A shiver ran down his spine as he recalled another troubling detail: nearly three weeks ago, Anthony Sculati, a dear friend and priest in training, had gone missing. Anthony had lived in East Bryndelle—the very town from the vision. A terrible certainty gripped Santino now: Anthony's fate was inexorably tied to this revelation. The pieces were falling into place, and they demanded action.

Santino moved quickly, his hands trembling only slightly as he made a series of calls. Sunday services would need to be covered. Meetings would have to wait. His final call was to Father Peter Mallory, now living in San Francisco.

"Peter," Santino began, his voice steady despite the storm raging within him. "I need your help. It's not something I can explain over the phone, but it's of grave spiritual importance. Something... something God has called us to do. You and I. I'm heading to East Bryndelle, in the mountains northeast of Redding, and I need you to meet me there...tonight. This can't wait, my brother. I'll explain everything when I see you."

Santino ended the conversation with a short request, admonishing Peter to keep silent to his peers about this whole thing, the chance for misunderstanding and ridicule being great when it came to trusting visions.

The phone call was a success, Peter Mallory had agreed to help him.

Packing was swift, but one final task remained. The cross. He couldn't leave without it. Slipping unnoticed into the church, Santino made his way to the vault without raising an eyebrow. The cool, still air inside the vault carried the faint scent of incense and polished wood. Opening the secure compartment, he retrieved the *Cross of Saint Paul*, wrapped in red felt, its weight both literal and symbolic as he cradled it reverently. He slipped the 5 inch long cross into the inside pocket of his coat, the comforting pressure against his chest reassuring him, as though God Himself had placed it there.

Moments later, he was in his car, the engine rumbling to life. He placed a hand over the cross, whispering a prayer for protection before setting off. The road ahead stretched long and uncertain—more than nine hours of driving ahead of him—but doubt never touched him. His purpose was clear. The vision had spoken, and he would follow its guidance, no matter how tired his old body would get. As he pulled onto

172

the highway, the relic resting over his heart, he whispered a final plea:

"Lord, guide my hand and steady my heart. Thy will be done. Amen."

The cardinal drove northward, carrying with him the weight of his years, the burden of his calling, and the shadow of the vision that now propelled him into the unknown.

Chapter 32

The sun blazed high in the sky above, but deep within the vast, winding cave system of the coven, time seemed suspended in eternal night. Shadows danced on limestone walls as Gaeldritch moved alone through narrow tunnels, her path illuminated only by the flicker of an ancient iron lantern she held aloft. Its flame cast a cold, white light, contrasting against the dark damp walls. The lantern itself, square and sturdy, bore the marks of centuries, its iron edges worn smooth by countless years of use.

The path descended gradually, twisting and turning as if the earth itself sought to conceal the destination. At last, after descending deeper and deeper, Gaeldritch emerged from the stone passageway into a cavern of breathtaking beauty. It was an open grotto where the air was filled with the soft tinkling of dripping water, the sound echoing in the stillness.

Before her stretched a tranquil lake, its surface faintly rippled by the continuous droplets falling from unseen cracks in the lofty ceiling above. This was a wonder in the dark depths of the mountain Gaeldritch had named *Lacus Luminis Stellarum*—the Pool of Starlight.

The cavern ceiling was studded with countless quartz crystals, each emitting a never-ending gleam and refracting faint phosphorescent light by some arcane chemical process. Blue and white pinpoints glimmered like distant stars, their reflections shimmering on the surface of the lake. The effect was otherworldly, a sacred tapestry of light and shadow that seemed alive. Gaeldritch paused at the shore, holding her lantern high to drink in the scene, her expression one of reverence and possession. This place was hers—hers alone, save for Hiktilda. No other witch was permitted to disturb the sanctity of this grotto. Gaeldritch had poured decades of her soul into it, weaving her mind, emotions, and spirit into its essence.

Fifty feet from the shore, in the lake's center, was a small circular islet of stone and sand. Stalagmites jutted upward at odd angles, casting jagged shadows in the lantern light. At the heart of the islet stood a square iron cage draped in a black sheet designed to divert the ever-dripping water. Within the cage sat a small black bed, raised on short stilts, and on it perched the figure of a small pale child.

The child was small in size, a boy, no larger than a four-year-old, with skin as white as moonlight. Shoulder-length white hair framed his delicate features, and his thin black robe accentuated his ethereal presence. Gaeldritch's lips curved into a faint smile as she gazed upon him.

Setting the lantern down on the shore, Gaeldritch stepped into the lake. Despite the water rippling softly around her feet, she sank no more than an inch—beneath the surface lay a hidden stone causeway, her hidden path to the islet. Each step sent gentle splashes outward, the sound blending with the cave's ambient rhythm.

As she neared the islet, the boy stood and moved toward the bars of his cage, his pale blue eyes wide with anticipation.

Gaeldritch stopped just before him, her bony hands resting at her sides.

"Patience, albino, patience," she said in a tone laced with condescension, though her gaze held a flicker of admiration.

Kneeling to meet his eye level, Gaeldritch reached into her robe and retrieved two small items: a red vial and a slender blade. The flame of her lantern caught the glint of steel as she extended her hand.

"Your arm," she commanded, her voice cold yet measured.

Without hesitation, the boy obeyed, slipping his delicate arm through the iron bars. Gaeldritch grasped it, her fingers icy against his skin. With practiced efficiency, she drew the blade across his pale flesh. Blood welled immediately, its crimson stark against his alabaster skin. She squeezed his arm lightly, angling it so that each drop fell cleanly into the vial she held beneath.

"Yes, albino," she murmured, her tone softening with genuine admiration. "Your blood is so pure, so untainted. A child of the moon and stars. Skin the sun has never touched, and eyes so pale they've never known the burn of daylight."

Once the vial was filled, Gaeldritch released his arm and swiftly capped the container, tucking it into the folds of her robe. From another pocket, she pulled a piece of black woven cloth, wrapping it around the small wound with precision. Her motions were gentle, almost tender, as though handling a rare treasure.

Reaching into yet another pocket, she withdrew a second vial, this one filled with a pearly, opalescent liquid. She held it out to the boy. "Here's your reward, albino," she said, her tone brisk but not unkind.

The boy adeptly uncorked the vial with small, nimble

fingers and drank its contents in a single gulp. The moment the liquid touched his lips, a wave of ecstasy washed over him, his body swaying with its power. He handed the empty vial back to Gaeldritch before staggering back to his bed and lying down, the narcotics taking quick effect in his small body. His pale eyelids fluttered shut as he succumbed to a deep, restorative slumber.

"Eat when you awaken, child of the stars," Gaeldritch spoke, knowing the words weren't heard, tossing a bundle of cloth-wrapped food into the cage. Her voice softened, almost wistful, as she added, "Where would I be without your innocence?"

She answered herself in a hushed, almost reverent whisper. "I'd never know what the zealots see in their visions."

Straightening, Gaeldritch turned and began her journey back across the submerged causeway, the vial with the sacred blood of the boy secured in her robes. She retrieved her lantern and ascended the path leading away from the twinkling pool, her footsteps fading into the darkness, leaving only the quiet drip of water and the glimmer of the cave's stars behind.

Chapter 33

Peter Mallory, age 53, navigated the serpentine roads into East Bryndelle as the sun sank behind the jagged hills. His car, a compact model that hummed and rattled with each twist and turn, felt cramped but sufficient—a symbol of the modest life he had grown accustomed to. Every mile he drove further into the mountains carried him away from the predictable routines of his world, his comfortable existence as a history professor at the University of San Francisco slipping further into the rearview mirror.

For more than three decades, Peter had devoted his life to teaching. His lectures on the complexities of religious history had captivated students and sustained him through lean times. Academia was not lucrative, especially in the shadow of San Francisco's skyrocketing living costs, but it was rewarding in other ways. He thrived on the rhythm of semesters, the hum of campus life, and the comforting certainty of facts meticulously etched in the halls of time. But this—this was something else entirely.

He shifted uneasily in his seat, trying to focus on the road ahead. East Bryndelle, a remote mountain town tucked away in the middle of nowhere, had never surfaced in any of his research. It was a name without context, a place too obscure to hold historical significance. Yet, as Peter wound deeper into its forested edges, an inexplicable weight settled in his chest. There was a darkness here, a sense of something veiled beneath the surface.

His knuckles whitened as he tightened his grip on the steering wheel, his mind circling back to the call that had catapulted him from his carefully ordered life into this strange and urgent journey. It had come without warning this morning, disrupting his plans for office hours and a quiet evening with a new translation of some obscure medieval text. The caller's voice had been unmistakable— deep, deliberate, and tinged with the calm authority that only years of leadership could impart. It was Cardinal Santino Tarvaldi, a man Peter had not spoken to in years.

Santino's name alone was enough to transport Peter back decades. They had first met during Peter's month-long research visit to the Vatican in his younger days. It had been a rare privilege, a chance to study in the archives of the Holy See, and Santino, then a younger cleric, had taken an unusual interest in the budding Jesuit scholar. Their evenings had been filled with spirited discussions about history, theology, and the mysteries that bound them to the divine. Santino had an encyclopedic mind, a rare match for Peter's curiosity, and their bond had lingered in Peter's memory as a kind of intellectual touchstone. Over the years, their paths had diverged, Peter returning to academia and Santino rising within the Church's ranks. But their connection had endured through occasional letters and the unspoken recognition of shared purpose.

This morning's call, however, had been unlike anything Peter could have expected.

"Peter," Santino had said, his voice steady but urgent. "I need your help."

The words had jolted Peter from his usual morning calm, leaving him momentarily speechless. "Help? With what?" he'd managed, though the Cardinal's tone suggested something far beyond the ordinary.

"It's not something I can explain over the phone," Santino had replied, his voice laced with gravity. "But it's of grave spiritual importance. Something... something God has called us to. You and I."

Peter had tried to ask more questions, but Santino's words were as firm as they were cryptic. "I'm heading to East Bryndelle, in the mountains northeast of Redding, and I need you to meet me there tonight," he had instructed. "This can't wait, my brother. I'll explain everything when you arrive. Can you do this for me? Good. And Peter, don't tell anyone where you're going or what you are doing. I think it best that we perform our duties in silence, otherwise we will likely be misunderstood by our peers in performing our calling."

And with that, the conversation had ended.

Now, hours later, Peter's mind raced with questions as he steered his car along the darkening road. Santino's tone had carried a weight that Peter couldn't ignore. Grave spiritual importance. What could be so urgent, so dire, that it warranted pulling him from his comfortable, predictable life and driving across the state that same day? The Cardinal had been adamant about secrecy, about the need for haste. Peter, unaccustomed to being summoned like a soldier to the front, had been a reluctant to accept doing this but unable to refuse his old friend of such a powerful and rare request.

Ahead, the rugged silhouette of East Bryndelle began

to emerge against the fading light. Nestled in a bowl of dense forests and scattered meadows, the town seemed almost otherworldly, a pocket of civilization carved into the wilderness. Its small cluster of lights flickered faintly, fighting back the encroaching night. Peter felt a chill run down his spine as he entered the outskirts of the town. Despite the quaintness of its appearance, something about East Bryndelle felt off—its edges too sharp, its shadows too deep.

Santino had given him precise instructions: meet at the parking lot of the town's Catholic church. The Cardinal, ever cautious about his prominence, had insisted on discretion. Peter pictured the old man in his brown suit and old fedora, a deliberate contrast to the robes that marked his high station. Santino was never one to flaunt his authority, especially in a strange matter like this.

As Peter navigated the town's narrow streets, a strange mix of curiosity and dread churned within him. He had faced countless intellectual puzzles over the years—enigmas hidden in ancient texts, mysteries bound by history and faith—but this felt different. This was not an academic exercise, not a debate to be resolved in the safety of a library. Whatever awaited him in East Bryndelle, it was real. Tangible. And possibly dangerous.

Peter Mallory spotted a single car in the church parking lot as he pulled in—a modest, older sedan with a man in a fedora sitting behind the wheel. Even in the dim light, Peter recognized the figure. It was Santino. The Cardinal waved to him through the windshield, beckoning him to join him in the car.

Peter parked his car next to Santino's vehicle and climbed

181

out, the cool night air prickling his skin. He opened the passenger door and slid into the seat beside the Cardinal, the worn upholstery creaking under his weight. As soon as the door shut, Santino spoke.

"Peter, my dear friend," Santino began, his voice warm and earnest. "You don't know how much it means to me that you came. I haven't spoken to you in three, maybe four years, yet here you are. You've put your life on hold, driven across the state without a word of complaint."

Peter offered a faint smile. "Of course, Santino. I figured if you were asking for help, it must really be serious."

"God bless you," the Cardinal replied, his expression softening for a moment. Both men shared a brief smile, but it was fleeting. Santino's face grew solemn, his tone dropping to one of urgency. "Peter, I've had a vision. A vision that involves you and me—here, in this town."

Peter's brow furrowed. "A vision?" he echoed. "Go on."

"Tomorrow night is the full moon," Santino said, his voice steady but heavy with significance. "We must be at a certain house by then. I don't know where it is yet, but I'm certain we'll find it. We have to."

Peter nodded, though unease was already gnawing at the edges of his resolve. "Alright. This town is small enough. I'm sure we can find it. And once we do?"

"We wait," Santino replied, his gaze fixed on some unseen point in the distance. "We wait until we are called to act. The spirit will guide us." He paused, then added with difficulty, "My vision... it showed you protecting a man. This man was unconscious, lying on the ground."

Peter's stomach tightened. "Protecting a man? From what?"

"I don't know," Santino admitted, his voice carrying the

weight of uncertainty. "But you were holding a cross—a relic—and you were shouting at something, a shadow in the darkness."

Peter's palms sweated, his mind racing. "A shadow? Santino, what are we talking about here?"

"I don't have all the answers," Santino said gravely, turning to meet Peter's gaze. "But I do know this: it's God's will that we are here. And tomorrow, we will be at that house."

Reaching into his coat, Santino produced a bundle wrapped in red felt and placed it gently in Peter's hands. "This is for you, Peter," he said. "You must take it now, and you must return it after tomorrow evening. It cannot be lost under any circumstances."

Peter unwrapped the felt bundle, revealing the small but exquisitely crafted crucifix. Its silver and gold surface gleamed even in the dim light of the car, with the large ruby glinting at its center. He turned it over in his hands, thumbing a string of intricate engravings on its surface. The weight of it felt profound, almost otherworldly.

"It's incredible...it's a beautiful cross." Peter muttered, his voice hushed.

"This is no ordinary cross," Santino explained. "We in the church call it the *Cross of Saint Paul*—it's very old—cherished by all who know of its existence. It is a relic, one of the holiest objects in the Church's possession. And tomorrow, I believe it will serve its purpose: to ward off evil."

Peter's unease deepened as he studied the cross. His eyes fell on the Latin inscription running down its stem. "What does this mean?" he asked, tracing the lettering with his finger.

Santino raised an eyebrow, his voice low as he recited the phrase from memory. "'*Maleficos non patieris vivere.*' It translates to: *'Do not allow the evil to live.'* The inscription was added centuries after the cross was made, a testament to its purpose."

Peter leaned back against the seat, the weight of the relic feeling heavier now. "This is... a lot, Santino. Are you sure you're feeling okay?"

Santino chuckled softly, brushing off the implied concern. "I'm fine, my brother. But I need you to lean into your faith. Trust me. Better yet...trust in God."

Peter took a deep breath, nodding reluctantly. "Alright. What do I do with this cross? What do I say?"

"You'll know when the time comes," Santino said simply. "When you are called to act, it will be crystal clear. Faith, my brother."

"I'm no fighter, Santino," Peter protested, his voice tinged with doubt. "I'm a history teacher. What do you expect me to do?"

Santino placed a hand on Peter's shoulder, his grip firm and reassuring. "Brother Peter, you are indeed a holy warrior. You wield the Light of God, and that is the greatest weapon of all. This is not a test of books or debates. This is a test of faith."

Peter shook his head, still unconvinced. "The Lord admonishes me to never kill."

"You won't," Santino replied. "At least, not in the way you think. You cannot kill what does not live. I believe the shadow in the darkness is...well, that it is not a man we will meet—it is not human and not alive like us. *Bestia fictilis*—a beast of false life."

Peter's stomach churned. "A beast? What are we even talking about here?"

Santino's voice softened, yet it carried an unshakable resolve. "I don't have all the answers, Peter. But I know one thing: tomorrow, we will do our duty to God. You will know what to do when the moment comes."

Peter took a deep breath, closing his eyes for a moment as he tried to steady himself. "You're right, Santino. I must accept this is God's will."

Santino smiled, patting Peter on the shoulder. "That's right, my brother. Have faith. Tomorrow, we stand together with God as our support."

Peter looked down at the cross in his hands, its ruby glinting like a drop of blood in the dim light. He couldn't shake the feeling that tomorrow night would change everything.

Chapter 34

It was 4 a.m. when Santino woke with a start, his heart briefly fluttering at the disorientation of waking in an unfamiliar room. The dim outline of the hotel's furniture slowly came into focus, and within seconds, the events of the previous day settled into his mind, grounding him. He took a deep breath, feeling the weight of exhaustion pressing against him, but it was a sensation he knew well. For the past twenty years, waking at this early hour had been a sporadic but familiar occurrence, something he had long since accepted.

Lying still in the quiet room, he offered a silent prayer, his words echoing gently in the sacred space of his heart. Then, swinging his legs out from under the covers, he planted his feet on the floor and stretched, his joints creaking as if to remind him of yesterday's long drive.

Padding softly across the room, Santino made his way to the bathroom, grabbing the hotel Bible from the nightstand as he went. It wasn't his cherished leather-bound Bible—the one he'd owned since his twenties and left in his car—but it would suffice. In the bathroom, he turned the water tap on, watching as steam began to rise once the cold water cleared the pipes and hot water rushed into the tub.

As the room filled with warmth, Santino eased himself

into the bath. The hot water wrapped around his tired body, coaxing some of the soreness from his muscles. He opened the Bible to a random page in the New Testament, letting his eyes skim over the familiar words, their meaning washing over him like the water itself. Still, his mind wandered. He couldn't help but wonder about the day ahead, the uncertainty weighing heavily on him.

After finishing his bath, he dried himself and stood before the mirror. His reflection stared back at him, tired but resolute. *Okay, here I am, Lord. Please protect me and my friend Peter today,* he prayed silently, gazing deeply into his own eyes as if to find reassurance there.

He went to his bed and continued reading verses, but the words meant nothing as his mind repeatedly considered his vision and it's implications.

By 7:30 a.m., Santino decided to see if Peter was awake. They had a long day ahead—breakfast first, and then they had to search for the house from his vision. He stepped outside his front door into the chill morning air, the early morning dawn giving the sky a red-blue ambiance, and walked a few feet up the sidewalk to Peter's door. Pulling his coat close to trap his body warmth, he reached out and gently knocked, the sound echoing softly in the stillness.

After a quick breakfast at the small diner beside their hotel—a place where the scent of burnt coffee mingled with the sizzle of bacon—Santino and Peter stepped out into the cool morning air, the weight of their purpose pressing against them like an unseen force. Without a word, they climbed into the car and drove a few blocks to a modest grocery store, its neon "OPEN" sign flickering slightly, as if struggling to maintain its glow.

Inside, they moved with quiet determination, their footsteps muffled against the linoleum floor. The fluorescent lights overhead buzzed faintly as they navigated the narrow aisles, scanning the shelves for enough provisions to last them through the long, uncertain day ahead. Once they found the house from Santino's vision, they wouldn't be leaving—not for food, not for anything. Better to be prepared than to risk missing something vital.

They gathered their meals with precision: ripe fruit, stacks of bread and cold cuts, bottled water, and a few bags of snacks. Santino, without thinking, reached for a familiar favorite—pistachios—the repetitive motion of cracking the shells a ritual that steadied him.

With their supplies secured, they returned to the car, the plastic grocery bags rustling softly as they placed them in the backseat. Santino slid into the driver's seat, adjusting his grip on the wheel before glancing toward Peter.

"Well, Peter," he said, exhaling slowly, "let's find this house. I'll rest easier once I know we're in the right place." His gaze flicked to his companion. "You have the cross, right?"

Peter tapped his coat pocket, his fingers brushing against the weight of the object within. "Right here."

Santino nodded, the tension in his shoulders easing slightly as he turned the key in the ignition. The engine rumbled to life, steady and sure. He shifted into drive.

"Let's go."

They wound their way into the quiet suburbs, where tree-lined streets stood still in the hush of the early hours. Neatly trimmed hedges and sleeping houses passed by in a slow, deliberate procession. The world outside was calm—almost too calm—an eerie contrast to the focused intensity that buzzed between them.

Santino's vision had been clear about one crucial detail: the house they sought would bear a statue of a saint in the front yard. That was the key, the marker that would confirm they had arrived.

So they drove on, eyes scanning porches and lawns with an almost predatory sharpness, waiting for the sign that would pull them from uncertainty into absolute knowing, waiting for the moment when the path before them would be revealed.

They had only been driving for about an hour, winding through the sleepy streets of town, when they saw it.

There, in the front yard of an otherwise unremarkable house, stood a two-foot-tall concrete statue of St. Augustine. Weather-worn and unassuming, it rested amid a bed of bishop's weed, its carved features softened by years of exposure. Yet to Santino, it was as vivid as the moment he had first seen it in his vision.

"There it is, Peter! That's the exact statue," Santino breathed, his voice laced with something between astonishment and reverence.

Mallory leaned forward, studying the stone figure with a scrutinizing gaze. "You're sure, Santino?"

Santino exhaled, shaking his head slightly, not in doubt, but in quiet wonder. "Even after all these years... after all these visions proving themselves so precise... it still astounds me." His fingers tightened around the steering wheel as he gazed upon the statue, a tangible confirmation of the divine whispers that guided him. "Yes, that's it. That's the sign. We're here, Peter."

Without another word, he eased the car forward and brought it to a stop in front of the house, aligning it perfectly with what he had seen in his premonition. Every detail matched—the angle, the position, the feeling in the air, thick with unseen gravity. A shiver ran through him as he cut the engine. Silence settled over them, deep and absolute.

Mallory shifted in his seat, letting out a slow breath as he lounged back a few inches, trying to find a more comfortable position. "So... now we wait?"

Santino didn't take his eyes off the house, his fingers still resting lightly on the wheel. His voice, when it came, was low, measured. "Yes. Now we wait. But we stay vigilant, my brother."

The weight of his words hung between them, mingling with the stillness of the street. A breeze whispered through the trees, rustling leaves against pavement. Somewhere in the distance, a dog barked once, then fell silent.

Time stretched, elongated, as they watched and waited.

Chapter 35

Detective Smalls strode into Bryndelle Insurance first, his gray blazer hanging just loose enough to hint at long hours on the job, the faint wrinkles on his button-up shirt lending him an air of calculated indifference. His sharp eyes scanned the office, but they settled quickly on Greg Warren, lounging in his glass-walled office as if the world outside didn't matter. Greg's feet were propped lazily on his desk, his laugh faintly audible through the glass as he chatted on the phone. The moment he spotted Smalls, his demeanor shifted; the two men locked eyes like opposing forces in a chess match. Greg could sense he was law enforcement by the way he carried himself.

Trailing a step behind, Detective Hastings entered with quiet intensity, his gaze sweeping the room like a searchlight. Every detail caught his attention—the faint hum of the refrigerator, the faint aroma of stale coffee, and finally, the chaotic sprawl of papers on Holly Child's desk. It stood out like a beacon of disorder, and Hastings was drawn to it like a bloodhound picking up a scent.

Inside the office, Greg hastily ended his call, swinging his feet to the floor and straightening up as if to restore some semblance of professionalism. "I'll call you back," he muttered into the receiver, his tone sharp and clipped. "Something's come up."

Smalls wasted no time, pushing the glass door open with a deliberate, forceful motion. "No need to rush on our account," he said, his voice smooth but laced with a warning edge. "Finish your call. We'll wait."

Hastings, already at Holly's desk, had no such patience. He opened the first drawer without hesitation, rifling through its contents with practiced efficiency. The faint rustle of papers carried across the office, drawing Greg's attention like a siren's call.

Greg shot to his feet, his voice rising with indignation. "Hey, there! What do you think you're doing? Those papers are confidential!"

Smalls met Greg's protest with a calm but unyielding tone, his words cutting through the tension in the room like a knife. "Relax, sir. We're detectives with California State Law Enforcement, and we're here on official business. I'm Detective Smalls and this is Detective Hastings. Our intention is to conduct a thorough search of this office— with your permission, of course. Rest assured, our oath to confidentiality ensures that none of your customers' privacy will be compromised."

Greg blinked, clearly caught off guard by the detective's assertiveness. "Don't you need a warrant or something? What is this even about?" His voice slipped between confusion and irritation as he sat back into his chair again.

Hastings, who had been idly flipping through a stack of papers on Holly's desk, chimed in with a measured response. "Technically, yes, we'd need a warrant—if you refuse to give us permission. But time is of the essence in cases like this."

His words were casual, but there was no mistaking the edge of urgency beneath them.

Smalls let the conversation pause, locking eyes with Greg in a way that made the manager fidget uncomfortably in his chair. "We're here about a missing person," Smalls said, his voice dropping to a tone both grave and deliberate. He let the words linger in the air for a moment, weighing their impact. "Holly Childs. Your employee. She hasn't been seen for a few days and we urgently need to speak to her."

Greg's face paled, his mouth opening slightly before snapping shut again. "Holly's missing?" he stammered. "I didn't... I didn't know. I had no idea. I figured she quit without telling me. What happened?"

Hastings stepped forward, his presence amplifying the pressure in the room. "That's what we're here to find out. So, let me ask you directly—are you going to deny us permission to search this office for evidence that could help locate your missing employee?"

Greg's mind seemed to race, his eyes darting between the two detectives as he tried to process the situation. Finally, he exhaled sharply, throwing his hands up in defeat. "No, no— I'm not denying anything. You can search. I just... I had no idea Holly was missing. What—what do you think happened to her?"

Smalls gave a tight nod and stepped past Greg, his attention already shifting back to the chaos of Holly's desk. "All I can tell you is that we have reason to believe she may be in danger. Beyond that, I'm afraid I can't share details—confidentiality, you understand."

Greg sank back into his chair, looking stunned. "Right, right. Of course. Well... I guess you'll be here for a while, then."

Hastings, already pulling open another drawer, glanced up briefly. "We're quick. Won't take long."

Smalls turned back to Greg, his tone softening slightly. "Mr. Warren, if you wouldn't mind, perhaps you could take a seat outside or grab yourself a coffee while we work, give us about ten minutes. We'll need to speak with you afterward—just a few quick questions."

Greg hesitated, glancing toward the door, before nodding. "Yeah, sure. I'll… step out for a bit. Be back in ten." He grabbed his coat and walked out the front door of the office and down the sidewalk, leaving the detectives alone.

As soon as Greg was out of sight, Hastings glanced at Smalls with a wry smile. "That was easy."

Smalls chuckled faintly, already rifling through the mess of papers. "Let's get this over with."

It didn't take long for Smalls to uncover something unusual. Beneath a haphazard pile of folders and papers, he found an envelope, the envelope… with the corner protruding from the stack. It was unmarked, its placement almost deliberately obscured. He slid it out from underneath the stack of papers and opened the unsealed letter pulling a single sheet of paper from it.

As his eyes moved over the text, his expression shifted—first to confusion, then to something darker.

"Hastings," Smalls called, his voice low and steady. "You'll want to see this. Come check this out."

Hastings straightened from his search, walking over to peer at the paper. Smalls held it up so they could both see it's contents.

The letter was venomous, each word dripping with malice. Smalls read it aloud, his steady tone unable to mask the disgust simmering beneath the surface:

I'm going to give you this warning once and only once: stay away from Greg. He's mine. He's leaving his wife for me, and your pathetic little flings with him are over. You need to find a new job while you're at it. I won't tolerate your cheap, sleazy attempts to seduce him anymore. Enough is enough.

Quit your job now and never contact Greg again, and I might consider letting you go without the punishment I owe you. I can even forget your past slutty behavior. But if you don't listen to me, there will be consequences. You'll regret every second of your miserable life if you choose to ignore this warning. I'll make sure you suffer, I'll make sure your family suffers. I'll ruin your life piece by piece.

This isn't a joke, Holly. Don't test me.

Believe me

Anna

When Smalls finished, the silence in the office was deafening. Hastings exhaled sharply, his expression dark. "That's not just a clue; that's a goddamn loaded gun waiting to go off. The tone, the threats, the name… Anna's practically daring us to find her."

Smalls placed the letter carefully on the desk and snapped a photo of it with his phone, ensuring every word was preserved as evidence. His movements were precise and deliberate, his mind already processing the implications of the letter. He stuffed the paper into his coat pocket, and then slid the empty envelope back underneath the papers where he had discovered it, maintaining the appearance of the desk.

"This changes things," Smalls said, his voice low but charged with intent. "We've got motive, a direct threat, and a name. Anna just shot straight to the top of our list of persons of interest, along with her boyfriend here."

Hastings nodded, his sharp gaze scanning the room. "If Greg's mixed up in this, we'll nail him. But for now, let's keep digging. He's not back yet, and we might only get one shot at this."

With renewed focus, the detectives dove back into their search. Hastings rifled through file cabinets, while Smalls meticulously sifted through the piles on Holly's desk. The earlier ambiguity of the case had hardened into a sharper clarity, the pieces beginning to align. A tangled web of jealousy, obsession, and potential violence was unfolding before them.

When Greg walked back into the office, he found the two detectives standing near Holly's desk, with Smalls leaning casually against its edge, exuding a calm but authoritative presence.

"Mr. Warren, good walk?" Hastings asked, his voice light but with an undertone that suggested he was already analyzing Greg's response.

"Yeah, it was fine. It's cold out there," Greg replied, rubbing his hands together briskly. His gaze flicked toward the desk, then back to the detectives. "Did you guys finish your searching?"

"Yes, we did," Smalls replied smoothly. "We'd like to ask you a few questions, and then we'll be out of your hair. Can we go to your office and sit down for a moment?"

Greg nodded, his expression guarded as he led the way into his office. Once inside, he took his usual spot behind the desk, visibly trying to project an air of control. The detectives followed, settling into the chairs across from him with the precision of men used to commanding a room. In near-perfect synchronization, they pulled out small black leather folders and clicked their pens, the subtle sound cutting through the stillness like a metronome.

"How long has Holly worked for you?" Smalls began, his tone steady and professional.

Greg leaned back slightly, crossing his arms. "I guess it would be about three years now," he replied, his voice measured but lacking warmth.

"How old are you, Mr. Warren?" Hastings asked, the question casual but purposeful.

"I'm 36," Greg answered, sitting up a little straighter, his body language subtly defensive.

"You're married?" Hastings continued, each query building on the last with deliberate precision.

"Yes, I am. I have two kids."

"Ages?" Hastings pressed, his tone unchanged.

"Two boys, 11 and 8 years old," Greg said, his voice tinged with the faintest trace of impatience.

Smalls, unfazed, picked up the thread. "Would you say Holly was a good employee?"

Greg hesitated, his eyes flickering briefly toward the desk outside. "Yeah, sure. I mean, she had some issues," he admitted, his tone shifting as though trying to downplay the statement. "I had to really push her to work faster sometimes. You can see how far behind she was," he added, gesturing toward Holly's desk, still piled high with papers.

The detectives exchanged a brief glance, their pens moving steadily across their notepads, recording every word, every hesitation. The atmosphere in the office grew heavier, the unspoken tension thickening as the questions continued.

"Please don't take offense at any of these questions, Mr. Warren. It's simply a procedural formality we're required to follow," Hastings said, his hand raised in a calming gesture, his tone smooth and measured, designed to put Greg at ease.

"Okay," Greg responded cautiously, his voice laced with unease. He shifted slightly in his chair, his fingers brushing the edge of the desk as if searching for an anchor.

"Did you and Holly have a relationship outside of a professional one?" Smalls asked, his voice steady and direct, his sharp gaze fixed on Greg with the weight of expectation.

"No," Greg blurted out, the word escaping with an almost rehearsed swiftness. He paused briefly, his eyes darting away before continuing, "You know, she was…is cute, but way too young for me." A nervous chuckle followed, thin and unconvincing, as he added, "She just isn't my type anyway, you know?" He tried to shrug it off casually, but the subtle tension in his shoulders and the faint sheen of perspiration on his brow betrayed the discomfort that the question stirred under the detectives' piercing scrutiny.

"Sure, sure. Okay," Smalls said, tapping his pen lightly on the edge of his folder, the rhythmic sound amplifying the tension in the room. "How long did you know Holly's brother?"

Greg leaned back in his chair, letting out a short, dismissive scoff. "I didn't even know she had a brother… has a brother." He caught himself mid-sentence, his words clipped and defensive.

Smalls didn't miss a beat, his tone smooth and conversational. "He was quite a bit older than her. You don't recall knowing him?" Without waiting for a response, he pressed on. "When did you first meet Hannah Childs, Holly's mother?"

Greg's brow furrowed, a flicker of irritation crossing his face. He shook his head emphatically. "You know, I barely knew Holly. I never met anyone in her family. Frankly, I didn't care. As long as she did what I told her, I didn't give a…" He stopped abruptly, then quickly added, "I mean, I never cared, so I don't know anything about her."

"So, to be clear, you never met Holly's mother or her brother. Correct?" Hastings interjected, his voice colder now, with a precision that left no room for ambiguity.

Greg's gaze flickered uneasily between the two detectives. He shifted in his seat, his discomfort growing into a tension that was almost tangible. "No, I never met any of her family. She was just an employee—and not a very good one, I might add."

Smalls and Hastings exchanged a quick, knowing glance, a subtle communication between seasoned partners. Smalls leaned forward slightly, his pen still in his hand. "Mr. Warren, you say you're happily married?"

Greg straightened up defensively, nodding quickly. "Yes, of course."

"Mr. Warren, tell us about your relationship with Anna," Smalls said, his voice calm but edged with an intensity that cut through the room like a blade. His narrowed gaze locked onto Greg, unyielding.

Greg froze, the blood draining from his face as his mind raced. *How'd they know about Anna?* Panic flickered behind his eyes, and his fingers gripped the arms of his chair.

"Look, Mr. Warren," Hastings interjected, his tone sharp

and no longer masking his impatience. "It's going to go a lot easier for all of us if you cut the crap and start being honest with us."

Greg hesitated, his lips pressing into a thin line as he weighed his options. Finally, he sighed heavily, his shoulders slumping under the weight of his admission. "I've been... well, I'm... yes, I am happily married," he said, stumbling over his words, "but I also have a relationship with Anna."

"For the record, Mr. Warren," Smalls said evenly, his voice steady but firm, "we need you to tell us Anna's full name, address, and occupation." The soft tapping of his pen on the folder punctuated the gravity of the request.

Greg swallowed hard, his nerves visibly fraying. "Sure. Anna Holden. She's 34 years old. Lives at... uh, 2220 West Sunny Way Drive. She's a medical assistant at the Emergency Clinic just down the road... 1st West and Main." His voice faltered slightly, and he exhaled deeply, as though trying to rid himself of the tension. "Look, guys, I didn't think it mattered in relation to Holly being missing. That's why I didn't think it was important..uh..pertinent to tell you about Anna."

Smalls' gaze didn't waver as he leaned forward slightly, his voice dropping to a sharper, more commanding tone. "It *all* matters, Mr. Warren. This is a very serious matter, and we could charge you with obstructing justice right now." He let the weight of his words hang heavily in the air, the silence pressing down on Greg like a vice.

Greg opened his mouth to protest, but Smalls cut him off, his voice cooling slightly but losing none of its authority. "But I think we'll let that be for now." The implication was clear—this was a reprieve, not forgiveness.

Hastings leaned in, his gaze sharp and threatening as he

addressed Greg. "Mr. Warren, you're not planning on traveling today or anytime soon, are you? Because let me be clear: you are now involved in an active investigation. Legally, you cannot leave the city limits of East Bryndelle without our express permission. Do you understand?"

Greg's face flushed crimson, his discomfort radiating through the room. "Yes, I understand," he said quickly, his voice trembling just slightly. "Look, guys, that's fine. I'll be here. I'll cooperate one hundred percent. I promise." He hesitated for a moment, his eyes darting nervously between the two detectives. "Actually, I really wanted to ask you guys a favor…"

The detectives exchanged a brief, knowing glance. Smalls raised an eyebrow, his tone wary. "Yeah? What's that?"

Greg swallowed hard, his face growing even redder as he leaned forward, lowering his voice as though the walls themselves might betray him.

"Please… don't tell my wife about Anna."

Chapter 36

Gaeldritch stood silently in the stone circle, Hiktilda at her side, the two of them enveloped in the mystical aura of the clearing. The carved stone altar at the circle's center seemed alive under the pale lunar light, its basin glistening with dew. The ancient pines towered around them like sentinels, their branches swaying slightly in the cool night breeze. The moon's silvery light, already in its fullness, bathed the scene in an ethereal glow. The quartz bevels embedded in the rock caught the moonlight and refracted it into a cascade of shimmering sparks, as though the stars themselves were rising from the earth.

"I remember this, Gaeldritch," Hiktilda murmured, her voice tinged with wonder. "Standing here beside you floods me with memories—my past. We stood in many stone circles like this back...back in another forest...another country... another time."

"Yes, darling," Gaeldritch replied, her smile soft yet tinged with a knowing sharpness. "Many a night we worked wonders of power together under this same moon, beneath these very stars, although in forests far, far away from here." Her words carried the weight of boundless experience, spoken as if the years between their gatherings had not diminished their purpose.

Hiktilda paused, closing her eyes and inhaling deeply, as though the very air held the echoes of their past. "Not long ago—less than a week—I was still shackled to the profane, trapped in their hollow existence. I played their game, waved at neighbors I neither knew nor cared for, and pretended at a reality that was never mine." Her voice wavered with the weight of her revelation. "It felt wrong. It was never real."

Gaeldritch turned to her, her gaze piercing yet compassionate. "Your body and mind held dominion over your spirit, darling. But now, your true self has eclipsed the falsehoods entirely. The black thread stirred your soul, awakening it from the deep slumber imposed on it centuries ago—before the flames consumed your flesh."

Hiktilda absorbed Gaeldritch's words, nodding slowly as their truth resonated deep within her. "Yes," she whispered, her voice thick with emotion. "I feel alive again, truly alive."

She breathed deeply, her chest rising and falling with renewed determination. "Now, I mean to express my spirit in its fullness—with power, with devastation. The world lies before us, ripe for the taking. I hold no remorse and no doubts. Those type of ideas are no longer a concern of mine."

Gaeldritch's lips curved into a sly smile. "Indeed, darling. These are my understandings as well. Let the sheep and cowards wallow in their pitiful lives, heavy with guilt and remorse. Such burdens are for the profane."

Hiktilda lifted her gaze to the heavens, the full moon now centered directly above them, its glow casting a pale halo over the clearing. "Now," she said, her voice laced with an icy resolve, "we divine. Let us see what stands before us."

Her words hung in the air, as chilling and sharp as the night breeze, as the two women stood poised to unleash their power, ready to reshape the world in their image.

"Yes, darling. Tonight we divine with the blood of innocence and see deeply," Gaeldritch intoned, her voice low and deliberate, as she drew several vials from the folds of her dark robe and placed them carefully beside the carved stone basin.

Hiktilda moved gracefully to the edge of the circle, gathering a small bundle of dry wood from beyond the stones. She carried it back and stacked the pieces neatly in the fire-pit a few feet from the altar. Gaeldritch selected a vial with a deep amber liquid, uncorked it, and poured its contents over the wood. The thick liquid shimmered in the moonlight, its scent sharp and metallic. Hiktilda, poised and methodical, scraped iron against flint above the pit, a single precise stroke. Sparks flew downward, and the wood erupted into a roaring blaze, casting flickering shadows across the towering pine trees that encased the circle.

The two witches returned to the altar, standing shoulder to shoulder before the carved basin. Their voices rose in unison, chanting a tumbling cascade of ancient and strange words, their arms moving in rhythmic waves and jerking motions that seemed both chaotic and deliberate.

"Teristi nox collum!"

"Inkulanti trecharis!"

"Nerbah kribah luna vidiyah!"

Gaeldritch reached for the vials, uncorking them one by one and pouring their contents into the basin. The liquids hissed and bubbled, some crackling like fire, others churning like water over stones. The moonlight gleamed off the basin's edge, amplifying the mixture within.

The witches' chanting grew louder, their voices alternating

as though each were answering the other. Gaeldritch finally retrieved the crimson vial she had set aside earlier, its glass glinting ominously. Holding it aloft, she bellowed, "*Sanguis pueri luminis stellarum!*" Her voice echoed through the clearing as she emptied the vial's thick, red contents into the basin.

The liquid hissed and frothed violently, the color deepening to a near-black as it swirled. Hiktilda, without hesitation, grabbed a flaming branch from the fire-pit and plunged it into the basin's churning depths. "*Ignis, da mihi visionem stellarum!*" she commanded.

The basin erupted in a flash of green light followed by a red afterglow, casting an eerie luminescence over the circle. Moments later, thick smoke billowed upward, curling into the air like spectral tendrils. It enveloped the two witches, swirling around them in a dense shroud.

Gaeldritch and Hiktilda stood still, breathing deeply of the acrid smoke. Their eyelids snapped shut as their minds opened to the shared vision—images and sounds flooding their consciousness in vivid, overwhelming clarity. Fragments of light and echoes intertwined, revealing secrets and shadows to behold as they shared a vision.

A thick fog rolled across the ground, cloaking grass covered ground in a ghostly shroud, its swirling motion curling around the feet of a thin man standing in the moonlight. He held something aloft in his right hand, an object radiating an intense light that pierced the haze like a blade. It was a silver cross—ornate and imposing—with a rose-red light emanating from its center, pulsing as though alive. The man's lips moved steadily, forming words of command, words that seemed to ripple through the fog, bending it to his will.

The vision flashed to a new picture, a new angle, a man

with a full head of silvery-white hair stood holding a book, a black leather-bound bible in his right hand. He bellowed out words, holy incantations towards a shadow in the distance.

Suddenly, the vision erupted into a chaos of every spectrum of color flashing in a torrent. The swirling smoke churned violently, and without warning, a blinding flash of golden light burst forth, striking the witches with an almost physical force. The impact sent them reeling, their feet stumbling backward as they struggled to regain their balance. Their breaths were ragged, their faces contorted with shock as they turned, their movements clumsy against the aftershock.

The basin's bubbling intensity ceased abruptly, its glowing contents collapsing into an opaque black stillness. The clearing fell into an eerie silence, save for the crackling of the fire nearby. Hiktilda turned to Gaeldritch, her eyes wide with a mixture of confusion and unease. She spoke in a hushed tone, her words carrying the weight of what she had just witnessed. "Our vision… our vision was destroyed!"

Gaeldritch's frustration boiled over as she gestured sharply toward the basin. "Did you see it? Did you see it?" Her voice was edged with anger and disbelief. "He held something—an artifact!"

Hiktilda nodded slowly, her expression darkening. "I recognize it. It was a weapon of the Crucia, a relic of the late Romans," she said, her voice thick with disdain. "I saw it clearly. There were men in Bryndelle—a real threat. That was our *Abominatio* who was in danger!"

The witches moved wordlessly to the rough stone seats near the edge of the circle, their movements heavy with the weight of what they had just endured. They sat in silence for several minutes, the quiet broken only by the occasional hiss of the dying fire and the rustle of the wind through the ancient pines.

Finally, Hiktilda broke the silence, her voice calm but tinged with a calculated edge. "This artifact blocks our clear vision. This is unexpected..." Her words trailed off, her gaze fixed on the distant horizon, as if searching for the answers now obscured from them.

Gaeldritch's jaw tightened, her hands curling into fists on her lap. "Then we must find these men," she said, her tone resolute. "We must find them before they find Tum-Grissell."

The two witches exchanged a grim look, the air between them heavy with determination. The night had taken an unexpected turn, but they were far from deterred. The men in the vision, the artifact, and their defiance would soon be brought to reckoning.

Hiktilda gazed up at the moon, visible behind the dissipated smoke. "We must remove this threat before they destroy Thomas. I fear this isn't a vision of a far off future...but is a vision of what is happening tonight! We can't afford to ignore this, we must go!"

Gaeldritch nodded slowly, her expression calm but laced with steely determination. "Yes, you're right, darling. We will need to be hasty, but fear not... fear not," she said, her voice carrying a soothing cadence, like the whisper of wind through the ancient pines.

Hiktilda's face darkened, her gaze distant as if she were peering back through the veils of time. "I recall, deep in my memories, a weapon such as what we just witnessed. It was wielded against me long ago—it was indeed the very same artifact used to put me to the flames." Her words were heavy, the bitterness of centuries past seeping into her tone.

"Fear not, Hiktilda. Fear not," Gaeldritch repeated, her voice soft yet resolute. She reached out as if to anchor Hiktilda in the present. "I am here with you, and together, we shall overcome this threat."

Hiktilda rose from the stone seat in a blur of motion, her energy crackling like a storm barely held at bay. The air around her seemed to hum with the force of her ire, the scent of charred wood lingering in her wake. She strode back and forth before Gaeldritch, her steps sharp and deliberate, her black hair writhing and twisting in the silvery moonlight as if animated by the fury coursing through her veins.

"I fear nothing, my dear Gaeldritch," she declared, her voice like the first rumblings of a distant tempest. "But I burn with rage that a couple zealots—some ignorant fools—dare to threaten my coven, threaten our construct. To threaten all of us!" She turned abruptly, her eyes gleaming with a fire deeper than anger—an old and terrible resolve. "I will not be deterred. I will see these men removed!"

Her pacing quickened, her breath shallow with the force of her conviction. The firelight caught in the strands of her hair, twisting its ink-black lengths into shifting tendrils of shadow and flame. She raised her chin, her voice no longer a mere declaration but a bellow of defiance.

"If you will, I'd have you at my side as we fly tonight," she said, her gaze locking onto Gaeldritch's with unwavering intensity. "These men will come to understand—too late— the cost of interfering with forces far beyond their feeble grasp. They will *learn* what it means to stand against us!"

The air grew thick with the charge of her fury, as if the very earth beneath them recognized the weight of her words. Even the flickering flames of the nearby fire seemed to twist in strange patterns, bending to an unseen will.

Gaeldritch, ever the steady flame to Hiktilda's wildfire, rose from her place and stepped forward, her expression calm but brimming with knowing. Without hesitation, she reached for Hiktilda's hands, clasping them gently within her own. The touch, though soft, carried a quiet power, a grounding force amid the tempest.

"Of course, darling," Gaeldritch murmured, her lips curving into a smile laced with both affection and unshakable loyalty. "I wouldn't miss our time together for anything in the world."

For a moment, silence stretched between them, charged not with anger but with something far stronger—an unspoken vow, the weight of centuries of sisterhood.

Hiktilda's brow furrowed as a thought crossed her mind. "Tum-Grissell is already in town," she thought aloud. "He's on his way to the woman's house... to retrieve her hair and the knife. The zealots of the cross must be there!"

Gaeldritch's eyes darkened with concern. "Yes... and we must fly into town immediately before they reach him. I fear for him—he may already be in dire peril."

Their gazes lifted toward the sky, the moon casting its silver glow upon them, illuminating their shared resolve. The forces that bound them—older than kingdoms, stronger than any spell—solidified in that moment. Whatever lay ahead, they would face it together.

A few minutes later, the two witches stood side by side, their dark forms barely distinguishable in the gloom, each clutching a small blue vial. Without a word, they uncorked the containers, releasing a faint, sweet scent into the night air. Slowly and methodically, they poured the greasy, congealed contents into their free palms. The mixture glistened under the moonlight, thick and unctuous.

With practiced ease, they smoothed the viscous salve over their bare skin beneath their robes, humming low, rhythmic chants—words that seemed older than the trees around them, older than the stones beneath their feet. The sound was less a melody and more a vibration, a resonance that seeped into the air and made the very shadows quiver. As the ointment soaked into their flesh, they moved with slow reverence, their eyes gleaming with an eerie light.

Once their bodies had been thoroughly anointed, they turned their attention to their staffs. Long and gnarled, with intricate carvings, the wood seemed to drink in the unguent, darkening as the witches rubbed it in with careful, deliberate strokes.

Gaeldritch's lips curled into a knowing smile. "The unguent of flight... Do you remember its making, my darling?" Her voice was silken, threaded with the amusement of one testing an old friend's memory.

Hiktilda's gaze flickered with recollection. She let out a slow, pleased breath, savoring the sensation of the oil seeping into her skin. "Indeed, I do recall."

She closed her eyes, speaking as if conjuring the memory itself. "Wolfs-bane, steeped in the juice of nightshade... and the fats of the profane—their oils, siphoned from their glands... all mixed with devotion, with reverence, with the proper words spoken with power."

Gaeldritch nodded approvingly, her pleasure evident. "Good."

They returned to their staffs, rubbing the last of the salve along the slick wood, before tucking them against the folds of their robes, pressing them firmly against the insides of their legs. Their fingers curled around the smooth, oiled grain, gripping the staffs with habitual familiarity.

And then, without warning, Gaeldritch disappeared.

No crack of thunder, no rush of wind—only the faintest distortion in the air, like a shimmer of heat over stone, and she was gone. A heartbeat later, she reappeared many yards away, standing still and silent, her dark eyes gleaming like embers.

Hiktilda smirked and followed suit. With a flicker, she vanished, only to materialize nearly eighty yards away, close to where Gaeldritch had reappeared. The two locked eyes, their lips curling in the unspoken delight of old sorcery.

Then—*flicker*—Gaeldritch was gone again, through the air like a phantom slipping between worlds. Hiktilda vanished in pursuit, their figures darting, disappearing and reappearing across the landscape in bursts of impossible movement.

They traversed the forest and canyon with terrifying speed, vanishing and materializing in eerie silence. No footsteps, no rustling of leaves—only the subtle ripple of the air where they had been. This was *witches' flight*, a mastery of motion that defied the chains of mortal travel. A mere twitch of the staff, a shift in stance, and distances collapsed beneath their will.

The night swallowed them whole as they soared toward the unsuspecting town, unseen, unheard.

Chapter 37

The sun had long since fallen, surrendering the world to night, but the full moon cast its pale, ghostly glow across the landscape, illuminating the earth in silvery hues. A vast shadow loomed near the back porch of the house, its form hulking, unnatural—covered from head to toe in a thick sheath of black bog mud. Only its orange eyes, cold and alert, remained untouched by the oozing film.

Tum-Grissell stood motionless, a statue of living darkness, nestled deep within the folds of the night. He did not breathe. He did not stir. He watched.

The house stood still, unassuming, as if unaware of the force lurking at its periphery. There were no lights on inside the house, but the outside front porch and back porch both had their lights on—just as Hiktilda had predicted. The woman—Anna—was not home, and Hiktilda had told him that she was not expected to be returning.

He had watched long enough to determine that if anyone else lived there, they were most likely fast asleep. But this woman probably lived alone. That made his task easier.

He had done his share of silent stalking through homes thick with slumbering prey, but there was a certain elegance in working unopposed, in moving through the empty halls of a dark house.

Hiktilda had given him his task earlier that day, whispering her instructions with the certainty of someone who knew her will would be carried out. Find one of Anna's hairbrushes. Take the strands of hair caught in its bristles. Find a kitchen knife—a large one, preferably part of a set, so that its absence would be keenly felt. That part was not optional; it was a requirement. If he failed to retrieve the knife, the entire task would be considered a failure. Then, bring both items to her.

The Grand-Witch had not explained why, but she didn't need to. For many past centuries, he had obeyed her commands, following her guidance without question. Her mind worked on a level beyond even his comprehension, weaving plots and schemes in intricate layers that no ordinary being could unravel. She was cunning, and Tum-Grissell had no concern to seek answers where none were required.

The time had come.

Like a wraith slipping between realms, he emerged from the shadows and stepped toward the back door. His massive, mud-slicked hand hovered just above the handle, fingers ready to grab the handle. But before making contact, he willed the blackened sludge coating his hand to retreat, drawing it back into his flesh as effortlessly as water receding into a tide pool.

His bare fingers met the metal—cool beneath his touch. He never worried about fingerprints. They shifted and swayed as he lived and breathed, like eddies in a swirling pool, changing with the passage of time.

A single twist, and the lock gave way with a pitiful snap. The knob spun loosely in its housing, yielding to his unnatural strength.

But the door did not open.

A deadbolt still held it fast, its resistance a mere inconvenience.

He placed one enormous hand against the wooden surface, braced his other against the doorframe, and slowly, deliberately, pushed.

The house groaned.

The splintering of wood filled the still night air, a deep, resonant crackling, like the sound of bones breaking under great pressure. The frame buckled. Shards of wood curled and snapped. The bolt, overwhelmed by his inexorable force, surrendered with a low, tortured creak.

The door slowly swung open on it's slightly bent hinges.

He stepped inside, the threshold of the house swallowing him whole.

With a mere thought, he willed the bog-mud covering his feet to seep back into his skin, leaving no trace of his presence. His massive frame filled the narrow laundry room, the ceiling pressing close, the walls shrinking around him.

The house was small. Cramped.

It barely contained him.

The kitchen lay just ahead, a modest space where a single wooden table was tucked against the far wall, leaving little room for movement. No matter. Tum-Grissell had spent lifetimes adapting to places that did not accommodate his form.

It was dark inside, but the absence of light meant nothing to him. He was a creature of shadow, a thing that thrived in the blackness of the deep bogs and the unlit corridors of the forgotten world. His eyes, alight with an eerie phosphorescent glow, cast an imperceptible veil of green over the space.

This was his world—the hush of the night, the stillness of a house in the silent darkness.

He moved through the kitchen like an apparition, slipping into the narrow hallway beyond.

The bathroom was his first destination.

Opening the top drawer of the vanity, he found it immediately—a hairbrush tangled with strands of auburn. The very strands he had come for.

A single pluck, swift and precise, and the nest of hair was his.

With practiced ease, he dropped it into the small black sack tied to his waist, pulled the cord closed, and returned the brush to its place as though it had never been touched.

One task complete.

He scanned the bathroom once more, his luminescent sight seeking out any remnants of his oily mud. Finding nothing, he stepped back into the hallway, heading for the kitchen once more.

The counters were empty. No knife block.

That meant a drawer.

He opened the one closest to the stove, and there it was—a large, blue-handled chef's knife with a ten-inch blade.

Exactly what the Grand-Witch wanted.

No hesitation. He grasped the larger knife, lifted it from its place, and slid the drawer shut without a sound.

Then—

A voice.

Muffled. Close.

His body tensed, muscles coiling with primal readiness. The sound came from the front of the house—indistinct words, but unmistakably human. A man was outside.

215

Tum-Grissell moved without pause, retreating into the laundry room. He pressed the broken door back into place, its shattered frame barely holding, but good enough to deceive the casual eye. Then he waited, ears straining against the silence.

Three seconds passed.

Nothing.

Without hesitation, he opened the door and, in a single fluid movement, stepped out into the night, pulling it closed behind him. He slipped back into the shadows a few feet away, crouched next to a hedge against the house. He faced toward the door, watching and waiting in silence.

Then—movement.

A figure rounded the corner of the house. A man, clad in a long coat, his stance rigid, purposeful. In his right hand, barely catching the moon's reflection, he carried a small snub-nose pistol.

He stood just a few feet from the back door. His body was positioned for action, every muscle taut, every breath measured.

And then—

A loud knock echoed from the front of the house.

Then, the sharp chime of the doorbell.

Tum-Grissell did not move. Did not breathe.

Chapter 38

Santino sat beside Mallory in the car, the two of them locked in the stillness of the stakeout, their bodies aching from the long hours spent waiting. They had been there since 10 a.m., and now, as the clock crept past 10 p.m., the strain of inactivity settled into their muscles like heavy stones. The air inside the vehicle was stale, thick with the mingling scents of old coffee and leather upholstery.

Earlier in the day, they had taken brief turns stepping out, stretching stiff limbs and wandering the quiet streets, hoping to spot something—anything—out of place. But there had been nothing. Just the same tidy homes, the same clipped lawns, the same empty sidewalks. A neighborhood that seemed untouched by urgency, draped in the mundane.

Until now.

The night lay draped in silver, the full moon casting its pale, spectral glow across rooftops and pavement. And then, finally, something changed.

Mallory saw it first.

A dark sedan pulled up two doors down from the house they had been watching for hours, its engine cutting out in a whisper. The doors swung open almost immediately, and two men in long coats stepped onto the street. Their movements were sharp, deliberate. They didn't glance around. They didn't hesitate. They walked toward the house with an air of quiet authority.

Mallory stiffened, his breath catching. "Santino! This has got to be it," he said, his voice edged with urgency.

Santino, jolted from his weary daze, sat up straighter, his senses sharpening. His eyes tracked the men, absorbing every detail—their posture, their stride, the way their hands hovered close to their coats as if prepared to reach for something unseen.

For a moment, he didn't speak. He simply watched. Calculating.

Then, his jaw tightened. "Peter, you're right," he whispered. "Now we move. We have to move now. Go slow, stay quiet, and be careful."

Mallory didn't wait for further instruction. He pushed open the car door, stepping onto the sidewalk with determination. His movements were swift, but measured—he didn't want to draw attention to himself too soon. Without looking back, he strode toward the house where the men had parked, his car door left ajar, a silent precaution against the sharp click of it closing.

Santino leaned forward slightly, voice hushed but firm. "Peter—remember the cross," he urged in a sharp whisper.

Mallory didn't acknowledge him, but Santino knew he had heard.

A long, tense beat passed.

Santino exhaled slowly, his fingers drumming lightly against the worn leather cover of the Bible resting on his lap. He had flipped through its pages earlier, letting the weight of its words fill the empty hours. Now, his gaze lingered on it, searching for an answer that he already knew.

Go. Follow him.

The hesitation evaporated.

With a steadying breath, he set the Bible down on the passenger seat and reached for the door handle. The night air was crisp as he stepped out, his shoes making the faintest whisper against the pavement. He moved with quiet purpose, keeping a measured distance—twenty feet behind Mallory, just enough to watch, just enough to react.

The house loomed ahead.

Something was happening.

Santino's pulse thrummed in his ears.

Stay vigilant. Stay brave, he told himself.

Chapter 39

K nock. *Knock. Knock.*
"Anna Holden. This is Detective Smalls with California State Law Enforcement. I need to ask you a few questions. This is very important—your life may be in danger."

Knock. Knock. Knock. Knock.

The sound echoed through the night, sharp against the stillness.

Detective Hastings shifted his weight, standing just a foot away from the back door, his revolver held steady in his grasp. He had done this many times before—one man announces himself at the front, and if there's a rat inside, they scurry out the back. He was here to catch that rat.

But there was nothing. No hurried footsteps, no whispered curses, no slamming of a door. Only silence.

"Anna Holden, this is Detective Smalls," his partner called out again, his voice calm but firm. "I'm with the police, and I need to ask you some questions. This is important. We have a warrant to enter the premises and will do so if you do not open the door." A beat of silence. Then, with even more weight behind his words, "We are here to protect you. Your life may be in danger."

Hastings remained perfectly still, his years of experience sending a warning through his gut. Something wasn't right.

His eyes scanned the back door.

The wood around the latch was splintered, raw and uneven as if it had been forced. And then—the knob. Broken. Twisted in its housing like it had been *ripped* rather than turned.

His breath slowed. His senses sharpened.

A scent hit him—acrid and damp, thick like something decaying deep in the earth.

He turned.

The shadows shifted.

"Is someone there?" he demanded, his voice low, steady.

Then—pain.

Like lightning through his nervous system.

A force like a vice clamped down on his hand. Not just squeezing—*crushing*. The bones in his hand gripping his pistol snapped like dry twigs, twisted grotesquely around the metal shape of his revolver. A guttural noise, barely a gasp, escaped his lips as his body seized in agony. His mind screamed at his fingers to pull the trigger, but they were gone—useless, mangled flesh wrapped around dead nerves.

Two glowing eyes stared back at him from the abyss.

Then, the knife.

Tum-Grissell moved like liquid shadow, silent and deliberate. In one swift motion, the stolen knife plunged deep into Hastings' chest.

The blade met no resistance. It slid effortlessly between his ribs, piercing his heart as if the body had been waiting to be opened.

A twist.

A pull.

221

A second later, the knife was across his throat. A precise, clean stroke.

Hastings' legs failed him instantly. He should have collapsed, his body limp, but Tum-Grissell held him up, gripping his broken hand like a puppet master keeping his marionette from the stage floor.

A wet gurgle came from Hastings' throat as his body struggled to function for a few more seconds. But Tum-Grissell did not watch.

He had already turned his head.

Another man had arrived.

"Stop right there! Lay down on the ground, now!"

The command rang out sharp as a gunshot.

Detective Smalls rounded the corner of the house, flicking the safety off on his pistol, ready to use the weapon, his stance rock solid. His eyes widened as they took in the scene—his partner, held up by a monster wrapped in shadow.

Tum-Grissell dropped Hastings' body with a dull *thud* as their gazes locked.

"I'll put you down!", Smalls threatened.

Then, the shadow moved.

A blur of motion.

Crack! Crack! Crack! Crack!

Smalls fired, each shot tearing into the mud-covered figure. Bullets struck flesh—or what should have been flesh. Each impact sent a sickening splatter of dark, viscous muck spraying outward, but Tum-Grissell never faltered.

No flinch. No pause.

No pain.

Smalls barely had time to widen his stance before a monstrous fist collided with the crown of his skull.

One hit.

Like a sledge hammer striking brittle glass.

The force sent Smalls downward, his body folding over itself as he crumpled to the pavement in a heap.

Tum-Grissell loomed over him, breath slow, measured.

He tilted his head, studying the man at his feet. His fingers flexed around the handle of the knife, its blade still slick with the fresh blood of Hastings.

Would the Grand-Witch want this one dead, too?

Or would she prefer another fate?

Tum-Grissell tensed, his hulking, mud-slicked chest rippling like the surface of a stagnant swamp disturbed by an unseen force. The slugs buried within his body, lodged in the dense, unnatural muck that formed his flesh, began to shift. Slowly, deliberately, he willed them out.

One by one, the bullets were expelled, forcing their way through the thick black sludge that had absorbed their impact. They fell, *clink, clink, clank, clink*, striking the concrete patio beneath him with cold finality, tiny remnants of a futile attempt to stop what could not be stopped.

He exhaled, the breath more an amused vibration in his throat than anything human.

Time to finish him.

His glowing eyes flickered with something almost akin to satisfaction. He'd use the knife on this man, too. He was sure the Grand-Witch would appreciate that.

"Tum-Grissell," he murmured in a low octave, the name rolling from his lips—neither a mere identity nor a title, but a confirmation, a validation of his existence. It was not just a name; it was a statement of being, a whispered acknowledgment of the dark force of which he was made.

Chapter 40

Santino remembered the thunderclaps from his vision—four distinct echoes rolling through the sky. But now, with his own ears ringing in the present, he understood. They had not been thunder at all. They were gunshots.

Mallory was already moving ahead of him, disappearing into the night as he ran toward the backyard of the house where the detectives had just faced something beyond mortal reckoning. A deadly encounter had unfolded here. And the incident was not yet over.

In the yard, beneath the cold gaze of the moon, Tum-Grissell loomed over the fallen detective, the stolen knife gripped tightly in his massive hand. The bullets that had hit his chest—mere surface damage. He had suffered no harm. And now, he would end this troublesome man.

Then—Mallory appeared.

The Jesuit priest materialized between the hulking shadow and the unconscious form of Smalls, his arrival swift and unexpected.

"Back! Stay back, foul beast of darkness!"

Mallory's voice rang out like a war cry, shattering the heavy stillness of the night. He stood firm, his lean frame rigid with defiance. In his outstretched right hand, he brandished the *Cross of Saint Paul*, the polished silver reflecting the moon's pale glow. The cross, a relic of sacred power, gleamed like a beacon in the darkness.

Tum-Grissell halted mid-step. A flicker of hesitation crossed his mind with doubt in his eyes.

Santino had reached the side of the house just in time to witness the scene. He saw Peter standing stalwart, the radiant cross held aloft, forming a barrier of light between himself and the monstrous creature. Smalls lay still behind Peter, his body crumpled on the ground, but still breathing.

Peter's voice rang with unshaken resolve.

"You will not harm this man, and you will not harm me! With the *Cross of Saint*—"

A deep, thunderous voice cut through his command like a blade.

"Your cross is nothing to me!"

Tum-Grissell moved with unnatural speed, his massive arm shooting forward. His blackened, mud-coated fingers clamped onto the top of the cross, gripping it with inhuman strength.

Peter staggered, his muscles burning with resistance, but it was like fighting against the weight of a mountain. The raw force behind Tum-Grissell's grip was beyond anything human, beyond anything mortal.

Then—something unexpected happened.

A snap. A shift.

The cross came apart.

Both Tum-Grissell and Peter froze in momentary confusion. The upper horizontal and vertical portion of the relic had detached from its base, slipping free in Tum-Grissell's massive hand. He stared down at it, puzzled by its unexpected fragility.

Peter's breath hitched as he glanced at what remained in his grip.

The lower half of the cross had revealed something hidden within—a crystalline shard, white as frost, sharp as the tip of a spear.

The sacred weapon had been waiting.

The moonlight caught its surface, and in that single flicker of illumination, Peter understood.

Tum-Grissell was confused.

And confusion meant weakness.

With no time to hesitate, Peter stepped forward, his heart pounding but his mind resolute.

The hulking mass stood surprised and open, still looking at the piece of the relic in his hand in bewilderment.

With every ounce of divine courage surging through him, Peter struck.

The crystalline shard drove into Tum-Grissell's chest, sinking deep, piercing not mud, not darkness—but something real. Something vulnerable.

A deep, guttural snarl erupted from the creature, not of rage—but of pain.

Real. Raw. Ancient pain.

Tum-Grissell staggered back, clutching his chest. His massive frame shuddered as a foreign, long-forgotten sensation flooded his body.

He fell to his knees.

A thick, wet sound hit the ground.

Blood.

Not black. Not oozing tar.

Red.

For the first time in over nine centuries, Tum-Grissell bled.

His trembling fingers smeared the warm liquid across his chest, his gaze fixed on it in horror, in disbelief. It was impossible.

Until now.

Peter saw the beast falter.

This was his moment.

With renewed confidence and determination, he stepped forward again, raising the weapon. This time, he would aim for its head. Right between those burning, orange eyes.

Then—

A scream from behind.

"Gorzunstrica!"

The voice was sharp, shrill, and terrible.

It cut through the air like a blade, freezing Peter's very soul.

His body locked.

Every muscle. Every nerve. Frozen.

His breath caught in his throat, his mind screaming at his limbs to move, to finish it—but his body refused.

His hands, his legs—paralyzed.

He could only stare.

Chapter 41

"Peter! There's someone behind you!"

Santino's voice rang out, thick with alarm.

Peter's mind barely had time to register the warning before the air around him shifted—thickened. A presence materialized behind him, warping reality itself as it arrived.

Gaeldritch.

She stood behind him in her flowing black robes, her ancient staff gripped firmly in one withered hand. There had been no footsteps, no movement to herald her coming—she had simply appeared. With a single whispered word of power, she had seized control of Peter's body, freezing him mid-stride.

He was trapped.

His muscles, his limbs—locked.

The night air hung heavy with malevolence as she turned her head toward Santino, her voice curling like smoke from her lips.

"You have no power here, old man."

The words slithered through the space between them, carrying an unnatural weight.

Santino's breath hitched. His body trembled violently, an unseen force creeping into his bones, into his mind, stripping away his will. The urge—the need—to reach for his Bible overwhelmed him. It was instinctual, desperate.

He had left his Bible in the car!

He had to move.

Had to run.

With the last shreds of his strength, he turned and bolted toward the car, toward his holy book, his old legs burning with effort, his breath coming in ragged gasps.

Gaeldritch barely spared him a glance. He was nothing to her.

Her attention shifted back to Peter, standing like a stone statue.

Her gaze flicked to his right hand—the cross-knife still gleaming beneath the moonlight.

With a single, effortless motion, she swung her staff. The relic was knocked away from his grasp, spinning through the air before landing with a dull clatter on the concrete patio.

Peter felt the staff snap against his hand and gasped inwardly, but his body refused to move.

Then, Gaeldritch stepped around him and stood before him, stretching her free hand toward him.

Her fingers, pale and skeletal, settled upon his scalp. It was a touch that mimicked a blessing—but there was no mercy in her hand, no sanctity in her gesture.

Her lips parted.

"Kneel before me." she spoke to his terrified eyes.

With surprising ease, she pushed down on his head, forcing his body to collapse to his knee.

"*Tang laskrow, ting laskrew, dread flood the blood,*" she intoned, her voice thick with dark power.

Peter heard her words and shuddered. The words were

wrong. They felt dark and evil.

A terrible sensation flooded through Peter's mind, his thoughts unraveling into darkness.

"Ario vextevio pustristii!"

Then came the threads.

Black tendrils slithered from beneath her fingernails—thin, writhing things, like ink given life. They burrowed into his scalp, weaving beneath his skin like parasites hungry for a host.

Pain.

A searing, mind-shattering agony, unlike anything he had ever known.

Peter's vision pulsed, his world tilting violently as the dark tendrils moved inside him, writhing through his flesh like living veins. Gaeldritch pressed harder, her hand tightening, forcing the corruption deeper.

His body went soft and weak.

His breath let out an enormous exhalation.

Then—he collapsed.

Peter Mallory crumpled onto the earth, his body curling into itself, while Gaeldritch crouched down with him, keeping her terrible hand grasping his head. He shuddered violently, then convulsed, his entire form quaking in erratic, inhuman tremors. Every inch of his flesh vibrated in rapid, micro-movements, making him appear blurred—distorted beneath the silver glow of the moon.

Gaeldritch threw back her head and laughed.

The sound was jagged, like broken glass scraping across stone.

Finally, with a whisper—

"Soma pix sunato."

The black tendrils recoiled, slithering backward, returning to the abyss beneath her nails.

Peter lay still.

His face was pale, his body slack, but he was alive. Bruised, battered—but alive.

Gaeldritch wasted no time.

She stepped over the unconscious Detective Smalls, her fingers stretching toward his forehead and grasping it tightly.

"*You shall not speak. You shall not think. Your mind is now riddled with confusion. Avidyasah!*"

Again, the black tendrils poured forth. Some slithered into his skull, burying deep within the folds of his mind, twisting, tangling his thoughts into a chaotic knot. Others writhed and curled just beneath his skin, leaving no trace—no wound— but ensuring that when he woke, his mind would be nothing but a labyrinth of disarray.

The work was precise. Flawless.

She withdrew her hand, the tendrils slinking back beneath her fingernails.

Now—the final piece.

She turned toward the massive, slumped-over form of Tum-Grissell.

The ancient creature knelt upon the cold concrete, his colossal frame hunched in agony, his breaths ragged and uneven. A crimson river spilled from his chest, thick and dark, pooling beneath him. He stared down at it, dazed— *real, red blood.* Not the blackened sludge of the bog, not the viscous, murky substance that had coursed through his veins for centuries. No. This was different. This was human. The cross-knife had somehow changed his constitution.

And the sight of his own red blood had undone him.

Gaeldritch advanced with slow, purposeful steps, the weight of authority in her stance. Her voice cut through the heavy night like the crack of a whip.

"Listen!" she commanded, her tone sharp with urgency. "Tum-Grissell, you must summon every ounce of your will—your very existence depends on it! Absorb the essence of the bog back into your skin, now!"

He lifted his massive, muck-covered face, his burnt-orange eyes flickering in the moonlight, unreadable. There was hesitation there, doubt. To relinquish his armor—to strip away the blackened coat of the bog—was to make himself even more vulnerable. And vulnerability was something Tum-Grissell hadn't felt for 800 years.

Gaeldritch's lips curled in frustration. Time was slipping away.

"I can save you, but only if my ointment and elixir can reach your human flesh," she snapped. "The sludge of the bog will reject what you need."

There was a sharp desperation in her voice, a brittle edge she had not allowed herself to use in centuries.

And Tum-Grissell—ancient, indomitable Tum-Grissell—flinched.

Then, without another word, he shut his eyes and obeyed. With a slow, pained exhale, he began drawing the sludge back into himself. It retracted in sluggish waves, slithering over his skin like living tar, seeping into the coarse fibers of his being. His raw flesh, streaked in red blood, was now fully exposed.

Gaeldritch moved swiftly, her steps light but precise. She reached for the black sack at his waist and plunged her long fingers inside.

From its depths, she withdrew three strands of auburn hair and,with deliberate care, she stepped toward the lifeless form of Detective Hastings, his bloodied chest exposed to the night air. She laid the strands across him like a whispered invocation, a thread of destiny woven into the fabric of death itself.

The plan was in motion.

Without hesitation, she bent low, plucking the cross-knife from the ground and tucked it into the unseen folds of her robe. Then, she pried the chef's knife from Tum-Grissell's slackened grip, sliding it beside the relic in her robe. She scanned the patio and spotted the four spent slugs from Smalls' shots—each one having struck Tum-Grissell and been effortlessly pushed out moments later. Lastly, her fingers curled around the broken upper half of the cross in his palm, peeling it away and secured it within the depths of the same deep pocket.

Everything was accounted for.

Her mind—so sharp, so meticulous—had always seen what others missed.

Now, the final step.

From within her robes, she retrieved a vial made of transparent quartz, its glass so thin it seemed to shimmer, almost intangible, beneath the pale moonlight. Within, a thick, silvery liquid churned, a substance that neither rested nor stilled, shifting like molten mercury, turbulent with unseen forces.

She uncorked it.

A soft hiss escaped the vial as the air kissed the sacred liquid, releasing the faint scent of burning herbs and iron.

"Lean back," she commanded, her voice cold and steady.

"Move your arms, open your chest to me."

Tum-Grissell obeyed, exposing the gaping wound that still wept scarlet rivers down his massive torso.

Gaeldritch tipped the vial.

The liquid poured in a slow, deliberate stream, cascading over his open wound. The moment it touched his flesh, a violent hiss erupted, curling upward in ghostly tendrils of pale smoke. The potion seeped into his wound like rain vanishing into parched soil.

His face was stern. His body jerked. His limbs went rigid.

With fluid precision, Gaeldritch retrieved a second vial—a small blue one, cool as ice against her palm. Uncorking it swiftly, she upturned it, allowing its thick, congealed contents to spill into her hand. The substance was greasy and translucent, its scent a mixture of crushed nightshade and turpentine.

With practiced hands, she rubbed the unguent between her palms, feeling its slickness against her skin. Then she set to work—her fingers pressing firmly, urgently, as she spread the oily concoction across Tum-Grissell's bare flesh. She worked quickly, coating his arms, his shoulders, his heaving chest—every inch of his body.

Gaeldritch's bony fingers then tightened around his glistening forearm, her nails pressing into his muscle, piercing his skin with her fingernails, in a vice-like hold.

She then spoke in a low, commanding tone of voice—woven with an undeniable force of will, gazing into his eyes, piercing deep into his core.

"You will fly with me now," she said, each syllable weighted with power. "Do not resist. You must submit your will to me and have no fear or you will die tonight. Do not resist!"

"I understand."

The night around them stilled, breathless, listening.

And Tum-Grissell—mighty, bloodied, and frightened for his life submitted.

With her left hand, she slid her staff between the folds of her robe, anchoring it between her legs.

Then—

"Terafi vaya rucha d'veshmai!"

The night twisted.

The air around her fractured, bending at impossible angles.

Then—she was gone. Along with Tum-Grissell.

In the blink of an eye, she reappeared down the street, moving in dark flashes of blackness, her form flickering like a shadow breaking through dimensions.

With each vanishing step, Tum-Grissell moved with her, his massive body shifting through the unnatural spaces between light and dark.

Flicker.

Gone.

Flicker.

Farther still.

And then—

They had vanished out of the town.

Swallowed by the abyss of the night, leaving only whispers of what had transpired.

Chapter 42

Santino ran, his body trembling, his breath ragged. Every step felt like wading through thick, clinging dread, unable to move at full speed, as if he were in a nightmare. The witch's voice still echoed in his ears—an unholy sound, raw with malevolence. It was not simply evil; it was the absence of everything good, pure darkness.

His car was in sight. Just a few more steps, and he could grab his Bible. Then he would turn back—he had to—to save his friend, his brother, Peter Mallory, from the unthinkable horror he had just witnessed.

He reached the car, heart hammering, and thrust his hand inside—

But his Bible was gone.

His breath caught. His stomach turned to ice.

Then—

"It's here, you pathetic pawn."

The voice slithered from behind him, sharp and jagged as shattered glass.

A tremor crawled up Santino's spine. He turned slowly—dreading what he would see.

And there she was.

Hiktilda.

Standing mere feet away, draped in endless folds of black, her robes moving like liquid shadow. Her hair—thick, black, and writhing—shifted unnaturally, as though each strand were alive, animated by an unseen force. Her skin, sickly pale, stretched tightly over the sharp bones of her face.

And in her sinewy, veined right hand—

She held his Bible.

The leather cover curled under her grip, as if recoiling from her very touch.

Santino swallowed, his voice barely a whisper.

"What do you want?"

Then, his world turned for the worse.

A searing orange glow erupted from her palm. The Bible smoldered instantly, its edges curling inward, blackening with unnatural fire.

Smoke billowed in thick tendrils from between her fingers as flames devoured the holy book—ravenous, merciless. The many pages crumbled to ash in mere seconds, dissolving into the wind, fluttering away into oblivion.

Santino staggered back, feeling the embers in his soul, his breath coming in short, panicked gasps.

"You cannot harm me! I have the power of light!" he screamed, forcing the words out, desperate to believe them.

Hiktilda's eyes darkened, an abyss that consumed the last inkling of his strength.

"*SILENCE!*"

Her voice struck him like a thunderclap.

"You shall speak no more to me!", she howled.

The words crashed into his chest like a physical force, ripping through his body.

His throat seized—his breath choked—his voice was gone.

His knees buckled. His body trembled violently. His mind screamed at him to resist, to fight back—but his limbs no longer obeyed.

With a slow, deliberate motion, Hiktilda raised her hand and waved it in a single arc.

"Kneel before your new deity! You are nothing! *Fiat umbra! Let there be darkness!*"

The command shattered what remained of his will.

His legs collapsed beneath him.

His knees crashed against the cold pavement with a sickening crack, a sharp jolt of agony shooting through his bones. The pain was real—too real—but there was nothing he could do to stop it. He let out a strangled gasp, his ears humming like distant thunder, his body bent forward, locked in submission.

The Grand-Witch had broken him.

Then, she reached for him.

Her long, skeletal fingers hovered above his skull, stretching toward him like the claws of a vulture descending upon its dying prey.

Then—contact.

Her fingers pressed into his scalp.

A grotesque squirming sensation erupted beneath her touch.

Then came the threads.

The thin, black tendrils slithered from beneath her nails— alive, twisting, writhing, coiling like worms searching for flesh to consume.

The oily strands burrowed into his scalp, piercing skin, diving beneath the surface.

Pain.

Indescribable.

It wasn't just physical—it was worse. It clawed into his mind, twisting, corrupting, unraveling. His memories frayed at the edges. Thoughts became distorted. His prayers—words he had spoken for decades—were stolen from him, vanishing into the darkness swallowing his mind.

He could feel her darkness inside him. He could hear her voice echoing from within.

"You are nothing," she whispered, her voice dripping with sadistic pleasure. "Nothing but a sad, weak old man."

His body convulsed. He shuddered. He gasped for air.

Then, the threads retracted, slithering back beneath her nails, vanishing as if they had never existed.

But Santino felt them.

Something had been left behind.

Hiktilda lingered for a moment, her fingers still pressed against his skull, savoring the moment. Then, suddenly, violently, she gripped his hair and yanked.

A sharp, blinding tear of pain exploded across his scalp.

A jagged scream tore from his throat.

She had ripped a clump of silver hair from his head—roots and all.

Blood pooled where the strands had been torn, the exposed follicles burning with raw agony.

Santino did not move, he could not move.

He remained kneeling, his body wrecked, kneeling humiliated before the Grand-Witch.

Hiktilda studied the silvery strands in her palm, then let them slip from her fingers into a hidden pocket of her robe.

She smiled.

"Go now," she murmured. "Go fetch your little helper and leave this place forever. Run away, with what little of yourself

I've left intact."

She shifted her staff in between her legs.

And then—

She vanished.

Flicker.

Gone.

The air where she had stood seemed to tremble and shimmer, as if the darkness itself had shuddered in her wake.

Hiktilda had faded into the night, leaving only the ruin of what she had touched.

Santino remained kneeling, his breath shallow, his body shaking.

The world around him felt hollow.

And for the first time in his life—

He felt truly lost.

Chapter 43

S antino collapsed onto his hands, his breath coming in uneven gasps. His body trembled violently, exhaustion and terror wracking him in equal measure. For a fleeting moment, the weight of everything crushed him, and he let out a strangled sob, his fingers curling against the cold pavement.

But he couldn't stop. He couldn't give up.

I must help Peter!

He clenched his teeth and forced himself to move.

Slowly, painfully, he straightened his battered legs, ignoring the fiery protests from his knees. His body swayed, weak and broken, but he planted his feet firmly, gripping his bleeding scalp with one hand to steady himself. Step by step, he limped forward, dragging himself back toward the house—toward the scene of the nightmare he had barely escaped.

Please, Lord... let Peter be alive!

He turned the corner—

And his heart nearly stopped.

Peter lay motionless, crumpled in a heap on the ground, his body eerily still under the moon's cold light.

He was astonished that there were two other bodies in the backyard, not just the one he'd seen earlier.

A choked gasp escaped Santino's lips. His vision swam. His knees nearly gave out again. This was too much.

His pulse roared in his ears as he rushed forward, collapsing beside Peter's unmoving form. With trembling hands, he gently shook him, his voice cracking with desperation.

"Peter! Peter! Please wake up! We have to leave! We have to get out of here!"

For an agonizing second, there was nothing.

Then—a faint, shuddering breath.

Peter's eyelids fluttered.

Santino sucked in a sharp breath of air, his chest tightening with adrenaline and relief.

He's alive.

Peter's lips parted weakly, his voice barely a whisper.

"I... I can't move," he murmured, confusion and fear clouding his eyes.

"You can move, you must move. Keep trying! I'll pull you up," Santino pleaded, gripping his arms. "It is too dangerous for us to linger! We are leaving, now!"

Peter groaned, his body sluggish, unresponsive. But then— a twitch in his fingers. A slow movement in his arm. His legs stirred weakly beneath him. Each second that passed seemed like minutes.

Then—the sound.

A distant wail, cutting through the night like a blade.

SIRENS.

Santino's blood turned to ice.

"The police," he breathed. Panic clawed at his throat. "We can't be here when they arrive. They won't believe what happened. We'll be in more trouble than we can imagine!"

He wrapped an arm around Peter and yanked him up with

all the strength he had left. Every muscle in his body screamed in protest, but he ignored it. They staggered forward, their battered forms barely upright, leaning against each other for support.

They had to move.

Every agonizing step toward the car felt endless.

Santino didn't know how he did it—how he got Peter into the passenger seat, how he forced his own broken body behind the wheel—but somehow, through sheer will, he did.

His hands shook violently as he jammed the key into the ignition.

The engine roared to life.

His heart pounded. His eyes darted to the mirrors.

Any moment now, he thought. *They could stop us. They could catch us.*

He prayed silently, but moving his lips, *Please, Lord, don't let the evil stop us! Save us from their darkness!*

He threw the car into gear.

The tires lurched forward, the headlights still off as he maneuvered down the street, his hands white-knuckling the wheel. Every turn, every shadow, every flicker in the night sent a fresh jolt of fear through him.

But then—

Nothing.

No whispers. No curses. No shadows rising from the earth to pull them back.

They were free.

Santino exhaled a ragged breath, his entire body shaking with exhaustion and disbelief.

"Praise the Lord," he whispered, his voice hoarse, barely audible.

He made the sign of the cross as they sped away, swallowed by the dark night, heading back toward the hotel.

They had escaped the evil.

They had avoided the police on their way to the scene of the crime.

They had survived.

Chapter 44

Hiktilda knew the night was far from over. There was still much to do—much to savor. The small encounter with the old man had been nothing more than a passing amusement, a fleeting indulgence. The old zealot, the frail weakling, had entertained her for a moment, but what truly thrilled her was the intoxicating power she wielded over the lesser creatures of the world. She had forgotten what real power felt like.

A feeble old Catholic—what was he to her? Nothing. Insignificant. She had laid a curse upon him with the ease of a weaver spinning wool, a wicked smile curling upon her lips as she envisioned the delightful torments she would visit upon him in the coming days. Let him run—yes, let him scurry into the shadows like a frightened rodent. It was all part of the grand design.

She had paused in her spectral ascent back to the forest of the coven, stopping halfway up the jagged canyon, the wind whispering through the chasm below. Beyond the towering trees lay the bog, shrouded in mist and moonlight, where she knew Gaeldritch had taken Tum-Grissell. She lingered for a moment, savoring the stillness, letting the weight of the night settle upon her like a velvet cloak. The full moon, vast and luminous, hung in the sky like a great silver eye. She tilted her head, murmuring to herself, *The poor fool Warren... He is next—once I see Gaeldritch, once I get the knife and the hair, his ruin is next.*

She knew she would need more unguent applied for the many flights she'd be taking in the remaining night hours. Reaching into the folds of her robe, she withdrew a vial of thick, glistening liquid—the *Ointment of Flight.* Standing in the moonlit canyon, she uncorked it with a practiced flick of her wrist, releasing the sweet scent of its ingredients. With deliberate reverence, she poured the congealed substance into her palm, its texture cool and viscous. She slipped her hand inside her robe, massaging the ointment into her flesh, ensuring every pore, every hair follicle, was bathed in its holy essence.

The wretched police had tried to interfere, stumbling blindly into matters far beyond their comprehension, but they had been powerless. The zealots—sanctimonious fools—had dared to challenge the will of the coven, to destroy her brother, the perfect golem, a true achievement of their dark craft. *Nothing can stand against me,* she mused, a slow smile unfurling across her lips. *Not with Gaeldritch at my side.*

With languid precision, she smeared the remaining ointment along the polished shaft of her staff, delighting in the ritual, in the promise of flight. She adjusted her grip, shifting the staff between her legs.

Flicker

She vanished—no longer bound by the burdens of flesh, no longer tethered to the earth. She surged forward, slipping between the threads of the world itself, flickering—seen and unseen through the cold night air. The canyon fell away behind her, swallowed by darkness. The scent of damp earth and ancient rot beckoned from the forest beyond. The bog awaited. Gaeldritch awaited.

The night was still hers.

Chapter 45

The streets were nearly empty as Santino and Peter drove back to the hotel on Main, the dim glow of streetlights flickering like failing sentinels against the suffocating darkness. The town was eerily still, as if holding its breath, as if it too sensed what had just unfolded.

Mallory slumped in the passenger seat, his breathing ragged and uneven. Every inhalation was a struggle, every exhalation laced with pain. His fingers trembled slightly as he pressed them against his side, probing the damage.

"I think my ribs might be broken," he finally muttered, voice hoarse, almost brittle. "I'm having trouble breathing."

Santino kept his eyes on the road, his jaw locked tight. The headlights cut through the night, carving a path through the silence, but his mind was far from the stretch of pavement ahead.

A long pause.

Then, Mallory turned to him, wincing as he shifted. "Do you have the cross, Santino?"

Santino's fingers tightened on the wheel. He didn't answer. For a moment, the only sound was the low rumble of the engine and the rhythmic thumping of his heart in his ears.

Of course, he had heard the question. And of course, he

didn't want to answer.

The *Cross of Saint Paul* was gone.

Lost. Perhaps still lying in that accursed backyard, glinting dully beneath the moonlight like a worthless trinket. Or worse—claimed by one of those demonic hags, spirited away into the shadows like some grotesque prize. He didn't know. And when the attack had come, when the world had erupted into chaos and blood, the cross had been the last thing on his mind.

Survival had been the only thought. Peter's life. His own.

Santino exhaled through his nose, finally breaking the silence. "It's gone, Peter," he admitted, his voice low, edged with frustration. "If the police find it, they'll probably return it to the church. But there will be questions. Questions I can't answer."

Peter inhaled sharply, absorbing the words, the reality of them. He let his head rest against the seat, his eyes shutting briefly as though the weight of the night had finally sunk its claws into him.

"I think I destroyed that beast," he whispered after a long pause. "The shadow... I think it's gone."

Santino nodded slowly. "Yes. The cross put the beast down, just as my vision foretold. But—"

"There was no witch in your vision, Santino," Peter cut in, his voice tinged with disbelief, with something dangerously close to awe. "She came out of nowhere and—" He hesitated, shaking his head as though he couldn't quite reconcile what he had seen. "I've never seen anything like it. She was so...terrible." His voice faltered, lost to the enormity of the memory.

Santino's expression darkened. "There were two of them,

249

Peter." His voice was grim, each word a stone dropping into a deep, black abyss. "Two demonic hags."

Silence hung thick between them, pressing against the confines of the car like a living thing.

Then Santino turned into the hotel parking lot, the tires crunching over gravel as he threw the car into park. The streetlamp overhead flickered weakly, its glow casting long, distorted shadows over the pavement.

"We need to leave town," he said, his voice like steel. "Tonight. Right now."

He turned to Peter, his eyes cold, determined. "Give me your room key. I'll pack your things. Can you make it to your car while I do this?"

Peter let out a slow, shuddering breath. Then, with a grimace, he gave a weary half-smirk. "Yeah..." he muttered. "I can crawl if I have to."

Santino didn't return the smile.

The night was still thick with danger, thick with unseen things lurking just beyond reach.

The next five minutes passed in a blur of aching limbs and weary movements. Santino gathered their belongings with methodical urgency, loading each piece into their cars as though he could pack away the horrors of the night along with them. The weight of exhaustion clung to him, a leaden presence pressing against his bones, but he forced himself to move, to finish what needed to be done.

Mallory, though battered and barely holding himself together, managed to stagger toward his vehicle. Every step was a battle against the searing pain radiating from his ribs, but he gritted his teeth and kept going. With a heavy groan, he

250

eased himself into the driver's seat, each movement sending fresh waves of agony through his body. His fingers trembled as he fumbled for the seatbelt, dragging it across his bruised torso and clicking it into place with a final, shuddering breath.

Santino finished clearing the rooms of their possessions and walked towards Peter's car door, standing by his window, his expression grim, his gaze steady. There were no wasted words between them—only the weight of all that had transpired. Finally, Santino spoke, his voice low but firm, intoned with both warning and reassurance.

"Peter, head straight home," he said. "Get your rest, and keep your faith strong. If you have no strength left in your body, then pray—pray the entire drive if you have to. And, Peter…" He paused for a moment, his lips pressing into a thin line before continuing, "Thank you. For fighting this evil. God understands what you did tonight, and that's what matters."

Peter swallowed hard, the words settling deep into him, a quiet balm against the ache of everything they had just endured. With a slow, weary nod, he turned the key in the ignition. The car rumbled to life, its engine breaking the fragile silence that had settled over them. Without another word, he pulled out of the parking lot, his taillights glowing like embers in the dark.

Santino watched him disappear down the road before turning back to his own vehicle. He slid into the driver's seat, resting his hands on the wheel for a moment as he exhaled a slow, measured breath. His fingers curled, knuckles tightening. He whispered a prayer under his breath—not just for himself, but for Peter, for the road ahead, for the unseen dangers that still lurked beyond the edge of his vision.

Then, with a deep sigh, he shifted his car into drive and pulled onto Main Street, the road stretching before him like an open wound.

As he left the town behind, the weight of the night sank into him fully, every ache, every bruise making itself known with merciless clarity. His knees throbbed, raw and swollen from the night's brutal trials. His muscles screamed in protest with every shift of his body. And his scalp burned with an agonizing sting—a cruel, searing reminder of what had been taken from him.

His once-perfect silver hair, the thick mane that had once gleamed under the light, was now marred by a gaping absence. A chunk had been ripped away, torn from his flesh, leaving behind nothing but exposed, burning skin. The pain was relentless, a sharp, stinging wound that pulsed in time with his heartbeat. He had no idea how he would explain this to any inquisitive minds, but for now, he just had to focus on driving home.

Without any conscious thought, he found himself speaking out loud, the words strung together but nonsensical, muttering.

"The thread twists tighter, winding through the gaps where burned paper crumbles into ghostly speech, its edges curling like the pulled hair of a forgotten doll, strands snapping under invisible fingers."

He clenched his jaw and pressed the gas pedal forward. The road stretched endlessly ahead, swallowed by darkness.

Chapter 46

S he knew exactly where Greg Warren lived.

She had been there before, back when she had played the role of Holly, the dutiful assistant, the unappreciated woman in the office. When she had been tame.

Mr Warren had sent her there a handful of times, tasking her with retrieving the papers he had so carelessly left behind in his morning haste. She had obeyed, arriving at his palatial home, knocking on the heavy oak door, waiting as his wife, Susan, handed her the forgotten files with a polite but dismissive smile.

That life—that person—felt like a dream now, a paper-thin illusion that had long since burned away, even though it was only a few days ago since the transformation had occurred.

Holly was gone now. In fact, Holly had never really been there to begin with.

Hiktilda had reemerged in her full glory.

She had always been Hiktilda. She had simply remembered the truth.

It was just past 12:30 a.m. when she appeared outside Greg Warren's bedroom window, her heeled boots sinking into the dewy grass. The house loomed before her, its grand structure bathed in moonlight, its walls brimming with the quiet arrogance of wealth and privilege.

With a slow, predatory gaze, she surveyed the yard, memorizing every detail, every shadow. Using her witch's flight, she would not set off motion detectors and their accompanying camera systems since she didn't perturb the light enough to trigger their sensors.

Then, gazing at a window above her she flew again, and with a subtle twist of her staff, the world shifted.

She was inside.

Standing in the dark upstairs hallway, surrounded by the hush of the sleeping house.

"Sharadi me jala ja laya manan, umbra silens, anoxi.", she hissed a spell of darkness, an unnatural shadow wrapped around her, an obscurity that would make her difficult to discern to any whom she didn't purposefully grant awareness—her willingness to be seen.

The words of power fell from her lips like drops of ink into water. Darkness swallowed her, coiling around her body, devouring her form until she was nothing but a void, a black absence that drank in every sliver of light. A living silhouette, impenetrable, unknowable.

She held her right hand to her mouth and breathed on her fingers, whispering, *"Umbra, digitis meis iungere et nullum signum relinque."*—her fingerprints becoming smooth under her command.

She reached for the main bedroom doorknob, her fingers curling around the cool metal.

She turned it slowly, deliberately, allowing the door to drift open with a silence so profound it was unnatural.

Hiktilda glided inside.

She did not walk—that word was too clumsy, too human.

She drifted, a weightless specter, slipping through the air with a quiet that did not belong in this world.

And there he was.

Greg Warren.

Lying in bed, his wife curled beside him, both of them lost in the gentle embrace of sleep. How peaceful they looked. How vulnerable.

Hiktilda stretched out a shadowed hand over Susan's sleeping form, her fingers weaving an invisible cage around the woman's mind, securing her in the depths of unconsciousness.

"Noli expergisci dulatia."

The spell was gentle, but absolute.

Susan would not wake. Not for the storm that was about to break.

Hiktilda turned to Greg, stepping around the bed, her form little more than a ripple in the darkness. She loomed over him, studying him, amusement flickering in her cold eyes.

Mister Warren, she mused, tilting her head. *How fragile you look in sleep. How small and weak you truly are. A maggot like you deserves not an ounce of pity.*

She placed her hand upon his head, her touch feather-light.

Then, her fingers tightened.

Black thread tendrils slithered from beneath her fingernails, writhing like eager parasites as they plunged into his skull.

Greg's eyes snapped open.

His mouth parted in a silent scream, his throat working, but no sound escaped. He trembled violently, his body rigid as the tendrils burrowed deeper, wrapping around his thoughts, sinking into the marrow of his mind.

Terror.

It filled him, drowned him, swallowed him whole. His soul

darkened, tainted by the dreadful filaments writhing inside his head, coiling, feeding.

Hiktilda's lips parted in a soft, breathy laugh.

Then, she spoke the words of the curse, letting them drip from her tongue like poisoned honey:

"A curse in speech, a muddled mind,

Only outlines of thoughts behind.

No longer will you see your kin,

But twisted eyes—black spiders in!

Parcloos! Cloo-Lu! Ferin-dar! Kerin-Krue!"

Greg's body spasmed violently. His eyes rolled back, leaving nothing but bloodshot whites. His jaw clenched, then fell open, and from his lips spilled a thick, black, oily liquid. It slithered down his chin, staining his skin like the bile of something ancient and rotten.

Hiktilda inhaled slowly, shivering with pleasure as she reeled in the black tendrils, drawing them back into her fingers.

A soft sigh of pleasure escaped her as they vanished beneath her nails.

"Stand.", she audibly spoke.

The word was not a request.

Greg obeyed.

With stiff, jerking movements, he crawled from the bed, his limbs no longer his own. He rose before her, his irises shifting slowly back into view. A husk of the man he had been just moments earlier. A puppet on invisible strings.

Beside them, Susan slept on, undisturbed, obedient to Hiktilda's words.

The Grand-Witch reached into the folds of her robe and withdrew something—the blue-handled chef's blade, still marked with the dried blood of its last victim.

The very same knife Tum-Grissell had used only hours before.

She pressed it into Greg's slack hand.

"You will need this," she murmured. "Soon, they will come for you. They will try to consume you."

She leaned in closer, whispering in his ear.

"You must fight them. You must defend yourself from the vermin."

Greg's fingers twitched, curling around the handle. His grip tightened.

Hiktilda smiled.

Reaching into her robe once more, she pulled free a few auburn hairs.

She let them fall to the floor, delicate as drifting embers.

Then, she moved to the other side of the bed, to where Susan lay, still under the spell of an unnatural slumber.

Hiktilda turned back to Greg, her voice low, urgent, dripping with conviction.

"Listen to me carefully, Greg."

She gestured toward the sleeping woman, Susan Warren.

"One of the creatures is here."

She saw the flicker of confusion in his glazed-over eyes, the way his fingers flexed against the knife's handle.

"You've caught the wretched thing in its sleep," she continued, her voice thick with urgency. "You see lying before you a huge, hideous, black spider! Now is your chance."

She took a step back, watching, waiting, reveling.

"Use the knife!" she commanded.

A pause. A heartbeat.

Then, softly, sweetly—she commanded him.

"Use the knife now."

Hiktilda drifted out of the master bedroom, her movements fluid, unhurried, like a specter gliding through the dimly lit hallway. The air around her seemed to thicken, the house itself growing heavy with an unseen presence, as if the walls could sense the darkness moving within them.

She moved down the hallway to the next door, and pushed it open without a sound, stepping inside.

A heartbeat later, a child's scream tore through the silence.

A young boy—not yet a teenager—stumbled out of the room, his face pale with sheer terror. His breath hitched in frantic sobs as he bolted down the hallway, his small feet barely touching the floor in his desperate flight. He reached his parents' bedroom and flung himself inside.

Hiktilda emerged into the hallway once more, her lips curling into a small, knowing smile.

The child's scream, and a great tumultuous sound came from the main bedroom where the child had run to for protection.

Without pause, she crossed the corridor and entered the next room.

Another child's scream.

This one was just as raw, just as panicked.

A second boy—slightly smaller, but no less petrified— burst from his room, his wide, tear-filled eyes darting wildly, seeking refuge. He, too, fled straight to his parent's bedroom, slamming the door behind him, disappearing into the chaos of the commotion within.

The house was alive with the sound of fear—muffled cries, a scream of terror from a grown man, the shifting of bodies in the master bed, the sound of bladed violence from within, the aftermath of silence.

Hiktilda stepped back into the hallway, inhaling the scent of terror lingering in the air like the aftermath of a storm.

Then, with a quiet chuckle, she tilted her head back slightly, inhaling deeply, savoring the moment.

Her fingers curled around her staff, drawing it into place.

And with a flicker—

She was gone.

Chapter 47

FBI Special Agent Roberts guided the silver sedan into East Bryndelle, the road stretching ahead like a ribbon of desolation beneath the cold glow of the streetlights. The clock on the dash read 1:45 a.m. Special Agent Thompson sat in the passenger seat, arms crossed, eyes heavy with exhaustion. They'd each been phoned at 10:30 p.m. and ordered to come to the crime scene immediately. They had gathered their trappings and left Redding within minutes of the order and were on the road, averaging over 80 mph since they started, and were just pulling into town.

"Well, this is definitely not my favorite way to have my night wrecked," Thompson grumbled, rubbing a hand down his tired face.

"I was in bed, barely falling asleep when they rang us and told us to drive out here. Yeah, the homicide of a state LEO is always bad news." Roberts muttered, gripping the wheel a little tighter. They both knew what that meant—pressure from the brass, local law enforcement on edge, and the unspoken weight of solving this before it spiraled into something worse.

"Ugly business. Let's get to the crime scene… uh, 2220 West Sunny Way Drive… off Main, up this way…" Thompson pointed toward an upcoming turn, his eyes fixed on the map glowing from his phone screen.

Roberts followed the directions in silence before finally speaking. "The other detective—he's still on scene?"

Thompson thumbed through the case file, scrolling past grim details illuminated in digital sterility. "Yeah, but apparently he's in the back of a black-and-white. Name is Smalls—Detective Smalls. They say he's pretty shaken up. Not exactly... coherent."

A few more turns, and the crime scene unfolded before them like a grisly painting under the flickering wash of red and blue police lights. Two squad cars sat angled in the driveway of an aging suburban home, their emergency lights splashing against the weathered siding. An ambulance idled nearby, its back doors closed.

After a quick exchange with the responding officers to get their bearings, the agents made their way to the patrol car where Smalls sat. The detective was slouched in the back seat, his silhouette barely shifting as they approached.

Roberts opened the door, crouching slightly. His voice was steady but firm.

"Detective Smalls, I'm Special Agent Roberts. I know you've been through a tragedy tonight, but it's vitally important that you pull yourself together and explain to us in detail what happened. We need to catch whoever did this—whoever hurt your partner. Do you understand?"

Smalls blinked slowly, his gaze unfocused. Then, in a voice like dry leaves rustling against pavement, he spoke:

"The blackened sludge seeped through the cracks of a world long abandoned by reason, where the sirens of duty wailed against the choking fog of futility."

Roberts and Thompson exchanged a glance. The words were coherent, but the meaning was lost in a feverish labyrinth of nonsense.

"Hold on, Detective," Thompson said carefully.

Smalls barely seemed to register the interruption. His breath hitched, and then more words spilled from his lips, faster, more frantic.

"Each badge weighed down by the gravity of unsolved crimes and the madness they carried. In the alleys, flickering signals were lost in the mire of decayed cognition. Each file stacked higher than the last."

"Okay, that's enough, Detective," Roberts said, exchanging another look with Thompson. He reached out, giving Smalls a reassuring pat on the shoulder before closing the car door with a firm snap. "We'll check on him later."

The night air felt heavier as they walked around the side of the house to the backyard, where the crime scene lay waiting in silence. The sharp scent of blood emitting from the concrete patio.

"Forensics still needs to comb this place," Roberts murmured, eyes scanning the scene. "We can't do much tonight. It's obvious—Detective... uh... Hastings was stabbed to death. Heart and throat." He exhaled, shifting on his feet. A large puncture to the body, the violent slash across the throat, the dark red puddles on the concrete—it was all so painfully obvious.

"Let's head to the station and talk to Sanders, get his case files. Then we'll get to the hotel, try to catch some sleep," Thompson said, stretching his neck. "Tomorrow's going to be a long day. Hopefully, Smalls gets his act together by sunrise. I have a feeling it's gonna get a hell of a lot worse before it gets any better. Let's go."

Without another word, the two agents turned away, the crime scene behind them offering no answers—only the quiet promise of more questions.

Chapter 48

The silver car was parked in the near-empty parking lot of the East Bryndelle Municipal Building, its sleek exterior reflecting the scattered glow of streetlamps. The hour was just past 2 a.m., and the town lay in a restless silence, the kind that clung to the air too thickly, too completely—as if something unseen was waiting to exhale.

Inside the vehicle, FBI Special Agents Roberts and Thompson remained still. The interior was quiet, save for the faint rustling of a federally stamped manila folder in Thompson's hands. Its edges were worn, its contents bundled neatly inside—thin paper shielding terrible truths.

Their composure was a mask. Beneath it, unease simmered, the weight of the case pressing against them like an unseen hand on their backs.

Roberts was the first to break the silence. His voice was steady, measured, but heavy with the gravity of what they had uncovered.

"So, Sanders didn't give us anything that wasn't completely obvious. We've got a State Detective—Hastings—brutally murdered. His partner, Smalls, is found at the scene, but the guy's a wreck. Babbling. Mind shattered. And here we are sitting in our car in a backwoods town in the middle of the night."

Thompson nodded slowly. "Yes, sir. Here we are."

Roberts exhaled through his nose, fingers idly drumming against the steering wheel, eyes locked onto the municipal building before them.

"A decorated officer butchered. His partner lost to madness. And we're waiting on forensics from the Holden crime scene—that'll be a few days apparently."

Thompson leaned back slightly, rubbing a thumb along the edge of the folder. "Smalls and Hastings weren't amateurs. They knew how to handle themselves. Whoever got to them... they weren't just some thug in a ski mask."

"Agreed." Roberts' voice was firm, but there was something else there, something beneath the surface. A hesitation. "And Smalls... his mental state doesn't feel like coincidence."

He gestured toward the folder. "Did you pull the historical case files? Local and state?"

Thompson flipped through the reports, eyes scanning quickly. "Yes, sir. Most of it's standard—small-town disturbances, domestic incidents, minor assaults. But I found two cases worth noting."

Roberts lifted a brow. "Go on."

Thompson tapped the folder meaningfully. "First case was fourteen years ago. A missing persons report—Graham and Samantha Beckstead—farmers. Elderly couple, lived right here in East Bryndelle. One night, they simply vanished. No signs of struggle. No financial withdrawals. No messages. Just... gone."

Roberts' expression remained unreadable. "Could've packed up and left without telling anyone."

Thompson nodded. "Maybe. But the second case? That's

what got my attention."

He flipped to another report. "Eight years ago, Father Neil Woods—the local priest—disappears. No travel plans. No sightings. Family swore he'd never abandon his congregation."

Roberts frowned. "Families always say that. What makes these cases stand out?"

Thompson's fingers brushed over the typed forensics notes. "The mud."

Roberts blinked. "Come again?"

"Forensics reported unusual traces of mud inside both homes—smeared across doorknobs, light switches, flooring. It wasn't footprints either—it was smeared in key locations. The forensics team thought it was odd enough to include in their notes, but there was no follow-up."

Roberts' frown deepened. He leaned back slightly, processing. "And the composition? Source?"

Thompson exhaled. "Never determined. The lab didn't analyze it in detail. It was ordinary-looking mud, at least at first glance, but it was scattered in strange places in the house, and we had that mud at the Holden house tonight, mixed with the blood." He shook his head.

The words hung in the air between them.

Roberts tapped his fingers against the wheel, his mind already working the angles.

"Anything else?"

Thompson hesitated, flipping through another set of pages. "I pulled missing persons reports from Redding down to Sacramento. But there were…" He let out a breath. "Hundreds. Over the last two decades. Too many."

Roberts' jaw tensed. "Too much to sift through." He nodded,

as if already expecting the answer. "I wouldn't waste time trying to connect dots in the valley. They've got..." He smirked faintly. "...their own explanations."

Thompson raised an eyebrow. "Explanations?"

Roberts let out a quiet chuckle. "Mount Shasta. Aliens. Lizard people. Yeti. Cults. You name it. You've been in Sac long enough to know that place attracts its share of lunatics."

Thompson huffed a short laugh. "Yeah. Fair point."

Roberts' smirk faded. His gaze hardened as he put the car into gear. "I call it desperate deduction. People trying to make sense of something they can't."

Thompson paused for a moment and then added, "The Danielson family is apparently unhappy that we've sent the body to Sac for autopsy. So no body for his funeral, but life is tough like that."

Roberts let out a small chuckle, "Yeah tough for them, tough for us too, we'll be waiting a few weeks for those results and they'll probably be worthless."

He glanced toward the folder. "Let's check out the old Beckstead farm. It's right next to, uh... what's-her-name's place."

Thompson quickly scanned the notes. "Yeah, that's Hannah Childs' house."

Roberts nodded. "There could be a connection. Maybe we'll find mud outside the burned out houses?"

Then—

The radio crackled.

A sharp, static-laced transmission cut through the quiet, and Roberts immediately grabbed the receiver.

The voice on the other end was hurried. Uncertain.

Something had happened.

Something bad.

"...Warren residence... multiple fatalities... suspect Greg Warren in custody... immediate response requested..."

Roberts' blood ran cold.

Greg Warren—according to the detective's earlier report, had no criminal record, no history of violence, nothing unusual—and had now just snapped.

Roberts' jaw tightened as he got the address from dispatch.

Then—in one sharp, fluid motion, he threw the car into drive.

The tires screeched against the pavement as the car tore out of the parking lot, headlights slicing through the cold morning darkness.

Chapter 49

2:15 a.m.—the master bedroom reeked of blood.

The scent clung to the air like a heavy, invisible fog, thick and inescapable, seeping into the walls, the furniture, the very bones of the house itself. The coppery tang mingled with something else—something darker, fouler. A rancid undercurrent that curdled the stomach, something even years of violent crime scenes hadn't quite prepared them for.

Special Agents Roberts and Thompson stood in the master bedroom of the Warren residence, their trained eyes methodically scanning the carnage. The forensic team worked in near silence, gloved hands sweeping across every bloodstained surface, cameras flashing as they documented the unspeakable.

Even for men who had long since become desensitized to horror, this was different.

This was butchery.

Thompson pressed a white handkerchief over his mouth, swallowing hard against the bile creeping up his throat, and spoke with a tremble in his voice, "What monster could have done this?"

Roberts stood rigid, jaw clenched, arms folded tight across his chest. He inhaled slowly, the sour stench of death coating his lungs before he finally spoke.

"Greg Warren and his sadistic mistress, Anna Holden... they completely lost it."

Thompson let out a low grunt—more acknowledgment than agreement. He wasn't ready to draw conclusions just yet. He only knew that the weight of the room pressed down on him, heavy and suffocating.

Roberts continued, his mind already working to assemble the fractured pieces.

"Warren was planning to run away with Holden. But something went sideways." His gaze darkened, his voice tightening. "I think she broke him—just like she broke Smalls."

Thompson gave a small nod, his eyes fixed on the sprawled remains of Warren's family. "Adds up, boss."

Roberts turned, his stare drilling into the evidence laid out before them.

"We have the letter found on Smalls threatening Holly Childs and her family. Now forensics confirms Holden's hair was found at the Hastings homicide scene."

His fingers curled into fists. "She got inside Smalls' head. Poisoned him—psychologically or otherwise, I don't know. But whatever she did, it worked."

Thompson exhaled through his nose. "Yeah. She seems to have wrecked his capacity to think straight."

Roberts swept his gaze over the room again, taking in the blood-streaked walls, the slashed bedding, the grotesque scene of a family slaughtered.

"Then she comes here." His voice was steady, but there was something heavier beneath it now. "Something goes wrong. Maybe Warren hesitates. Maybe she realizes he's not strong enough to follow through."

Thompson narrowed his eyes. "Lover's quarrel?"

Roberts gave a grim nod. "She wanted him to leave his wife and kids. He wouldn't. Maybe she wasn't alone."

A breath. A pause.

Then—

"So she poisons him.

Then she butchers his wife and kids."

The words dropped like stones into the suffocating silence, sinking into the blood-drenched carpet beneath them.

For a long moment, neither man spoke.

Then Thompson broke the silence.

"And the way she did it… But something doesn't sit right. They said Warren was holding the knife when they found him, acting like a maniac—wouldn't let it go until they shot him down." He shook his head, struggling to wrap his mind around the sheer brutality on display.

Roberts' jaw tightened. "Yeah. That's real strange. I can't remember a more disgusting set of killings in my entire career."

Thompson rifled through the forensic report, flipping pages with quiet urgency.

"Forensics said they found Holden's hair here too, most likely since it's an exact color match. They'll confirm in a few days. And the knife Warren was holding…" He glanced up. "Straight from her own kitchen set."

Roberts muttered a curse under his breath. "She didn't even try to cover her tracks."

He dragged a hand down his face, exhaustion momentarily breaking through the mask of professionalism.

"She didn't care if we could trace her." His voice hardened, his posture straightening as his anger overtook his fatigue. "She knew she'd be long gone before we got here. We need to examine every damn paper in here house, and check all her financial history, maybe we'll get lucky."

Thompson let out a short, bitter laugh. "She's probably halfway across the state by now. Maybe already in Nevada or Oregon."

Roberts inhaled deeply, nodding once. Then twice.

"We're done here. I need to get out of this room." He turned toward the door. "We'll put Holden on every wanted list we can. A.P.B. through all local law enforcement agencies in the western U.S."

Without another word, he strode out of the bloodstained bedroom.

Thompson lingered at the threshold, casting one last look at the horror behind them.

Then he exhaled, turned, and descended the stairs.

Chapter 50

The forest cradled many small swamps, scattered like forgotten pools among its meadows, but only one true bog held dominion over the land. A dense patch of thick, pungent, bubbling, mud sprawled across two hundred yards in length, its width stretching to nearly eighty. A putrid heart beating beneath the canopy of the ancient pines—the oldest in all the forest surrounding Thunder Mountain—its presence was primeval, untouched by time, an abyss where the earth itself seemed to breathe.

The bog was a living thing. Its surface, a swirling mosaic of black, brown, tan, and even ghostly patches of white, concealed layers of decaying matter, ancient and thick, brimming with such decomposition that it exhaled a reeking, acrid stench. It festered. It bubbled ceaselessly, as if some unseen force roiled beneath, struggling to escape. Across the expanse, clumps of wet field grass formed deceptive pathways—floating, shifting, never stable—twisting like the labyrinthine corridors of an abandoned mine.

This was the domain of Tum-Grissell.

His claim to the bogs across the world stretched beyond mortal years, beyond borders, beyond the touch of any hand for over 800 years. He had left the Old World, abandoning the lands of Europe, crossing the Atlantic's restless tides. From the shadowed forests of New England, he had wandered westward, traversing the vast bones of North America, until at last, he reached this place—a place that welcomed him, that whispered to him, that sustained him better than any home previously had done. The forest near East Bryndelle had become his sanctuary, and the bog, his cradle of rejuvenation.

For Tum-Grissell was no mere construct of clay and water. Though he was once an ordinary man, he was metamorphosed into an *Abominatio*—a *Bestia Fictilis*, a beast of mud and stone, a thing beyond nature yet wholly of it, and brimming with his iron will. He required neither food nor fire, only earth and water to sustain his existence. He was the vision of the coven's benefactor, Vizier Julian, the master craftsman, the great and terrible mind that had transformed his mortal flesh, and wrought him centuries ago from the elements themselves into the creature he had become.

And now, as the first pale light of dawn clawed its way through the mist, Gaeldritch sat alone at the bog's edge, her legs in a half-lotus, cross-legged position underneath her robes, sitting upon the thick swamp-grass.

The air was cool, still damp with the ghosts of night, but she did not shiver. The witch sat motionless upon the toughened grass, her fingers resting lightly upon the folds of her robe about her lap. She seemed at peace, as if she were merely contemplating the morning, but her thin, cold lips moved swiftly, whispering the sacred language of the Order. Words of power slid from her mouth like a serpent's breath, a hushed incantation carried upon the wind.

"Bhumeh putram samgrami, jalasya tantram punar jivanam."
("I call upon the child of the earth, the woven essence of water,

to restore life.")

She held her right hand in the air, fingers stretched out.

"Sarvay vyathay viliyantam, tamaso murtih punah jagtaym."

("Let all pain dissolve, let the form of darkness awaken once more.")

She pulled her index finger and thumb together, touching the tips tightly together.

"Murtikayaḥ tanum prabodhaya, nadyasya pran samvarda."

("Reawaken the clay of the body, strengthen the river's breath within it.")

She pulled her middle finger down to her index finger and thumb.

"Divyasoolam niskay sayatu, sravatoo paypam, sathiro bavatoo."

("Body of clay, soul of the flowing waters, return to your strength!")

She then pulled her remaining fingers into the others and tightened them down into a small ball of fist. and held it aloft above her head.

"Vajrasarīram bootvay stitim kuroo, nah punar patay tiloo, nay pinar kiyatam!"

("Become a body indestructible, hold firm, fall no more, be diminished no more.")

She paused. The air stilled. Her dark eyes flickered with certainty.

Tum-Grissell would survive.

Her incantations of healing had worked. She could feel it.

The attack that had wounded him—what lesser creatures would have called fatal—was a mere inconvenience. A liver-eating vukodlak would have perished under such an assault. But Tum-Grissell was something far greater. His flesh was

275

not flesh. His blood was not blood. He was beyond them all. Beyond mortality itself.

She inhaled slowly, deeply. A long, measured breath, pulling the energy of the earth into her very being. And then, just as purposefully, she exhaled across the bog's surface. A breath not wasted, but sent forth—a deliberate thing, a spirit cast into the air, weaving unseen currents that reached across the bog, flowing toward the one who slumbered beneath its surface.

She shut her eyes once more and resumed her incantations, repeating them over and over. Her voice, though soft, carried power, sacred words gifted by the only one worthy to teach them—the visionary Julian.

Then, her voice shifted. She spoke not to the bog, not to the morning, but to someone else.

"Hello, my darling," Gaeldritch murmured, her voice curling into the empty space around her.

There was no immediate reply, but the forest itself seemed to stir.

From the depths of the trees, where the shadows clung thickest, Hiktilda emerged. She stepped from beneath the low-hanging boughs of a colossal pine, her movements unhurried, purposeful. Her silhouette wove seamlessly with the shifting mists, as if she had materialized from the very essence of the forest. She crossed the grass without a sound and lowered herself beside Gaeldritch.

"Good morning, my lovely," Hiktilda greeted, her voice a rich, languid purr, though weariness laced its edges.

Gaeldritch turned her gaze toward her companion. "Did everything unfold as planned in town?"

Hiktilda exhaled, allowing herself a moment of respite. She had spent the last five hours tracking the town's authorities, watching them sift through the remnants of the night, verifying that the plan had followed it's course.

"Yes, darling. Such amazing experiences. Everything went perfectly—so perfectly," she replied. But then, her voice softened, her dark eyes narrowing. "Except for our dear Tum-Grissell... I worry for him but I have faith in his resilience and your knowledge."

Gaeldritch smiled, a slow, knowing curve of her lips. "He has survived the night, and he has healed. The ritual of rejuvenation was successful, so set your worry aside. In fact, he will emerge before us now."

Hiktilda let out a breath, half a prayer, half a murmur. "A true *Abominatio*, the most formidable golem ever created... bless him."

And then, the bog stirred.

Twenty feet before them, the water's surface trembled. The bubbling, once gentle, grew violent. Ripples widened, colliding, twisting into chaotic spirals. The ground itself seemed to tremble beneath their feet. And then—the surface broke.

A crown of mud-slicked flesh rose from the depths, thick ropes of blackened sludge slipping away as Tum-Grissell emerged. His head rose first, the slick, viscous mire cascading from his brow, revealing the burning orange of his eyes.

His form—hulking, monstrous, monolithic—ascended from the muck, his shoulders breaking the surface, his chest, his arms. And then, he stepped forward. The bog released him willingly, reverently, its clinging tendrils sliding from his body like adoring hands reluctant to let go.

And then, in mere moments, the transformation began.

The swamp's filth—thick, pulsating, almost sentient—

seeped into his pores, consuming, devouring, assimilating. The grotesque, amorphous mass of his form began to shift, softening into pristine flesh.

His body was perfectly built—a sculpted masterpiece of flawless symmetry. His dark brown hair, thick and luxuriously wavy, framed a face of striking perfection. His eyes, once murky and terrifying, absorbed the last flecks of orange silt lingering in his irises, transforming into an oceanic blue, deep and mesmerizing. His skin, cleansed of all impurity, gleamed with an unblemished radiance—fresh, pure, as if he had emerged from crystalline waters. The transformation was complete. He was no mere man, but the very image of a perfect human male.

Hiktilda inhaled sharply, her hand rising to her chest. "My Thomas! You rise anew, rejuvenated!"

Gaeldritch's gaze sharpened, the flickering light of triumph gleaming in her eyes. "Your face has changed... the bog and the words of the master have remade you perfectly. You are a true masterpiece, a pinnacle of creation."

Tum-Grissell stood before them, his enormous frame casting a shadow over the earth. He tilted his head back, inhaling the morning air. Then, as if to confirm what had always been known, his voice rumbled, deep, ancient, unshaken:

"Tum-Grissell."

A declaration. A truth. A being beyond time, beyond death, beyond reckoning.

Chapter 51

Hiktilda was alone in her private chambers, seated on the cold stone floor atop a small black mat. Encircling her was a ring of eight candles, each one aglow with a flickering orange light that danced like mischievous spirits in the darkness. Before her lay an assortment of enigmatic implements—a massive iron oil lamp whose roaring flame surged from its very heart, and beside it, an ancient wooden casting mold. The mold, worn smooth by time, cradled a candle wick secured by pins at its top and bottom. In her right hand, she clutched a pair of heavy iron tongs that firmly gripped a clay melting dish, while in her left she held a handful of silver hair—Santino's silver hair—its gleam a stark contrast to the shadows.

With deliberate care, Hiktilda positioned the melting dish above the lamp's fierce flame. As the wax softened into a molten state, tiny bubbles began to churn on its surface. In one swift, practiced motion, she withdrew the dish from the heat and dropped the clump of the old man's hair into the molten wax. Then, with an air of measured precision, she reached for a small glass rod and used it to nudge the silver strands deeper into the glowing, viscous pool.

In one fluid, almost mesmerizing gesture, she poured the

molten wax from the dish into the small wooden mold—a mold intricately carved in the shape of a standing figure, complete with a square base that lent it an air of solemn permanence. Satisfied with her handiwork, she set the tools aside and carefully extinguished the lamp's flame with a diminutive iron snuffer. Rising from her mat, Hiktilda methodically applied the snuffer to each of the eight candles, their flames going out one by one, until the room was cloaked in an expectant silence. A small, knowing laugh escaped her lips as she departed the room, leaving behind the flickering remnants of her ritual.

Chapter 52

When Mallory finally pulled into his parking space at his San Francisco apartment, he was beyond exhausted—this was a weariness that had soaked into his marrow, a heaviness that pressed against his ribs like a burial shroud.

The last two hours of the drive had been the worst. The strangest.

At some point, he had caught himself talking aloud—not in simple recollections, not in fleeting thoughts, but in full, unraveling tirades. He had spoken as if explaining the events of the previous night to someone else, though no one was there. Words had poured from his mouth like water from a broken dam, slipping between explanation and gibberish, his voice laced with something outside of himself.

His chest ached viciously when he finally cut the engine. He moved carefully, easing himself from the car, dragging his battered body toward the backseat where Santino had carefully placed everything.

As he reached for his belongings, his breath gasped—sharp and unfamiliar words slipped past his lips before he could stop them.

"The mud rises thick, swallowing motion, pooling in the

281

creases of paralyzed limbs where devotion has rooted too deep, too tight…"

He winced as the weight of his suitcase pressed against his battered ribs, pain lancing through him like a blade.

The words did not belong to him.

He slapped his own face.

Wake up!

He slammed the car door shut, pressing his key fob, locking it all away behind him.

He walked toward his apartment—slowly, as if moving through a thickened atmosphere, his body reluctant, heavy.

"…like a whispered command that never quite reaches the muscles."

He didn't know why he kept speaking.

Or what force was pulling the words from his chest like a puppet's string.

By the time he reached his door, he could barely stand upright. He fumbled the lock, pushed his way inside, and let the weight of his body drag him forward, collapsing onto the bed with the grace of a dying thing.

Even here—even safe—the pain did not fade.

It bloomed.

A living thing. A presence that curled itself deeper into the meat of his bones.

He exhaled, barely a breath.

"Somewhere, the earth hums…a whisper…a vibration."

He kicked his shoes off, one at a time. Even that took too much effort. His arms felt foreign. His fingers distant.

"…a low vibration, a shudder beneath the skin, shaking the air but leaving the statues untouched, their stone eyes locked in eternal reverence."

He didn't understand what he was saying, yet the words felt more real than his own thoughts.

Like something otherworldly was speaking through him.

He lay still.

For a moment, there was silence.

Then—

"Thread tightens around wrists, around ankles, invisible but unyielding, a quiet force pulling tighter with each breath, each pulse, each unspoken plea. The saints do not blink. The mud does not yield. And somewhere between stillness and suffocation, something listens."

The last words left him like a strange, twisted prayer.

His eyes shut. His body surrendered. And sleep swallowed him whole.

Chapter 53

Santino pulled into the garage adjoining his Santa Monica apartment, the engine's low growl fading into silence. He sat motionless for a moment, gripping the wheel, his knuckles aching from the tension, his breathing shallow and uneven. Beads of sweat dripped down his face. He could feel a fever overtaking him.

He had driven through the night to get home. It was now 8 a.m., and exhaustion clung to him heavier than it ever had in his entire life. He felt horrible.

The mission was over.

Or at least, it should have been.

But something had followed him back. Something unseen, yet oppressive, coiling around him like an unshakable presence.

With methodical precision, he unloaded the remnants of his journey—the battered suitcase, the sweat-stiffened coat, the weight of failure pressing down on his shoulders. He had barely survived. He and Peter both.

And the *Cross of Saint Paul* was gone.

He shut the door behind him, bolted the lock as he always did, but this time, the action felt hollow—a meaningless ritual. The walls of his home, once familiar, now loomed unnaturally large, as if the shadows had stretched them in his absence. All his senses felt warped and stretched, he felt ill—his fever rising.

Santino moved through the house in a daze, his mind tangled in thoughts darker than the night he had left behind.

The *Cross of Saint Paul?*

Lying.

He hadn't lied since childhood. Not truly. But what else could he do?

How could he face the diocese? The cardinals? How could he tell them the truth—that he had stolen the relic from the church vault, taken it not on impulse, but by divine command—a vision so vivid it had seized him? Would they even try to believe him?

And worse... that he had lost it.

Most likely he had lost it to the darkness he had been so certain he could defeat.

Would they excommunicate him? Condemn him as a thief?

Or would they see him for what he was now—a failure?

He staggered to his bedroom and collapsed onto his bed, still fully clothed. As he sat there, his breath slowing, he noticed something on his sweat-stained sleeve—a single black thread, four inches in length, clinging to the fabric.

He peeled it away, rolling it between his fingers before flicking it to the floor.

For a few minutes, he simply breathed, the weight of everything sinking into him.

Then, at last, his eyes shut. His breath steadied.

And within moments, he fell into a restless sleep.

Chapter 54

L ater that evening, Gaeldritch sat in a very dark patch of shade beneath one of the forest's most ancient, towering pines—one of her most cherished retreats— where she had meticulously stacked a few rugged stones to fashion a crude, yet solemn chair. Encircling her, a deliberate ring of weathered stones demarcated the sacred space, framing both her seat and the clearing before her.

Clutching her gnarled staff, she suddenly thrust its sharpened end into the rich, dark earth with a violent, determined motion. Her voice, low and resonant, broke the silence:

"At midnight, when the darkness rules! The man who pridefully thinks his supposed faith grants him the power to halt the thread— oh, blackness and shadow that are ever-present—as the motion of this staff circles..." she intoned, her words echoing.

With precise, almost ritualistic grace, she began to move her staff in small, deliberate circles, ensuring that its pointed tip remained steadfast in the soil where it had first been plunged. Her black, glossy hair, imbued with an otherworldly life, writhed like a thousand sinuous serpents—each strand seemingly awakened in a frenzy—as it danced and coiled around her pale, timeworn face. Her eyes, alight with a cold, spectral glow, betrayed a grim delight as she continued:

"...so thy mortal frame moves, ebbing and flowing into oblivion!"

With each passing moment, her movements grew faster, the circles of her staff expanding in both speed and scale. Her voice dropped to a rapid, hushed whisper that nonetheless carried an unyielding force:

"Vibratio mortifera! O mortalis corpus, audite vocem maledicti: śakti tremens, kaṭhina vibra! Let your sinews convulse and your bones resound with the relentless cadence of asuric fury!"

As her staff spun with furious abandon, her voice swelled, resonating powerfully throughout the dark glade:

"Ossa resonent in tumultu, et anima tua vibrate in incessant śabda—may every fiber shudder with dread!"

Then, pausing to draw in a deep, measured breath, Gaeldritch held the silence for several charged seconds before unleashing the final, fateful words of her curse:

"Tremorem perpetuum, exsurgite in te; in umbris noctis, let the curse shake your form into the silence of oblivion!"

In a final act of resolute finality, she yanked the staff from the earth and struck it one last time against the soil, the sound echoing like a death knell. For a long, trembling moment, all was enveloped in an oppressive silence.

Slowly, Gaeldritch sat and allowed herself to catch her breath, inhaling deeply before exhaling a forceful gust of breath across the stone circle. With the ritual complete, she rose gracefully and, leaving behind the sanctified ring of stones, walked away into the encroaching forest.

Chapter 55

The light of day had given way to the cold darkness of night when Hiktilda returned to her hovel. Clutching her small lantern, she approached the wooden mold to inspect her creation. The wax figurine had cooled and set with exquisite detail, every contour preserved in frozen elegance. Wasting no time, she retrieved a long match from a bundle hanging in a case against the wall, inserted it into a delicate opening on the side of her lantern, and lit it. One by one, she methodically kindled each of the eight candles, until the full circle was ablaze with a soft, enchanting light, and she seated herself in its center.

Securing the match in a small slot on the lantern that allowed it to burn freely, Hiktilda then used her free hands to remove the wooden mold. With gentle, rhythmic taps against the cold stone floor, she coaxed the figurine to budge until it slowly slid free into her waiting hand. A sly, sadistic smile curved her lips as she set the wax figure upright on its square base. Grasping the match once more, she lit the wick at the figurine's core, raised her arms high, and began to chant.

"The threads twist tighter, coiling through your mind!"

At that moment, her black thread hair seemed to awaken, twisting and writhing like serpents in a stormy sea, animated by some mysterious, otherworldly force. As her incantation filled the hovel, thick drips of molten wax began to cascade down the figurine, pooling at its base upon the cool stone floor. The wax, like frozen tears of fate, lent an eerie finality to the unfolding ritual.

"Your thoughts dissolve like ash in a storm, while the black keeps winding, winding, and WINDING!"

Chapter 56

Mallory's eyes flew open.

His breath caught. His ears rang with an unnatural silence.

The darkness pressed in, thick, absolute. His pupils adjusted, burning against the red glow of his digital clock.

12:01 AM.

He exhaled—relief washing over him in a sluggish tide.

No pain.

None.

Not in his ribs. Not in his back. Not in his limbs.

Nothing.

For the first time since the nightmare had begun, his body felt healthy.

And then he noticed his fingers.

His toes.

Moving.

At first, just a tremor.

A tiny, almost imperceptible twitch. Like the shifting of sand beneath water.

Then, faster.

His fingers and toes shuddered—a vibration moving through them like the hum of an unseen engine.

The feeling crawled up his limbs.

His heart hammered.

His breath came too fast.

He was shaking violently, his whole body moving relentlessly, with no regard for what seemed possible.

The tremors deepened, seeping into his bones, the vibration turning into a blur.

The small, subtle quivers turning into convulsions—stronger, deeper, faster.

His muscles spasmed, his arms jerking against the mattress—his body no longer his own.

His chest lurched, his lungs seizing—

Snap.

A crack. Near his foot.

A deep groan from within him.

The pain came back.

It came back louder than before.

A roaring torrent of pain rushed through him.

Then—

Another snap. A crunch.

His bones.

His bones were breaking.

His limbs writhed, bending at unnatural angles, the oscillation turning violent, merciless—

His ribs caved inward and then popped outward.

His shoulder dislocated with a sickening pop.

The pain.

Beyond human comprehension.

Beyond anything a body should feel.

His arms twisted backwards.

His knees buckled inward.

His jaw unhinged as his entire torso collapsed in on itself.

He tried to scream.

Nothing came out.

His vocal cords did not exist anymore.

The oscillation doubled.

Every molecule, every cell in his body began to shred apart.

His eyes rolled back as the force behind it ripped him out of reality itself.

SNAP.

Everything broke.

The moment was an eternity of splintering, rending, shattering.

His flesh became pulp. His bones became splinters. His organs liquefied.

One final, horrible convulsion—

Then.

Silence.

What remained upon the bed was unrecognizable.

Only a slick, gore-stained wreckage of human matter. A ruin of blood and shattered bone.

There was no body.

No face to identify.

No Mallory.

Chapter 57

I t was after midnight when Santino awoke from his turbulent and feverish slumber. He still felt exhausted but at least he now had enough energy to get out of his dirty clothing, get cleaned up, and then get some dinner.

Had it been real? Or was it still happening?

His body moved of its own accord, guiding him to the bathroom. His fingers twisted the bath faucet, and hot water poured into the tub, steam curling into the cold air. He barely noticed the heat, lost in the weight of his own thoughts.

Santino exhaled shakily, peeling away his ruined suit. Sweat and dirt clung to his skin, the scent of smoke still lingering in the fabric. He was stripped down to his undergarments when he caught sight of himself in the mirror—

And froze.

The wound.

His stomach twisted at the violent, raw patch where hair had been ripped from his scalp. The flesh was still inflamed, an ugly, jagged wound. The hag had done this to him—the thing that had bent his body, that had forced him to his knees against his will. She was very real, no matter how much he wanted to deny her existence—evil was out there, evil had hurt him.

He had knelt before her.

Not by choice. Not by weakness.

But because something had commanded him to.

The memory surged back, clawing through his mind. The fire, his sacred book burning before his eyes, its pages curling into blackened embers as her laughter pierced his skull.

His stomach lurched. Had it even happened?

He pressed a palm against the cold porcelain of the sink, steadying himself. *Get a grip*.

Then—

"The threads twist tighter, winding through the gaps where burned paper crumbles into whispers, its edges curling like the pulled hair of a doll, strands snapping under invisible fingers."

His own voice but in a forced octave lower than he normally spoke.

Spoken aloud.

His breath caught. His chest seized.

He hadn't meant to say that. The words just came out of his mouth without his volition.

He stared at his reflection, his pulse hammering against his throat. His lips had moved. The words had truly come from his mouth and been spoken aloud.

But he had not chosen to speak them.

He was awake but it felt like a dream, a nightmare.

The bathroom seemed to shrink. The air thickened, pressing against his skin. His own heartbeat pulsed too loudly in his ears.

He clenched his fists. He needed to shake this off.

Snap out of it!

He shut his eyes tight. Took a breath. *Focus*.

Then—

"Silver cross dangles from trembling hands, catching the flicker of unseen flames, the cold weight pressing against a body that shakes with breathless laughter…"

His voice using tones he would consider childish, growling, unusual, gritty.

His eyes flew open.

No. No, no, no.

His lips kept moving. The words kept spilling. Faster. Faster.

"…too high, too sharp, a sound that doesn't belong in the hollow hush of kneeling prayers."

His voice rose—not his voice, not his words. Something foreign from within.

A force had rooted itself inside him.

He couldn't move. He couldn't stop.

The tub overflowed.

Scalding water spilled over, cascading onto the floor, curling around his bare feet. The heat bit at his skin, but he felt nothing.

His limbs would not obey him. He stood, rigid as a statue, his mouth spewing words that made no sense, yet felt more ancient than time itself.

"The floorboards groan beneath bent knees, splinters biting into flesh as words tumble out, half-spoken, half-lost, dissolving me, like ash in a storm, while the thread keeps winding—tight as fate, loose as my lie."

Louder. Faster. A feverish tide.

He could hear himself, but he could no longer stop himself.

The voice inside him was taking control.

Faster and faster, he wailed the words with horrible intonations.

"She laughed through charred teeth, her gnarled fingers tracing the air as the burning book shrieked in tongues only the darkness could understand, pages curling into the shape of lies whispered in dark corners. Truth melted like wax, honesty slithered into the cracks of a forgotten grave, and the hand sang a hymn of deceit as it stripped away the last remnants of hair from a scalp that no longer belonged to anyone at all."

The words pounded through his skull like a ritual chant, an incantation not of faith, but of something older, something hungrier.

Time fractured.

The night faded.

The blackness stretched into morning, swallowing the hours.

The water had risen past his ankles. Steam billowed, thick and oppressive, curling like ghostly fingers around his body.

Still—he spoke.

Still—he raved.

Still—his voice was not his own.

"She is everything! I am nothing!", he bellowed.

And finally, his mind had snapped.

The thread had tightened too much.

And somewhere deep within his skull, winding through his very soul—

The black thread coiled.

And coiled.

And coiled.

And though Santino stood breathing, his mind was ruined. He was no longer.

Chapter 58

Gaeldritch moved through the winding tunnels of the coven's underground sanctum, her iron lantern casting hungry pale blue flames against the cold stone walls. The air was thick with the scent of damp earth and the weight of age, resonant with the whispers of incantations long since absorbed into the rock.

She walked without a sound, her steps precise, as though she belonged to the darkness itself. The tunnels wound and twisted—a labyrinth of secrecy—but she knew their paths as intimately as the veins beneath her pale skin.

Geometric shapes streaked in black adorned the walls, an ancient system of symbols momentarily illuminated in the flickering glow of her lantern. Down steep ramps, up gentle inclines, through narrow bends where time had smoothed the stone, she moved with unwavering purpose, her very presence imbuing the underground with a silent authority.

Then—

She reached it.

A massive wooden door loomed before her, its blackened surface bound in thick iron brackets, a sentinel guarding her private dominion.

She did not hesitate.

From within the folds of her black-weave robes, she retrieved an ancient iron key, its surface worn smooth by centuries of use, of secrets locked and unlocked. She slid it into the lock, twisted, and—

Thunk.

The iron latch disengaged.

With a low, guttural groan, the heavy door swung inward on massive, timeworn hinges, the weight of history pressing against its movement.

Gaeldritch stepped inside.

The moment she crossed the threshold, the door slammed shut behind her, sealing with a final, automatic *click*—a mechanism she'd constructed ages ago.

Her chamber was dark and cavernous, lit only by the soft glow of her lantern. The air carried the scent of wax and parchment, underscored by something older, something far more ancient.

The room held multiple doorways leading to other chambers, and at the far end of the room, another wooden door bound in a cross-grid of iron stood waiting. Smaller than the others. Less assuming.

Without pause, she withdrew a second key—slender, sharp, crafted from iron—and slid it into the intricate lock. One flick of her wrist, and the door surrendered.

She slipped inside.

This chamber was different.

Smaller. Denser. The air here sat heavier, thick with dust and the weight of forgotten history.

Shelves lined the walls—wood and iron—cluttered with boxes, bottles, and relics draped in the dust of centuries. Objects best left unspoken, unseen, and untouched.

But Gaeldritch was the keeper of such things.

Her pale, sinewy fingers reached for a large black chest resting on the cold stone floor—a thing of shadowed wood, so dark it seemed to drink in the lantern's light.

The latch that bound it shut was no ordinary lock.

It was an enigma of iron and ingenuity, a web of twisting mechanisms, gears layered atop gears, pieces coiling into themselves like an ancient riddle—one designed to yield only to the one who commanded it.

Her fingers moved effortlessly, flicking pieces into place, shifting iron plates in a dizzying blur of movement.

Then—

Click.

The lid released.

She breathed in, her cold eyes narrowing as she peered inside.

A slow smile curled on her lips.

So many trinkets. So many stolen relics.

Each one a story. Each one a failed attempt to destroy her.

She reached into her robe and withdrew four bullet slugs, letting them roll in her palm, her smile deepening as she regarded them.

Then, without ceremony, she turned her hand over, letting them fall—a brief, leaden rainfall clattering into the chest.

Her hand slid into her robes again, this time drawing forth a silver cross—the *Cross of Saint Paul.*

She lifted it into the lantern's glow, its pristine surface glinting like a dagger beneath the firelight.

How quaint.

How desperate.

A weapon concealed beneath the guise of faith.

Her fingers traced the golden inscription embedded along its spine.

Maleficos non patieris vivere.

She knew the words.

"Do not suffer the witch to live."

Her voice curled through the chamber like smoke, thick with amusement.

And then—without reverence, without hesitation—she let the cross fall into the chest.

Clank.

It landed among the others.

Among the daggers, the stakes, the scepters, the holy relics and shattered hopes, the weapons meant to end her and her kind.

Gaeldritch exhaled through her smirk, shaking her head.

"Another feeble attempt from the so-called righteous. Another crusade reduced to dust."

Her long fingers traced the rim of the chest as she murmured, "A fine weapon, though. Crafted in Damascus, no doubt. Perhaps by Arumel himself."

She chuckled softly, an almost fond amusement in her voice. Then—

With a flick of her wrist, the lid snapped shut.

The lock reassembled itself immediately, pieces sliding into place, twisting, binding.

The box was sealed once more.

The world had failed to end her again.

And Gaeldritch—

She remained.

Unbroken. Unbothered. Eternal.

Chapter 59

I t was Friday morning, 8 a.m., two days after the full moon, the investigation into the homicide of State Detective Hastings was fully underway. Questions had been asked, answers given, witnesses interviewed, and forensic reports analyzed.

And still—nothing added up.

Special Agents Roberts and Thompson sat slumped in their silver sedan, the weight of exhaustion pressing them into their seats. The bitter scent of stale coffee clung to the air as they sipped in silence, preparing for the drive to Redding to submit their report.

Roberts reached for the ignition—then hesitated. His fingers hovered over the key for a long moment before he let out a slow, frustrated sigh and dropped his hand back into his lap.

"It doesn't add up," he muttered, his voice thick with frustration.

Thompson, who had been rubbing his eyes, raised an eyebrow. "Go on."

"Mr. Warren could have been the one who busted open Holden's door—a jilted lover situation. She had moved on, found someone new, and everything between them shattered.

But there were no prints on the handle—maybe he used a wrench, busted the frame with a kick. But no hardware marks. So whatever he did, it left no trace."

His voice trailed off, his mind racing ahead of his words.

Thompson leaned back against the headrest, rolling his jaw. "My guess? Warren lost his temper over something. Broke in. Probably got violent with Holden, got her real good, and that pissed her off something fierce. She then came after him with the knife but lost that fight," he speculated.

Roberts drummed his fingers against the steering wheel—a habit when he was thinking, his own subconscious metronome. The rhythmic tapping filled the silence, a measured counterpoint to the unease gnawing at him.

"Maybe that was her blood in the dried mud next to Hastings' body," Roberts murmured.

Thompson's expression darkened. "So what are you saying? That Warren broke into her place, argued with her, took her knife, attempted to kidnap her, killed Hastings on his way out, then murdered her outside, took her body, dumped it somewhere… and then waltzed back home and slaughtered his own family?"

Roberts exhaled sharply, shaking his head. "Exactly. It doesn't make sense. Jilted lovers don't usually go home and wipe out their entire families. Which makes me think Holden is somehow responsible for Warren's family. Maybe she had a lover doing the dirty work for her and he got to Warren's family…" He paused, his voice lowering. "Then again, I half-believe she's not dead. And that blood? It's not hers, and then the clowns in forensics…"

A heavy silence fell between them.

Roberts twisted the key in the ignition. The engine rumbled

to life, but it did nothing to cut through the unease settling over him like a thick fog.

"They botched the blood sample. Contaminated during collection, I think—even though they say the whole puddle of blood is ruined. Either way, the analysis failed. We've got nothing DNA-wise. A pool of blood that's worthless... unbelievable! And get this—not one of the samples had a single strand of human DNA. Didn't match any animal genome they ran it against either. It's a dead end. Totally botched the blood—make note of the forensics "lack-of" findings on the case. But, even after that fiasco, we have Holden's hair. Found at both crime scenes. That evidence is irrefutable."

Thompson stared out the windshield, lips pressed into a firm line.

"And Holden left her car at work, like she was in a real hurry to get out of town and was picked up by another unknown person," Roberts went on, eyes fixed on the dashboard, as if the answer was hidden somewhere in the flickering lights. "So there's almost no chance state troopers will catch her on the roads—if she's alive. That gets my mind spinning... So maybe she's got a new man, and they're headed somewhere in his vehicle... or—" He exhaled. "Or she's in the ground somewhere—somewhere real muddy, I guess."

Thompson gave a slow nod. "Where do you think she'd go?"

"Anywhere but here."

Thompson rubbed his temples. "Well, at the end of the day we have connections. Warren ties to the Childs girl through work and them being involved and all, and the mom and brother in the Childs family connect by virtue of the

Childs girl's connection to him. That also ties Warren to the Danielson homicide, since the Childs girl connects to him, too—lovers…again…violent lovers. The teacher, Julie Winthrop, also connects to Thomas Childs—once again…they were a thing. So, it looks like Warren did in the whole Childs family and the Winthrop girl, then beat Danielson to death—a major jealousy situation. Then he killed Holden, yet another of his lover girls, took the three Childs' bodies, plus Holden's, and buried them somewhere. Probably up in these mountains. Like you said, probably somewhere real muddy."

He hesitated before adding, "And then there's the priest."

Roberts turned his head sharply.

Thompson continued. "Yeah, Anthony Scolati also missing. His front door was broken into the same way as Holden's— handle twisted open with leverage, frame kicked in, not a finger print to be found besides Scolati's. Cell phone shattered across the kitchen floor. A violent altercation. And once again—the same damn mud, in this case, small flecks splattered all over the kitchen."

Roberts frowned, absorbing it all.

"Then," Thompson went on, voice tightening, "after an insane murder spree like that, Warren loses his mind and takes out his own family. 'If he's not going to live, nobody is' type of insane thinking."

Roberts scratched his chin, considering. "Yeah, maybe you're right. Add a cross-link reference to all these case files with the mud. That's the biggest case-connector we've got. Note the failure for forensics to analyze the blood, too."

"Already did, boss," Thompson replied. Then, almost as an afterthought, "Oh—forgot to mention. Detective Smalls hasn't stopped spouting gibberish for two days straight. The orderly in his psych ward said they found a small black feather in his mouth. Had to fight him for it."

Roberts blinked. "A feather?"

Thompson nodded grimly. "Yeah, a small feather from a crow—wedged between his gums and lips. Like a dog with a bone, he wouldn't give it up until they sedated him. Creepy stuff."

Roberts let out a long breath, his fingers gripping the wheel. "If that's a clue, I don't know what it's a clue to."

"Clear as mud?", Thompson quipped

"Note it. I want to connect all crow's feathers with the mud and blood. Strange connections are big clues."

He fell silent for a moment before muttering, "We've been on this case for two days, and it's already a done deal—time to close it. I'm already getting pressure from above to wrap this up. Probably should remain open as unsolved, but we'll charge Warren since he was literally holding the weapon used against his family and Detective Hastings, and all the connections to the victims are there."

Still…

Something didn't sit right.

A jolt of anger shot through Roberts, hot and electric. Without thinking, he slammed his palm against the steering wheel. The sudden impact rattled the entire car, but it didn't shake the feeling gnawing at his gut.

Chapter 60

It had been a week since Holly's transformation into Hiktilda.

Gaeldritch sat in her dimly lit hovel, the wooden beams above her sagging with the weight of many years. Wisps of thick incense curled through the air, mingling with the aged scent of parchment and dried herbs, a perfume of knowledge, power, and something dark and ancient. Shadows flickered from the single oil lamp, stretching long shadow fingers across the stone walls.

Then—

A knock at the door.

It was not the random rapping or the hesitant tap of a messenger. It was precise, deliberate. A rhythm known to only one.

Hiktilda.

Gaeldritch did not rise. She merely lifted one pale, sinewy hand and, with slow, deliberate precision, contorted her fingers into an intricate, unnatural gesture. Each joint twisted unnervingly, bending beyond the limits of human anatomy.

Her lips barely parted as she whispered the command:

"Reseri et aperi."

The heavy wooden door shuddered. The locks groaned,

latches clanking free as unseen forces slithered through the mechanisms. Metal bolts slid back with slow, deliberate clicks, the sound resonating through the chamber like the ticking of some infernal clock.

With a deep, resonant creak, the door swung inward. The darkness beyond yawned wide like the mouth of a waiting beast.

And there Hiktilda stood.

A cruel smile curved her lips, a sliver of malice shaped into something deceptively beautiful.

In one hand, she gripped a black iron chain, its links thick and old, worn with use. At the end of it, bound in crude iron cuffs, was a woman.

The captive was naked, save for the coarse black sack draped over her head, its fabric hanging in limp, miserable folds down her back. Her skin, exposed to the chill of the room, was dirty and bruised. She trembled—whether from fear or cold, it did not matter.

Her breath came in quick, shallow gasps.

Hiktilda took a step forward, tugging the chain.

The hooded woman stumbled, her knees nearly buckling. Bare feet met the icy stone with a muted slap.

With a flick of her wrist, Hiktilda swung the door shut behind them. The lock snapped back into place with a resolute, final click.

Gaeldritch rose, her robes billowing like ink dispersing through water.

"Good evening, darling," she purred, her voice rich and raspy, coated with something both velvety and venomous.

Hiktilda smirked. "My most cherished... I've brought you a new specimen."

Gaeldritch's gaze flickered to the woman in chains, her cold eyes drinking in the sight.

"How divine of you."

Together, they moved through the chamber, gliding toward an arched passageway carved into the rock. The corridor beyond yawned, its throat narrow and damp, exhaling stale, earthen breath.

They descended down an arched ramp-way.

The dim lanterns along the walls flickered, shadows stretching and contracting in unnatural movements. Water dripped somewhere in the unseen depths below—a slow, rhythmic *plink, plink, plink*, a heartbeat in the belly of the underworld.

Twenty feet down the passageway, another door awaited—iron-bound and scarred by time.

Gaeldritch reached into her robes, drawing a key blackened with age and tainted by use. A single twist of the wrist, a whispered word—

The door groaned open.

And the moment it did—

The muffled screams began.

Not loud. The gasps, the ragged inhales of many filled the chamber like the first moan of wind before a storm.

They had entered Gaeldritch's laboratory.

The air here was thick, suffocating—a perfume of alchemy, of brew and bile, of life stolen and distilled. The scent of dried herbs barely masked something metallic. Blood. Or something close to it.

Tables littered the chamber, cluttered with beakers filled with fluids of shifting color, distilling tubes twisting in unnatural spirals, cauldrons of iron bubbling with thick, viscous contents. Shelves lined the walls, bearing jars filled with things—things human, things bestial, things that had never belonged to this world.

And against the walls—

They hung.

Poor, wretched creatures, bound in iron and leather, shackled to the cold embrace of the stone. Each one hooded, mouths exposed just below the fabric's edge.

This room had been built for them.

Metal grates lined the floor beneath their feet, catching the runoff—the excess of suffering. Water trickled constantly from spouts bored into the stone wall behind them, washing away what the body could no longer hold.

Some were flayed, ribbons of flesh peeled back, revealing the gleaming sinew and pulsing muscles and organs beneath. Others maimed, left incomplete—a missing hand, a severed foot. Yet they remained, clinging to life by forces far crueler than mere iron shackles.

Thin glass tubing threaded into their torsos, pulsating fluids siphoned away, dripping into sealed basins at their feet.

They were not prisoners.

They were ingredients.

Hiktilda strode to an open iron ring set into the wall, dragging the chained woman behind her.

Gaeldritch moved with eerie grace, her presence effortless yet overwhelming. Taking the chain from Hiktilda's grip, she threaded it through the ring. With a decisive tug, she snapped the iron clasp shut.

The hooded woman gasped, her body jerking as the cold stone pressed into her bare skin.

Gaeldritch leaned in, her breath warm against the woman's trembling ear.

"Calm yourself, Anna. You won't feel a thing."

The woman flinched at the mention of her name.

Gaeldritch only smiled.

"None of my specimens suffer. I administer only the finest anesthetics." Her tone was almost maternal. "Soon, you'll forget everything."

Hiktilda let out a low laugh, the sound curling through the air like a serpent. She turned, striding toward another captive hanging from the wall a few feet away.

This other captive was mostly intact—save for her missing right hand, severed just above the wrist, the wound cauterized with blackened char. A blindfold of tight, black fabric covered her eyes.

And her mouth—

Sewn shut. Thick, black thread had been woven through her lips, binding them into a grotesque, silent seal.

Hiktilda crouched beside her, her voice too calm for the moment.

"Hello, Julie."

Julie jerked, her bound body spasming against the chains. A muffled, strangled scream tried to claw its way past her sealed lips.

Hiktilda reached forward, stroking her damp forehead.

"Shhh, shhh. Calm yourself," she cooed. "You're not going anywhere. Best save what little vital energy you have left."

Gaeldritch chuckled softly. "Don't mind her, darling. She's only fit for the most basic concoctions. Her remaining fats will serve our needs soon enough."

Hiktilda tilted her head.

"You don't like what's happened to you, do you, Julie? Losing. Suffering."

Julie trembled.

Hiktilda exhaled slowly. "Following visions of a weak, cowardly saint is always dangerous. You've learned that lesson the hard way. I'm sure you still think your visions were from some god or spirit... but trust me, there was a very human mind behind them. You were used, unsuccessfully of course. Just a pawn to a cowardly old nuisance to the order."

She leaned in, lips curling at Julie's ear.

"Take solace in your sacrifice. Your end will give us an ecstasy beyond mortal understanding. So, for that... thank you, Julie."

Gaeldritch grinned, her teeth glinting in the dim light.

"Tonight, our threads feed well."

The two Grand-Witches laughed, their cackles rising into a riotous chorus—one that slithered through the corridors, filling the labyrinthine depths with the promise of ecstasy to come.

Chapter 61

The revelry and ecstasy of the feeding had been divine—intoxicating and transcendent. Hiktilda relished the rapture of it—the exquisite sensation of herself and Gaeldritch allowing their black threads to slither, coil, and pierce through the fragile veils of their new specimens, drinking deep from the well of their essence. Julie and Anna had provided hours of unbroken bliss, their mortal bodies writhing in exquisite futility beneath the grasp of something far beyond their comprehension.

Hiktilda had sat beside Gaeldritch, their hands resting upon the victims—one hand each—anchoring them, sharing in their twisted delight. The Grand-Witches had sat in silent ecstasy, perched upon their black mats, smiling, eyes glistening, their cheeks slick with tears of rapture. The pleasure had been unspeakable—a sensation so pure and resplendent that no profane creature of the lesser world could ever conceive of it, let alone endure it.

A day had now passed. The excitement had subsided, and silence had reclaimed her hovel. Now, she sat alone, seeking rest—not through sleep, as ordinary creatures must, but through something far deeper. A Grand-Witch does not sleep. A Grand-Witch does not surrender to the unconscious abyss like common beings, dissolving into meaningless dreams. Instead, she enters a mode of simply being—a state of perfect stillness, where the illusions of flesh and thought are abandoned, and all that remains is the essence of self-knowing.

Lowering herself onto her black mat, Hiktilda adjusted the folds of her robe, allowing it to drape gracefully around her as she settled into the timeless posture. Her long, gnarled fingers traced her knee before she lifted her right foot and rested it atop her left thigh. The room exhaled with her, darkness pooling in the corners like black ink poured upon the fabric of the world. Her breathing was steady, flowing in and out through her long, crooked nose—inhale...exhale...unbroken, unshaken, untouched by the thought of lesser things.

And then, it happened.

A voice.

Clear. Sharp as sunlight on a blade. It did not pass through her ears; it resounded in the center of her—in the core of her being. There was no doubt. This was no stray whisper of thought. This was him.

The words carried tonality, warmth, an undeniable presence. And within them, a trace of something almost forgotten. An accent... a French accent.

"Hiktilda, Grand-Witch of the Elbynelem Clan, the Grand-Weaver of our sacred black thread... I have missed you for so long. So many years without your beautiful presence."

Her lips remained still. Her breath did not waver. She answered as only their kind could—through something beyond thought, through the boundless corridor of her heart.

"I missed you, Julian. I missed you so much. To be with you again makes my soul overflow with joy, my beloved." Her being poured forth, rich with longing, laced with desire. She paused in the silence for a few breaths and let her heart speak again. "Though your lessons have begun to return to me, your most sacred teachings still elude me, and I grow anxious for the deepest knowledge. Your teachings... I reach for them, but they slip like shadows beyond my grasp."

Julian's voice resonated again, its timbre like the brush of silk against her consciousness.

"My darling, I know what you seek, and that is why I am here in communion with you."

A thrill passed through her—subtle, yet full.

"I am ready and listening, my beloved... my Julian."

And then, like a river breaking its banks, his knowledge surged into her.

"Hiktilda, you are truly a rare wonder. You are a single diamond shining amongst the countless sands of humanity. You, along with myself, Gaeldritch, and the chosen few... we are *Maha-Devi*. We shine above the rest. We are the divided few. As *Maha-Devi*, we shine apart, with a radiance the profane simply cannot comprehend."

The words wove through her like an incantation—ancient and unshakable.

"My dear," he continued, "you will recall...in creation, we exist in an absolute sense—as One—without division. This entire universe exists in holiness, in the boundless, immovable field beyond names, concepts, and forms. To understand this ultimate knowledge is to wield true power. In fact, it is beyond even the concept of power. But in the world, with this knowledge, we move through time and space, experiencing... Experiencing is really what it all is, isn't it? We move in a world that exists only in division—in polarities, in the illusory separation of names and places, of 'this' and 'that,' of 'before'

314

and 'after.' Here, we are distinct from one another. Here, we forget we are one, we forgot we are Absolute."

Hiktilda's heart pulsed with recognition.

"I understand this truth," she replied.

Julian continued, "We, the chosen, shine with extreme individuality. We have nothing to do with the lesser creations—those drowned in ignorance, those captured in frivolous pursuits—for we few chosen fly above them, crowned with the ultimate knowledge... the knowledge of what we truly are. Even in darkness, we shine. Our halos burn with a radiance filled with both light and darkness."

A pause. A breath.

Julian allowed her to absorb the magnitude of what had been spoken.

"As *Maha-Devi*, we are the perfect expression of desire, and the fulfillment of that desire. We exist for the self—eternal, unshackled, sovereign. All is done in separateness, without regard, without remorse, without concern, without regret, and without pride."

Hiktilda shivered—not with fear, nor hesitation, but with something deeper, more visceral. The words were familiar, ancient echoes ringing in the corridors of her soul. She had always known these teachings. Even before they were spoken, she had known them deep in her core.

Julian continued, his voice weaving through the fabric of her existence.

"My love, listen for the next step in your journey as your destiny unfolds and accept it with no hesitation, but with pure openness. It is a beautiful sequence written in the great tapestry of existence, my darling—the one great dream of experience! For all of this... everything with a name, everything that has form, every concept, and every illusion…"

And then, as if from the depths of some unfathomable abyss, something broke loose within Hiktilda.

She burst out in laughter, and as she cackled, Julian spoke again in a commanding and loud bellow.

"Everything, darling—it is all for the experience, the tale to tell!"

Hiktilda stopped laughing and caught her breath for a few seconds. And then, with a broad smile, she clapped her hands together with a snap and opened her eyes—filled with tears of joy—and burst out, "All of this…all of it…it is *all* for the story!"

Ayduxia sakshi kachia

Appendix / Notae Arcanum

Admonitio de Lingua In Hoc Libro - A Important Note on Language in this Book
The **coven** (pronounced with a hard "O" — cō-ven, not "cuv-en") employs a ritual language forged from fragments of ancient and reconstructed tongues. Its roots draw heavily from Proto-Indo-European, shaped primarily by Classical Sanskrit, Latin, and Greek, with occasional echoes of Old Germanic dialects.

These incantations are not direct translations of any existing esoteric work, but rather a deliberately fractured and guarded ritual lexicon—evolved through secrecy, oral tradition, and intentional obfuscation in order to deter the profane from misuse.

> *Warning from Gaeldritch — Chapter 1:*
> "Do not mispronounce our spells! I admonish all of you now—speak with precision! There is no leeway to this command, and mispronunciation will be met with dire punishment."

In this world, sound carries weight. Power lives not only in the words themselves, but in *how* they are spoken. Even the smallest deviation in articulation invites consequence.

Glossarium Obscura - Glossary of Incantations

Ayduxia sakshi kachia

"Watch the wood burn."

An acceptance of destiny unfolding with a sense of adoration as it transpires.

Elementa creationis, facite iussa mea, datva me durstim, sudarsanam

"Elements of creation, heed my command—grant me truth and spirit-sight."

Bayani ye sudha balam pariva rayanti

"Those encircled by divine power."

Ostende mihi visionem

"Show me the vision."

Gou-zistrica

"Be stricken with sleep."

Sit metamorphosin fieri cursim, ut cumque sumptus

"Let the transformation come swiftly, no matter the cost."

Factum est

"It is done."

Vanki tayeef exuldi!

"Become your exalted self!"

Nunc carmen pulchritudinis canemus!

"Now we sing a song of beauty!"

Bibe totum

"Drink it all."

Darifex prozeefus! Veneficium pulchritudinis, virgo feruzstisio!

"Grant the spell of beauty in illusion—as the perfect natural maiden, hold fast!"

Taristti lilswar gribe!

"Let the hidden powers awaken!"

Incantatio formosa finire!   Sharadi me jala ja laya manan!

"Charm of beauty, conclude! Cast these words into a mirage of reflected light!"

Teristi nox collum

"Wear down the passage of night."

Inkulanti trecharis

"Press into the passage."

Nerbah kribah luna vidiyah

"By moonlight's gaze, grant great visions."

Sanguis pueri, luminis stellarum

"Blood of the boy, light of the stars."

Ignis, da mihi visionem stellarum!

"Fire, grant me the vision of stars!"

Gorzunstrica!

"Be stricken with paralysis!"

Tang laskrow, ting laskrew

"The piercing sting—the ecstasy of sensation."

Ario vextevio pustristii

"Let the mind unravel into confusion."

Soma pix sunato

"Darkness has claimed the body."

Avidyasah!

"Ignorance reigns! Confusion complete!"

Terafi vaya rucha d'veshmai

"Let spirit, soul, and body wander the earth."

Ahnox!

"The power of night!"

Sharadi me jala ja laya manan, umbra silens, anoxi

"Bend the light around me, cloak me in silent shadow—by the night's power!"

Umbra, digitis meis iungere et nullum signum relinque

"Shadow, cling to my fingers—and leave no trace."

Noli expergisci dulatia

"The bound mind will not awaken."

Vibratio mortifera! O mortalis corpus, audite vocem maledicti: śakti tremens kaṭhina vibra!

"Vibrations of death! Mortal flesh, hear the curse—tremble with unyielding shaking power!"

Ossa resonent in tumultu, et anima tua vibrate in incessant śabda

"Let bone echo in roaring tumult, let the soul tremor in eternal sound."

Tremorem perpetuum exsurgite in te, in umbris noctis

"Let endless tremors rise within you, in the shadows of night."

Maleficos non patieris vivere

"You shall not suffer the wicked to live."

Reseri et aperi

"Unseal and open."

Gaeldritch on *De Constitutione Entis Terreni*

On the Construction of an Earthen Being

Tum-Grissell possesses an intelligence far greater than any other earthen construct. *Far* greater. That is why he is so exquisitely dangerous… and why we of the coven hold him in such reverence. He completes our tasks with wit sharper than steel and a cunning that never dulls. And yet at the same time, he is physically beyond what most minds can even begin to comprehend.

He travels hundreds of miles without pause—no fatigue, no hesitation—slipping through wilderness and forgotten paths as if the world bends out of his way. Often he carries three to four hundred pounds in the black-thread sacks draped over his shoulders… woven expressly to bear our offerings. *The Sack-Man, the Bog Man, the Bag Man*—such quaint names the frightened townsfolk whisper. They have no idea how many centuries he has walked among them, unseen or half-seen, doing what must be done.

The Order's appetite has always been insatiable, you understand. Fresh ingredients… the calamities of the sheep… all necessary. And the creation of a being like Tum-Grissell is an ordeal of exquisite labor, with success never assured. The slightest miscalculation means failure—sometimes explosive failure.

He is fashioned from the clay and mud of the earth, yes, but bound with properly sublimated blood, generous amounts of lipids, and a very delicate array of fine particulates and potent liquids. These are united to form *Argilla Vivificans*—the Clay That Gives Life. It is a substance both sacred and treacherous, and it must be handled with careful hands and an unwavering mind.

Once the *Argilla Vivificans* is prepared—every incantation spoken, every gesture aligned with the ancient pattern—a portion of the human's blood is taken and purified. It must be done while the body is still alive, still aware, still… listening. Then, with the proper mantras, the living flesh—its final hours flickering away—is meticulously covered. Every inch. Every fold. Every secret place. Attention to detail is everything. Emotion is not optional; it is required in great, heaving waves.

And then comes the most delicate act. The chest is opened. The heart is removed—quickly, cleanly, reverently—and replaced with the Stone Heart, which is reactive beyond describing. The chest is sealed with eight sigils, and the remainder of the *Argilla Vivificans* is pressed into the flesh until it gleams.

The final step is what our benefactor calls *the Submerged Rising*. A charming name, really. The body is taken to a consecrated swamp and submerged entirely, like a baptism of the grotesque—yet pure, in its way. Death always comes at this stage. But death is irrelevant when the salve holds the energies tight, like a clenched fist around a secret.

Then we wait. Sometimes a day. Sometimes weeks. The creation either awakens into consciousness... or falls into the final oblivion, never to rise. But if consciousness does bloom—ah—then the creature climbs from the bog, reborn in mud and certainty.

Tum-Grissell is a marvel because he retained *all* of his intelligence through the transformation. Not a fragment lost. Even more miraculous, unlike the common earthen beasts—those pathetic creations that must gorge on livers and organs just to maintain their shambling forms—Tum-Grissell endures on the base elements alone: earth and water. He is the only true *Abominatio* ever achieved.

The failed ones still wander the world, a few of them. Horrid things... immortal, dim, hungry. But Tum-Grissell? No. He is perfect. And he is ours...

Hiktilda on *De Effectibus Sacri Fili Nigri in Corpore*
On the Effects of the Sacred Black Thread upon the Body

As a member of the Inner Order, you will recall the moment you were administered the sacred Black Thread with the proper dosage and the accompanying words of power. Once the Black Thread is released to move freely through the body, it begins a profound cleansing. This process will lead to one of two outcomes: either the mind collapses into madness and the body dies, or the mind and body accept the Black Thread, and from the human shell rises something grand and terrible—a true witch, one of us, no longer human and no longer condemned to suffer as they do.

The Black Thread amplifies the powers of the body and mind beyond comprehension—but only when properly guided. Its deeper workings will be taught in due time to those who prove capable and worthy. Even with the small measure of Black Thread now coursing through your veins, you wield immense power. With discipline and training, the Black Thread will grow alongside your abilities, and in time you may ascend to the rank of Grand Witch within the coven.

You will not suffer the diseases or frailties of the profane human. You have shed the weakness of that fragile form. Aging no longer takes its horrible toll. We may appear older or younger when working certain incantations, forms, spells, and spirits—but do not concern yourself with appearances. The coven possesses many methods to restore youth and vitality, and such rejuvenation is easily achieved through our extensive knowledge of the secret arts.

The Black Thread transforms the corruptible, miserable human body into something perfected—an immortal vessel, a marvel of creation. Age will no longer bring suffering or the slow collapse of life. Though the passage of centuries may alter your outward appearance, the Black Thread will never allow you to die, so long as it is properly fed.

The human body is a bag of filth. The Black Thread cleanses that filth. It is that simple.

The skin of the human body is filled with blood contami-nated by foreign bodies, parasites, caustic chemicals, and toxic wastes. It encases organs and the digestive tract—perhaps the most revolting system of all. The profane can consume what they believe to be clean food, yet even the purest meal is soon expelled in the most foul forms imaginable. One may drink the clearest water, yet within hours it becomes ammonia and acid, expelled with a stench that betrays the corruption within.

The body, before it is cleansed, is a revolting and abhorrent thing.

But it is purified through the Black Thread.

At first glance, this magnificent wonder may resemble a parasite, perhaps even a worm. It is neither. The sacred Black Thread is pure. If you accept it—and if it accepts you—it becomes your faithful partner in existence: in strength, in sanctity, and in connection. It is truly symbiotic with your being. It feeds with you and for you. It draws sustenance only from the purest essence of our victims and grants you an immense capacity for power.

You will no longer consume the food of the profane. You will no longer drink impure, unconsecrated waters. Such waters, unless brewed into proper concoctions, are worthless. You will no longer require sleep but will instead learn to flow with your breath in a state of pure being, an experience that is much more rejuvenating that sleeping as a human body ever could be.

Yet the world still holds dangers, both physical and unseen. But lesser creatures cannot harm you. Disease and sickness are no longer to be feared once you and the Black Thread become one—entwined, inseparable, and beloved.

Now you may ask: *from whence did the Black Thread come?*

It was fashioned by a master craftsman long before the time

of Julian. Yes—a man created the Black Thread. Yet he did not work alone, for he was aided by a most unusual creature, of which I will soon speak.

The man's name was Arumel, and he is ancient even by our reckoning. He is the same master who first instructed Vizier Julian in many of the alchemical arts and secret practices our benefactor now employs so skillfully. Arumel came from the civilization we know today as the Hittites. In his own time he was regarded as both mystic and priest, a man deeply practiced in what we call Red Zalma and Black Zalma—more on *that* later.

During one of his countless experiments, Arumel obtained a strange mutation of a desert arachnid. It was a black spider of unusual size, larger than a man's hand. Its body was thick and swollen, its legs long and thin like those of the black widow, and its glossy exoskeleton was covered in fine black hairs that seemed to absorb the light surrounding it.

Over time Arumel fed the creature countless brews and alchemical concoctions from his workshop. With each passing month the arachnid grew larger and larger, until at last it reached a size beyond any expectations. Due to its venomous and vicious nature, Arumel kept the mutation secured within a sturdy wooden cage for his own safety.

Yet despite its terrible form and disposition, the creature and Arumel formed a strange companionship. Day after day, month after month, they shared the same workshop, the same dim lantern light, and the same endless experiments.

For years he continued force feeding the beast mixtures drawn from his vast collection of potions and tinctures. The creature grew grotesquely swollen with the effects of these substances until, one fateful day, Arumel noticed something unusual. The thing's abdomen had become distended and heavy, so bloated that he briefly wondered whether it carried offspring. Yet he knew the creature had never known a mate.

Thus he concluded something else entirely.

The creature, he reasoned, had become overfull.

With careful preparation Arumel administered powerful sleeping agents to the beast. Once the creature lay unconscious, he donned thick leather gloves and lifted the monstrous arachnid from its cage. Holding it firmly above a large black iron cauldron, he applied steady pressure to the creature's swollen abdomen.

And then it happened.

From the spidery spinnerets there burst forth a torrent of thick black silk—wet, glossy, and darker than pitch. The strands spilled into the cauldron in tangled coils, glistening like oil beneath the workshop flames.

Yet what astonished Arumel most was not the substance itself, but its movement.

The silk did not lie still. It was alive.

It writhed and undulated in the bottom of the cauldron, twisting and coiling upon itself like living tendrils of an unseen horror.

The mutated arachnid remained deeply asleep as Arumel continued pressing the creature's abdomen, expelling every last strand the bloated body contained. Soon the bottom of the cauldron was alive with a swirling mass of black silk-like thread, shifting and writhing like a nest of serpents.

When he was satisfied the creature had yielded all it could, Arumel returned his dreadful companion to its cage and secured it once more. He then carefully gathered the living strands from the cauldron and sealed them within several glass vessels for further study.

Yet Arumel was not a patient man when confronted with discovery.

He waited scarcely an hour.

Opening one of the freshly filled bottles, he placed his fingertips into the damp coils of the Black Thread. Instantly the strands awakened, clinging to his skin. In a matter of moments they burrowed into his flesh and began moving through his body with alarming speed.

Many years later Arumel told Julian that he lost consciousness almost immediately after the first contact. He believed he remained insensible for two or perhaps three days.

When he finally awoke, he did so with a strength and vitality he had never known before.

Much more could be said of Arumel and the first days of the Black Thread—but that knowledge must wait for another time.

Yet there is one final tale that should be told.

Among the coven it is remembered as both a great tragedy and a great cleansing.

Arumel first administered the Black Thread to Julian, and the result was a resounding success. Julian accepted the Black Thread, and the Black Thread accepted him in return.

Under Julian's instruction, eight witches were initiated into the deeper arts. He trained them carefully, teaching them the secrets he himself had learned from Arumel. Julian believed in them completely, regarding each of them as a daughter of his own making. Their powers were already formidable, and the coven prospered under their growing strength.

Yet Arumel, ever the architect of greater designs, advised Julian that the time had come for these witches to receive the true gift. The gift of the Black Thread.

Thus, on a night of full moon and heavy silence, Julian prepared the ritual. A great iron cauldron was placed at the center of a sacred circle, and into it he poured a mass of living Black Threads gathered from Arumel's stores. One by one the witches were brought into the circle, standing evenly around the cauldron beneath the pale lunar light.

Julian spoke ancient words of power over the vessel. Into the cauldron he poured various elixirs and dark infusions, stirring the writhing threads as the moon climbed higher into the sky.

By Julian's command, the eight witches stepped forward and plunged their hands into the cauldron.

The Black Threads awakened instantly, lashing around their fingers and burrowing into their flesh. What followed was swift and merciless.

Four of the witches collapsed within moments of contact with the sacred filaments. Their bodies convulsed briefly before falling still upon the stone floor of the circle. They had proven too weak, their bodies and minds unworthy of the communion.

But four endured.

Those who survived rose again from the ordeal changed— stronger, awakened, and forever bound to the living power of the Black Thread.

On that night they became the first Grand-Witches of the coven. Their names are spoken with reverence among us even now: Gaeldritch. Skeinlace. Dorylibb. And me.

Further instruction is contained within the continued writings of the Order.

www.ingramcontent.com/pod-product-compliance
Lightning Source LLC
Chambersburg PA
CBHW030246120726
47903CB00005B/1647